STRANGE PLEASURES 2

STRANGE PLEASURES 2

EDITED BY

JOHN GRANT & DAVE HUTCHINSON

PRIME BOOKS
Canton, Ohio

STRANGE PLEASURES 2

Published in the United States by **Prime Books, Inc.**
P.O. Box 36503, Canton, OH 44735
www.primebooks.net

ISBN: 1-894815-08-4

CONTENTS

"We Really Liked This, But . . ."
John Grant & Dave Hutchinson

How do you go about putting together an anthology?

We'll let you into a little secret: the first thing you do is get in touch with your mates.

You phone them. You write to them. You e-mail them. You bump into them at parties and maybe an awards do. You ask them to put you in touch with *their* mates. You pluck up courage and approach writers you don't know but whose work you've admired from afar for years.

"We're doing an anthology," you tell them. "Fancy being in it?"

"Sure," they say. "What's it about?"

"Well, you know. Book. Short stories. That kind of thing."

"No," they say. "What's it *about*?"

Oh, right.

Second little secret: you have to decide what *kind* of anthology you're doing. And that might not be as easy as it sounds.

For instance, you might decide to put together a collection of stories that will annoy, offend and flat-out disgust as many people as possible. That way, you stand a chance of being hailed as the editors of a bunch of stories that are cutting-edge, ground-breaking. Dangerous, even.

Or you can go the theme-anthology route. You pick a subject — a social trend or another art-form or something — and tell your stable of authors that you want stories written around that theme. So you wind up with, say, an anthology of science-fiction frisbee stories, or stories about the threat of globalization or how bloody *awful* London's transport system is. And maybe you're hailed as the creators of a brand-new subgenre, parents of a New Wave which, in a few years, everyone and their dog is going to be writing in. Yeah. You wish.

(The obvious drawback here is that your writers might not necessarily *want* to write about frisbees; they might get partway through a story about globalization and think, "Ah, the hell with *this*. I want to finish my novel about Frenchmen in outer space." They might take *a very long time* to write their magnum opus about London Underground. Then you're left with a big book to fill and not enough stories to fill it with and you start buying litre bottles of Pepto-Bismol and shouting at the cat.)

Or you can go the *shared-world* route, where you rough out a few ground rules and some backstory, hand it over to your writers and say, "There you go, write us something around that, please." When that works, the results can be spectacularly good . . . but you don't see all that many shared-worlds anthologies these days, for some reason.

Or you can just collect a bunch of stories that you *like*. No theme, no shared world, no intention to go out and shock people and bust down barriers. Just a bunch of good stories.

Which is what we did.

And the surprising thing is, there's an awful lot of very good fantasy and science fiction — not to mention stuff that isn't *quite* fantasy or isn't *quite* science fiction — just floating around out there, unpublished.

Now, a lot of people think that if you write a really good story the world just comes beating a path to your door.

Doesn't happen.

What happens is you write your really good story and you send it out to various magazines and publishers, and a lot of the time what you get back is: "You know, we really liked this, *but* . . . "

There are a number of reasons for this. Your really good story might not fit the magazine's profile. (You wrote a delicate fable about elves and trees and unicorns and you sent it to a magazine that only publishes Goth splatterpunk; well, it was worth a try.) It might, no matter how good it is, be too long for the magazine. (The magazine typically publishes six two-thousand word stories in an issue and your story's seventeen thousand words long; well, they *might* have turned the whole of one issue over to you, even added a couple of pages, you never know.) It might, no matter how good it is, just not be to the editor's taste. (The editor's a big fan of gritty urban cyberpunk and you send him a finely crafted space opera about the rise and fall of galactic empires; he can see it's well written and all that, but it just doesn't ring his bells. On the other hand, he's got this absolutely *cracking* gritty urban cyberpunk story sitting on his desk...) It might not fit genre expectations — that business about not being *quite* fantasy or *quite* science fiction, but something that, although manifestly fantasticated, can't be neatly popped into a genre pigeonhole.

And so on. Every writer will tell you how one (or more) of the very best stories they ever wrote has just never, for some reason — and usually the reason isn't nearly so obvious as the ones we've cited above, and may indeed be totally incomprehensible — sold. The writer can't understand it; the writer's friends have read the manuscript and *they* can't understand it; when we were sent some of these "unsaleable" stories *we* couldn't understand it either. (Though in many other cases we, er, did.)

Some stories just don't *click*, no matter how good they are, no matter where you send them to. So they sit in drawers and on disks and occasionally, when it's late at night and your latest novel's come to a grinding halt, you take them out and you tinker with them and you sigh and you put them away again.

And then we come along. "Well, you know. Book. Short stories. That kind of thing. No theme, really. Just stuff we like."

There is, as we said, a lot of good stuff out there, looking for a home. Some of it lives here now.

And then there were the writers who sat down and wrote something specially for us. We told everyone that we weren't going to include any "passengers" — if we weren't sent enough good stories we'd rather not produce the anthology at all. Every story would have to have a special *something* — even though we weren't too articulate about saying what that special *something* was. The title of this series of anthologies is, after all, *Strange Pleasures*; if a story didn't have a touch of the strange about it, something that marked it out in our own minds as unique, then we weren't interested. (We turned down a number of very good stories

9

because, despite their many virtues, they didn't seem to us to have that touch of strange.) Thus many of the writers we asked to contribute looked at the contents of the legendary desk drawer and found them wanting, but realized that what we were offering was the chance to write *that* story — the one they'd never written before, however much they'd desperately wanted to, because *they'd known from the outset* that no orthodox editor would touch it with a bargepole.

We told them that this was exactly the sort of story we wanted to see.

It was only later it struck us that maybe editors aren't supposed to do that. We're glad we did, anyway.

Word got about. Submissions started arriving from writers we most certainly hadn't informed about this anthology we were editing. In one instance a story was sent to John Grant whose author had had no intention of offering it for publication at all and had never heard of the anthology — he was simply asking for it to be given a look-over by a friend. John Grant (some "friend", you might think!) liked it so much he covertly passed it across to Dave Hutchinson, who liked it a lot as well, and so . . .

We are, of course, only human. We have our likes and dislikes too, and we had a finite amount of space to play with. It soon became obvious to us that we'd accidentally tapped a far richer vein than we'd realized. So several stories we absolutely adored, we ruefully concluded, just couldn't be crammed into *Strange Pleasures #2* — even though our kindly publisher upped the book's permitted word-count considerably from his original figure. Some of these stories, hopefully, will turn up in subsequent *Strange Pleasures* anthologies — assuming they're not snapped up elsewhere before then.

As for those future volumes . . . well, we decided at the outset that we'd edit *Strange Pleasures #2* jointly and thereafter take turns, so that from now on each of us will be editing one *Strange Pleasures* anthology a year — quite enough for any editor, we think. If you feel you those have one of those *special* stories — one with that touch of strange — inside either your desk drawer or your brain, just desperate to burst out, by all means e-mail us and tell us about it: the e-address is papersnarl@snip.net. Make the subject line of your e-mail STRANGE PLEASURES SUBMISSION, and it'll go to the appropriate editor. Please *don't* send us full manuscripts out of the blue, without that preliminary query; we're as wary of viruses as the next person, so e-mails with unheralded attachments will just be zapped.

#

So there you go. That's how you put together an anthology. You could even do it yourself, if you felt like it . . .

Balzac

N. Lee Wood

I had Balzac in mind when I started out. "Either I have or I have not genius; in either case, I am laying up a store of sorrows. Without genius, I am done for. I must then pass my life in feeling desires I cannot satisfy, in miserable envy, cruel pain. With genius, I shall be persecuted and calumniated; and I know very well that Mademoiselle Fame will have to wipe away abundant tears."

He grossly overstates it, I think. There's something so smugly romantic to think that one must suffer for greatness, because the inverse logic also infers that, if Genius Suffers, then those that Suffer must be Genius. And, if one doesn't Suffer, then one can't be Genius. Uh-huh. Sounds like horseshit to me. Smug horseshit at that. In retrospect, Mademoiselle Fame didn't have to knock herself out wiping away any crocodile tears Monsieur Balzac may have squeezed out from time to time in proof of his Genius. The adoring French were pretty damned quick to forget the incredibly inane plays and hysterical melodramas he cranked out in his callow youth (I suppose that was before he became a Genius). And any tears *he* shed were from troubles caused by his non-Genius at business and half-hearted romances with married Polish countesses.

I never claimed to be a Genius. I had to look up "calumniated" and, while I've managed to muddle my way half-assed through about five languages, mostly those printed on menus, it was a bastard to read Balzac in his original nineteenth-century French. I've been called many other things; "well read" is one (why else, you see, would I be ruminating on the musing of a long dead Frog?), and another is "down to earth". I've been labelled as having "horse sense", which never has made much sense as horses must be among the stupidest animals ever evolved from protean slime. I've been acclaimed for having "business acumen", a "cool head for financial markets" and "a sharp nose for money", but never, ever have I been accused of Genius.

Although without Genius, I've always had the desire, an *honest* desire for Genius rather than the perceived rewards of Genius. Money, power, sexy lovers, your picture on the cover of *Rolling Stone*. These are the laurels supposed to be accorded to Geniuses, while those of us Without must languish about in . . . what was it? Oh, yeah, "miserable envy and cruel pain".

What a laugh. Go on, check out the *Rolling Stone* April issue two years ago. Then peruse a few back issues of *Esquire, GQ, MONEY, Financial Times, Business Week,* the *WSJ,* the society page of the *Post* in the archives of your local public lending library. See that straight white-toothed grin surrounded by those square jaws? The little crinkles around the baby-blues the giggle girls tell me are "cute"? Does this look like the face of a man who suffered in miserable envy and cruel pain?

Not me, brother. I didn't need to write decades' worth of long letters to get laid by Polish countesses. I didn't sink my capital into worthless fly-by-night business ventures, either. For the most part, I've been perfectly satisfied with my life. I've never been burdened by the artificial angst my generation manufactured to excuse their lust for money and status symbols. I've never been consumed by wild undying romantic passion, but I've had one acceptable and enjoyable marriage to a single, lovely lady. Widowers are somehow sexier than divorced men, so my sex life never stagnated much in the years after Emilie's death.

I've also had Luck. Anyone who tells you Luck isn't necessary for those with "real business acumen" doesn't have any real business acumen. Same for those who'll snort that business acumen is *all* luck. Luck is the right combination of the right things at the right time. Business acumen is recognizing it and taking advantage when it happens along. Luck isn't, contrary to popular belief, a rare commodity. Chances pop up all the time, but somehow most people blunder along, blindly ignoring them all. Or at least all but the damned few that pound your door down like Ed McMahon clutching a sweepstakes cheque in his sweaty fist.

I suppose if I'd been a Genius I'd have seen other chances I was blind to, the very subtle ones that slip by unnoticed by all but the most sensitive. Like the guy who dreamed of snakes biting their own tails, woke up and discovered he'd discovered the hexagonal chemical structure for rings of carbon atoms, which was considered a Big Deal by other Genius Chemists of the day. No shit, he literally dreamed it up! I waited forever for something like that to come to me in the wee hours of slumber, but no. Dream on.

I've been very lucky. Born in the Yoo Ess Aye, a child of middle-class parents cheerfully aspiring to upper-middle-classdom, heavy on the XY pair of chromosomes and light on the melanin genes. Lucky enough not to grow up too blond, or too rich, or too heavily affiliated with a long line of esteemed dead ancestors, either New England thin-bloods or Jewish aristocrats. Just white and bright enough to attract the best from everyone else while smart enough to be aware my own packaging was not synonymous with performance.

Like Emilie. Emilie was perfect for me. I was lucky enough to get a scholarship to Princeton (after having enough "horse sense" to scour the records in search of that dusty scholarship I finally qualified for), where we met at one of those sorority dance things. She'd come downstairs fortified with a bunch of her friends, clustered together and giggling. It was sort of sad, in its eternal way. The girls stood in clots to lend each other the courage to meet the boys, and the protection to ward them off. Like buffaloes standing in a ring with their deliciously meaty asses pointed at the wolves.

The "wolves" for their part were lounging in the chintz print overstuffed sofas and chairs scattered around the reception room of the sorority house in somebody's old maid conception of "casual" decorating. Or they slouched in doorways, or leaned against stereo cabinets and antique end-tables, smoking cigarettes. They talked in bored voices about cars and money and classes, and ignored the girls to show how cool they were while standing with their hands jammed in their pockets wondering how in the hell they were gonna get laid at this fucking dance. A few couples swayed and grabbed each other in time to the music on the "dance floor", a section of hardwood exposed by rolling up an antique Persian rug, but these were upper classmen and their steady girls.

When Emilie came down that staircase, I happened to be the spineless twit slouched over the top of a chintz easy chair discussing Latin American politics (a subject I knew just enough about to sound like I actually knew anything at all) with a kid trying to hide his genetically inherent computer-nerdism behind a pair of contacts and non-designer jeans, the latest fad. I looked up at this slender, blonde girl smiling nervously and saw Luck.

Emilie Stouthwick, of Stouthwick, Andrus & Chaney, old and well bred blue-blooded New England money family and prestigious law firm, was a pale-skinned girl with straight hair cut blunt at her small chin. Her lips were barely saved from being too thin by curving in a shape like the Mona Lisa's. She was reserved rather than truly shy, and spoke with an almost affected nasal accent that put a lot of people off. It came from spending too much time isolated in prep schools and snotty social circles than from any real conceit of her own. Emilie was many things, most of them good, and conceit was not on her list of failings.

I knew who she was, of course I did. She wasn't the most popular girl, nor the most beautiful, nor the richest. In a place like Princeton, she was pretty much the usual run-of-the-mill upper class rich bitch preppie. I knew most of the upper class rich bitch preppies, at least by sight if not by name. I also knew I wanted to marry one.

Yeah, yeah. So I'm an asshole. But I'm not so much of an asshole that I'd marry just *any* ol' upper class rich bitch preppie. It's an old but true saying that those who marry for money earn it. So, I'd dated a couple of girls who filled the basic requirements, rather like half-hearted sorting through the white bread chaff in search of some whole wheat. There were some nice ones, don't get me wrong. It was more personal incompatibility than any class prejudice on their part. There are a lot more people of my 'umble background than those in the upper class rich preppie set, so it's far easier for "us" to blame "them" for the failure. In any case, my background was just acceptable enough for the preppie set to associate with, so I couldn't really blame it on that either.

15

Lest you get any sentimental ideas that I was secretly longing to find the Girl of my Dreams and Fall Deeply in Love, I'd already found her. Literally the girl next door. Lusted insanely after her from the day she moved in when I was thirteen and riddled with acne and hormones 'til the day I finally managed to seduce her, parked behind the high school football field in the back seat of my father's aged Toyota. We were both barely sixteen. Spent the rest of high school walking around with a hard-on just thinking of her. She fell in love with someone else my freshman year of college, we argued bitterly, made up and fucked like crazed cats, then started the process all over again. Most of our relationship, then and after, was pain, wonderful mindblowing sex, tearful fights and despair. I finally lost her.

Thank God.

No, I wasn't looking for love when I met Emilie. I'm not sure I would know exactly what to call what I was looking for, except, maybe, Luck. Emilie *radiated* the stuff.

Our eyes connected across that room, my deep philosophical arguments about Latin America died an abrupt demise, and the calcium returned to my spine in one strong surge. I mumbled something to the latent nerd and left him trying to figure out how to untangle his fashionably clad legs from the arms of the chintz chair. I could feel the envious stares of the wolves as I courageously walked straight at the herd at the base of the staircase.

"Hi," was the witty, original pick-up line I'd come up with. And a smile. I'd had some practice with the girls of the preppie set, so when she turned red and smiled back I knew exactly the amount of bashfulness to put into nodding and clutching my beer. Even at that tender age, I knew what worked and how to make it work for me.

"Hi," she said, and the buffaloes giggled approvingly. Home run, boys. I got laid that night, and you didn't. I got more than laid, I got Emilie.

Emilie's mother was (is) a socialite, the kind of woman who would have been a girl scout leader and won ribbons for her apple pies at the County Fair if her parents hadn't had an Old Name and Lotsa Money. So, instead of girl scouts and county fairs, she sat on the Arts Council and gave garden lunches at the Stouthwick estate. She had married exactly right, an ambitious, talented law student with enough family connections for him to Get Ahead. Yet he was never a man who could allow himself to devolve into a jerk enough to get roped into Washington politics after he'd mellowed into the senior partnership of Stouthwick, Andrus & Chaney. He was (is) quite literally above that sort of slime, and did more than his fair share of pro bono work out of a real sense of social obligation and an idealistic desire to create a better world. That a better world is not something about to happen in the near future hasn't made him bitter or disillusioned. As you might tell, I rather liked Emilie's parents, and they rather liked me, which fit in rather well with my personal requirements for a marriage partner.

Emilie herself was a fine, fine lady. I don't know if I ever actually loved Emilie, but I did like her tremendously. We were good friends, and I believe I made her happy, which is a lot more than can be said for many marriages, love or not. She was supportive and understanding, tender and responsive in bed, and we fought just sufficiently to keep a little spice in our lives. She was intelligent and independent enough to have her own life apart from mine, which satisfied both of us just fine. In any way you want to cut it, she was the ideal wife for an ambitious young businessman. When she died of a sudden cerebral stroke, I did a good deal of honest weeping, and I missed her a lot. Whether or not that ends up qualifying as love, I don't know. I really don't.

After her death, her parents sort of adopted me into the family, in a warm, offhand way, the same way they treated Emilie and her two brothers. Now, it was "the boys", and they did for me as much as for their own blood. The brothers were a lot like Emilie, no surprise there, and didn't seem to feel either jealous or threatened by me, nor overly distraught when I gradually bowed out of their financial and social circle, making it discreetly clear I wouldn't claim any of Emilie's share in their quite substantial inheritance. I still go "home" on the occasional Christmas holiday or various birthdays, and they're still as friendly as ever. They're a good family, with good people. I simply didn't have any further need for them, and my life got too busy for sentimental entanglements.

Yes, I know, I'm still an asshole.

But by that time I'd made my own fortune. With Emilie's blue-blooded money connections, and her father helpfully introducing his beloved son-in-law to various wheeler-dealers, it wasn't too difficult to pick and choose between Lady Luck's droppings in my lap. I'd always had a "nose for a good deal" (another description not quite reaching the Genius level) and rode the rise and fall of the financial tide like the Silverplate Surfer.

Emilie's death did affect me in another way, I think. See, I'd started out wanting to make my very own fortune, while not being too above using Emilie's family connections to help it along, for reasons I hadn't even thought out too well myself. I'd never been exactly the driven workaholic type, nor was I a true philanthropist like Emilie's dad. I wanted to make a Big Pile of Money (with as little strain or pain as possible) just to see if I could do it.

I could.

I started out buying a tiny, run-to-the-red investment company (with a little assistance from Pop-in-Law), and quickly caught on to the game of taking other people's money and making it create more money for them and their clients, with a big, healthy percentage left over for myself. I knew which investments were good, solid deals and which were wet paper sacks ready to burst when the first whiff of wind come along. I didn't go for junk bonding or hostile takeovers, never forgot that beneath all the paper games there'd damn' well better be a quality product keeping the gold standard. So when the Mike Milkens of Wall Street and the S&L fiasco hit the fan, my prestige kept me floating clean and pretty on that vast ocean of sewage.

Within ten years, I'd paid off Emilie's father, with interest in the form of a small but attractive sailing yacht, and squeezed my little lemon into Fortune 500 world-class lemonade. Even got asked to serve on the President's Economic Advisory Committee, what a joke. Best advice I could give was to shitcan all those Washington Nobel Laureates busy blathering about free market mechanisms and macroeconomics and hire a room full of working single mothers and average housewives on a budget. No one else would know more about real economics. But that's not what they wanted to hear.

It wasn't as easy as I'm making it out, you know. Yeah, I had the knack of knowing when and what to buy and when and what to sell, but a lot of it was simply long hours of hard, drudgy work. I may indeed be the asshole you suspect me of being, but I've never been a *lazy* asshole. Then

Emilie had her stroke.

So, while I was in that hospital watching plastic bellows push air in and out of Emilie's comatose lungs, staring at the tubes shoved down her aristocratic nose and clutching her limp cold hand as if I could physically drag her back to consciousness, something happened inside me. It was like I suddenly stepped outside of myself, watching *me* from a distance going through the motions of Doing the Right Things.

I stayed near Emilie for the five days it took her to die. I slept with my forehead pressed against her hand, and chain-smoked with her father in the waiting room. I held her mother and patted her back while she wept. And all the time, it was like I wasn't really there at all. I knew Emilie was gone. That limp body lying in those crumpled white hospital sheets wasn't Emilie. I didn't want Emilie to die, but I didn't love her enough to delude myself into believing in miracles. My overwhelming feeling when she finally coded, and a flurry of doctors and nurses descended on the room in a theatrical display of Heroic Medicine, was one of impatience and relief.

But after I'd buried her I found I didn't want to go back to business any more. The firm was well designed, if I do say so myself. I had an extremely competent and loyal staff running the place, ambitious workaholic career ladies and gentlemen all. All I really had to do was go to a board meeting once in a while, sniff the air to see that everything was still on track, and go home. Invitations to lunch at the White House get turned down only once, but I didn't give a shit. Emilie's death was very convenient for me, although I never once personally used it as an excuse — you can do wonders with a slight sad smile, a distracted nod here and there at the right time, and people can assume whatever they want to. I started looking around for Something Different.

That's when I realized I wanted to be a Genius.

I went after that goal the same way I'd gone after everything I'd wanted before in my life. I took a long hard stare at all the symptoms of Being a Genius. Hell, I was no moron, but I wanted to believe that there was maybe some secret untapped part of me that if I only delved deep enough I'd find, and so release the latent Genius inside me. All I had to do was fig-ure out what it was I was a Genius *in*.

Science, as much as I enjoyed it in my younger days, seemed definitely out of the question. Everyone knows the probably apocryphal story about Einstein's big break (and this is one of those cases of Luck bopping him over the head with a baseball bat). He answered only one question in his college entrance examination, and failed because he didn't answer the rest. See, he spent so much time being fascinated with that first question that he just kept scribbling and scribbling until time was up.

But, and this was the Luck part, instead of the usual dimwitted basketball coach filling a seat with his ass and checking off numbers, he got a guy who actually *read* his answer, and was fascinated by it too. So this guy took Einstein under his wing, coached him through another exam, noodging every time the bushy-haired boy got too distracted, and the second time around, the whizkid passed. The rest is history. Or mythology, which is often just as good as the truth.

Colleges have changed since then. Geniuses aren't discovered like that any more. Now, if you want a Nobel prize for discovering a cure for herpes, you gotta start out young, grind your way through the expensive and bureaucratic monolith the American educational system has become, be savvy and disillusioned and conservative enough to survive internal politics, cynically drudge your way through ho-hum laboratory work, and *maybe* at the end of it you'll be left alone enough to let your Genius come out and play once in a while.

I didn't have the time nor the patience for that kind of bullshit any more. I really didn't think it too likely I was going to dream up a cure for cancer or AIDS or broken hearts, for that matter, anyway. Nope, forget sciences.

Well, most of Genius is Art, right? It's just a matter of which Art.

So there I was down in New York, figuring that this was supposed to be the navel of the Art world, checking out the scene, man, looking for, like, y'know, a happening. The New York art scene gets pretty depressing after a while, and, at the end of one hard day of dragging my ass around half-heartedly looking for inspiration, I wanted a drink.

Ended up in this weird joint near the Village, watching spiked-haired kids wearing a hell of a lot of black cowskin and incredibly tasteless jewellery jiggle and wriggle to music. Up on a tiny platform in a corner, behind a plexiglass window, was a tall, thin kid with a stringy ponytail and bloodshot eyes doing a bump and grind with himself while clutching a set of headphones to one ear and fiddling with a stack of records two feet high.

The music wasn't what Emilie and I had wriggled and jiggled to at her sorority dances, but I rather liked it. It had a strong, hypnotic beat. Actually, that's about all it had, but occasionally one or two of the tunes would jump out and scream Talent. Hot damn, I thought. I found it. I'd be a Genius musician!

I can laugh about it now. Barely. I'd never studied music other than the three years of junior high school trombone my mother forced on me, and my Sunday school choir leader had made it gently clear that I had a voice like a castrated walrus. But I figured, hell, that didn't seem to be stopping a lot of the acts I began watching and listening to for almost a year. The thin kid behind the plexiglass at first found it annoying, and later amusing, that this slightly over-forty pin-stripe wanted to learn the Biz.

I learned to deejay house music at a couple of minor clubs he bullshat into accepting me as his "apprentice". I learned how to count the beats and sync the tunes flawlessly, and designed a couple of sets myself that I was even rather proud of. I learned the difference between disco (old hack shit, man) and punk rock (adolescent kitsch to shock your mommie with), and heavy metal (the good, the bad and the totally synthetic). Within a couple of months, I could rattle off the pros and cons of every group making the charts and a lot more who weren't.

This aberrant behaviour, of course, did not go unnoticed by my erstwhile country club and tennis partners. While they were too genteel and well bred to actually come right out and tell me I was out of my fucking goddamned mind, I raised a few eyebrows and heard a few faint sniffs from wrinkled noses. My wardrobe (ever see Punk Puke Pink Pinstripe?), my pierced ear and my beribboned ponytail (short, but getting there) were less than enthusiastically received, and I countered the kindly mutterings that Emilie's death must really have sent me over the edge with the same sad smile and offhand shrug that kept my business partners at a respectful yet prosperous distance.

And, I began to have my doubts about it all, too. After all, I'd just spent the better part of a year soaking up everything I could about the latest music trends and taking lessons fiddling around with a guitar or a set of drums and even (give me a break, I was trying for something *original*) an accordion, but my latent music Genius had yet to reveal itself. My punk music teachers were giving me exactly the same sort of raised eyebrows and wrinkled noses that my former confreres had, with the exception that they *did* come right out and tell me I was out of my fucking goddamned mind, man.

I was soloing as the weekend jockey at Harry Mammoth's on the side of the street where the elegant funk Village turns into the grungy punk Lower East Side, and doing a particularly uninspired set. My mind kept drifting alarmingly back to the last venture proposed at a stockholders' meeting while, on the other side of the dance floor, the live band was setting up their equipment on the grimy pile of cobbled-together packing crates that served as a stage. The band unfurled their banner with their name, looked around for somewhere to hang it and finally draped it over the ears, tusks and nose of Harry's trademark plastic mammoth head.

NORMA GENE AND THE REFORMED SLEAZEHOUNDS, it said, printed in runny red letters with the usual obscene decorations added around the borders. The mammoth's blinking red eyes backlit the sign nicely, I thought. I dubiously sized up the three long-haired, sullen and slightly fey looking men. Their lead singer was a nearly skeletal woman with pasty white skin and green hair. I yawned, and drifted the music into Yuzed Kondom's "Standing Erect in the Shower", and watched the dance floor undulations through half-open eyes. The tune came to a gratifyingly thunderous close, ending my set for at least the next twenty minutes, and I started sorting through the records as the band struck up to play. The girl had her head bent over the microphone as she waited for her cue. She opened her mouth and Luck fell out.

The guys, well, they were decent musicians, still are. But *her*! The chick had a voice that could rip the boxers off your hide without taking your pants off first. Rich, deep, throbbing, all the usual adjectives don't even come close to how this wan, skinny girl could sing. She sang like she had a combined case of stage fright and palsy, head thrown back, eyes squeezed shut, bony hips jerking the rest of her attached body around in spasms. The sound electrified me straight to my chair, and I knew ten seconds into her music that this kid was 24-carat gold star material.

The brain dead wrigglers on the floor couldn't tell the difference between me scratching records back and forth and the phenomenon belting it out on that rickety stage, and they didn't care. All they wanted was to pop more XTC and dance. But I could barely keep my attention on getting through the night. I raced out the back door after the band without bothering to turn off my equipment just as they were packing up the last of their second-hand instruments into a banged-up minivan.

I grabbed her by the elbow, and she twisted around so fast and hard I'm sure she thought I was going to hit her. All I could see in that pale face were frightened wide eyes and an open mouth as I babbled as quickly as I could.

"I'd like to see you, talk to you, do you think we could go someplace, getta cuppa coffee . . . ?"

The fear in her eyes was replaced by suspicion. She thought I was trying to climb into her skinny pants. "You're that deejay . . . Dr Pinstripe, aren't you?" One of the sullen boys came up behind her, brushing a thick tangle of dyed black hair out of his eyes so he could glare at me warningly. Boyfriend, no doubt. I treated them all to an outrageously expensive late night dinner at an exclusive restaurant near Central Park West. They got a kick out of walking through the forest of grey suits and designer evening gowns in their chrome studded leather outfits and cheap junk trinkets. It also helped me get my point across as they watched the miracle of my business card transform the sneer of the maitre d' into one of baffled if cautious respect.

The rest you obviously know. I managed that pathetic little group jamming for free in no-name clubs into one of the top ten rock megabands in the civilized world. I had the right group. All I did was make sure they played the right clubs before the right people at the right time — my speciality. Even the friends I had before Emilie's death now winked and slapped my back instead of giving me polite cold smiles, as if they'd known all along that this had been my real goal, making another name and another fortune for myself, if somewhat unconventionally.

Except it wasn't. I hadn't found my Genius. I'd found Norma Gene's. Norma Gene was (is) a Genius, a true Genius when it comes to writing and singing the hits. She doesn't know jack about business, and doesn't have the sense to care. It didn't take Genius to propel her and her little band to stardom. It just took me.

Did it bother me that I wasn't on the stage with them? Yeah, sort of. I mean, if Mick Jagger, Phil Collins, Madonna or Norma Gene walks into a restaurant, every eyeball in the place will swivel instantly in their direction. Put any of the managers of Mick Jagger, Phil Collins or Madonna, or me, into that same room and not an eyebrow will rise a mere centimetre. It wasn't that I wanted to be famous, actually. I just wanted to be a Genius and this weren't it.

After their third runaway platinum album, the Sleazehounds started their World Tour. Without me. Norma Gene kicked and screamed her now imperial way into my corporate headquarters office (I'd dropped the "Dr" and gone back to plain old pinstripes by then). She slammed the door theatrically and burst into tears.

"You can't fuckin' do this! You *gotta* go on this fuckin' tour, you're our fuckin' *manager*, man!" She started slapping her thin palm against the top of my eighteenth-century English Regent inlaid desk, making dents in its impeccable finish with her death-skull rings. "You're part of this fuckin' band, too, you lousy prick! You can't fuckin' bail out on us now. Whatta we gonna fuckin' do without you?"

"Just what you've been doing, Norma. Fuckin' rock and roll." I sounded pompously wise and old even to myself. She squinted at me, wiped a wet bubble of snot against the back of her hand and threw herself into the brocaded wingchair near the desk to sulk.

I gave her some bullshit rap about her being the command module at the tip of a rocket, and me being a booster unit. I'd carried the band as far as I could, which is what they needed at the time. Now, while I would fall back gracefully to earth, she and the boys would go where I never could, out on that stage, up to the stars.

"Besides," I pointed out, "my company will still handle all the business details, and I'll still get 30% of all your royalties on all the songs you write and record until the day we both drop dead. Trust me, I have your best interests to protect."

She tried a last attempt to dissuade me, one I took advantage of. I've already told you I'm still an asshole, so go ahead and sneer self-righteously if you want, but I got laid by *Norma Gene*, and you didn't. Not only that, we're still friends.

OK, so that's the story of how I *didn't* find my Genius in the world of music. I'd gotten discouraged and pretty much given up on finding my

Genius after that. I kept the earring and the ponytail but went back to my nice, comfortable old life. Once in a while, when I couldn't stand the boredom any more, I'd go look up my weirder friends in the clubs, even sit in on a set as Dr Pinstripe for old times' sake.

That's how I met Sarah. I won't tell you Sarah's last name 'til later, but I think you can see this one coming already. I'd gone down to watch my old mentor DeeJay (whose name really *was* Delwyn Jerzinsky) premiere his music magic in a better than usual club in SoHo. After the club closed, he took me over to Gear Strippers on West 18th to meet some friends of his. His friends turned out to be Sarah and DeeJay's latest squeeze, Melissa or Melinda, something like that.

We sat as far removed from the speakers as possible, and still had to shout to be heard, while up on stage beefy thighed Hell's Angel mommas stripped slowly down to their black leather and chrome studded G-strings and pierced nipples. Melissa/Melinda, DeeJay explained to me as he sat in a booth with his arm draped around her shoulders futilely searching for enough of one anorexic tit to squeeze, was a comic book artist, while Sarah was a serious artist. To him, it meant that Melissa/Melinda's art was Avant-Garde, a Socially Relevant Phenomenon, while Sarah was hopelessly encumbered with the petit bourgeois affliction of an education. Melissa/Melinda explained at some length that nobody who was seriously into the field called it "comic books" any more, the term was now "Graphic Novels", capital letters. She even knew the French term, *bandes dessineés*, although her pronunciation was hilarious. Sarah didn't say much of anything.

OK, fine. This obviously was an excruciatingly embarrassing but well-meaning attempt at a blind date. I looked at a couple of sketches Melissa/Melinda had brought along, and had to admit that "comics" certainly had changed since I was a bubblegum snapping adolescent reading *Terry and the Pirates* and *Uncle Scrooge*. She seemed to have a pathological fixation on extreme sexual violence and carnage that was mildly titillating, but eventually tediously dull. Sarah eyed them with equally polite attention.

"So," I managed to mumble out, "what kind of stuff do *you* do?"

Sarah smiled weakly. "Why don't you come up and see my etchings sometime?" It was an awful line. She went back to studiously stirring the whipped cream into her Irish Coffee. DeeJay looked back and forth at the two of us, shrugged with a shit-eating grin, and paid the bill like a gentleman.

I didn't see Sarah again for months.

But it got me to wondering about my Genius again. Maybe I was an artist, deep down inside, and my longing for Geniushood was the repressed feelings I had from not splattering paint onto a stretched chunk of cloth. After all, if badly drawn black-and-white ink sketches of men flayed alive with their eyeballs hanging out of their skulls and women's heads exploding as their impaled guts spill across their hands are an Avante-Garde Socially Relevant Phenomenon, then I might as well take a shot at it myself.

It was much easier getting ready for being an Artist than actually being one. I had all the furniture removed from the second largest room in my house, the largest having windows facing east rather than north — the ideal direction for lighting conditions, or so I've heard. Then I bought a brand-new massive easel weighing about as much as my Porsche, four dozen tubes of top-quality oil paint, twenty sizes of paintbrushes, assorted cans of thinner, turpentine, linseed oil and varnishes, and bought an entire wholesaler's supply of pre-stretched canvases, 200 of them to be exact, in various sizes.

I tore down the curtains from the bay windows for maximum natural northern light, put on my old sneakers, a ripped pair of jeans and a white smock I presumed looked like something Van Gogh might have worn, and waited for Inspiration.

Ever see a four foot by six foot absolutely blank white canvas? It's one of the most terrifying sights in the world. I sat there and stared at it for at least five hours, trying to imagine what in the fuck I was going to do with it, making doodles in the neatly laid out (and colour-coordinated) blobs of paint on my solid walnut pallet. Once in a while, I'd smear a finger of paint on my white smock to make it more Artist-like. Then I put everything away, took a bottle of Glenfiddich down to my private lake, and got stinking drunk.

My glorious Artist's alcove went neglected for months as I checked out art galleries, museums and libraries for books on art. I created my own crash course in art history and styles, searching for something that would inspire me.

Modern art, I knew, was an absolute must. It just didn't pay to paint like da Vinci or Raphael or David any more, even if I could. Impressionism appealed to me, but the critics seemed to think Impressionist painters were all quite dead, for some reason. Modern art was definitely *the* art of the very late 20th century.

What exactly "modern art" is I never quite determined. Some things I liked. Other stuff I loathed. But what it *is?* I tried, believe me, I really tried to figure that one out.

I started going to seminars, which left me more than a little cynical and disgusted. At one of these intellectually stimulating debates, I listened to a pair of so-called artists argue about the merits of their work. One created pictures by shooting live cockroaches he'd smeared with primary shades of paint out of a high-powered airgun, splattering them onto a canvas. For some unexplained reason, he found it necessary to import a species of large, fat cockroach from the Philippines rather than make do with the common roach infesting New York. The other did something he called "negative sculpture", which involved digging holes in various things, like buildings or the ground out in the middle of a desert, and then selling the immovable empty space as "art".

After insulting each other, they heatedly debated the work of another so-called artist in Paris who carefully preserved her new-born baby's first dozen used diapers in acrylic for them to be displayed in a prestigious gallery. (The argument wasn't about whether or not this was "art", but whether she should have sealed them in plastic or left them "au naturel".) Between the two of them, the random smears and blobs being touted in far too many Manhattan art galleries seemed venerably conservative.

It was at one of these random sojourns into the SoHo galleries that I met Sarah again. I'd dressed up in my best designer tux, tied my ponytail (much longer with a sexy curl to it now) with a matching silk ribbon, and mingled with the movers and shakers of the art world at yet another gala opening show. In one hand I held a plastic cup of too-sweet California champagne while balancing my Art Deco plastic plate of cheese cubes (plastic Monterey jack and cheddar with brightly coloured toothpicks sticking out for handles) in the other hand. Of course, there's never any place to set a glass down, which makes it impossible to eat the damned cheese cubes even if you wanted to.

I was standing in front of the artist's huge centrepiece, entitled *Sunset Over Alcatraz Reflecting on the Surface of a Rotting Persimmon, or How I Learned to Eat My Mother*. Like the title of the work, the painting was not only pretentious and incomprehensible but boring as well. I was considering dumping the cheese cubes into the nearest garbage can and going home to burn everything in my second largest room to ashes when Sarah walked up beside me and smiled.

"Well?" she said, nodding toward the painting, "what do you think of it?"

It dawned on me (bright boy that I am) that I'd completely forgotten her name, and, now that you mention it, I hadn't a clue as to the name of the artist I was being asked to pass judgement on. With a horrible sinking sensation, I realized this must be *her* art!

"It's . . . interesting," I burbled. "A fascinating use of texture and colour, actually. I see it as a kind of synthesis between Organic Abstract and Formal Irrationalist, with overtones of maybe Paul Klee combined with a Kandinsky-ish influence . . . " I rattled on this way for maybe a minute or two before my brain stuttered dry. I ended up staring dumbly into her solemn expression, clutching my plastic glass of champagne like a second-hand talisman to ward off disaster.

Her face trembled for a moment, then she grinned, unable to repress it another moment, so it seemed. "That was the best line of complete bullshit I've heard in a long time," she said, laughter in her voice, "and this is *not* my work."

At that very moment, Luck jostled my elbow, sending a cascade of too-sweet California champagne down the front of my tuxedo.

"Ah, shit," Luck said, and proceeded to brush ineffectively at the darkening stain with large, fat fingers, knocking my plate of cheese cubes over and smearing cheese-coloured streaks on top of the champagne spill. "Ah, bloody hell, hey, 'scuze me, ah, shit," Luck continued to mutter while batting drunkenly at the mess on my tux.

I happened to notice the expression on Sarah's face in time. It's a peculiar look I've often seen before, a sort of blank watchfulness that says: *Were this any other drunken asshole, I'd look disgusted.* So, instead of getting pissed off, grasping this fumbling idiot's wrists and shoving him away to keep him from doing any more damage, I chuckled as if having Number Two Yellow dye from the plastic Monterey jack massaged into a nine hundred dollar custom-tailored Ralph Lauren was mildly amusing. "No problem," I said. "Dry-cleaners do miracles these days. You *will*, of course, pick up the bill?"

Sarah's eyes went very slightly wide at that, then slightly wider as the man apologetically pulled out his business card.

"Hey, sure, of course! Shit, man, I'm real sorry . . . "

Luck's name was Aldo van Derayne-Dorrego. You know, as in Pascal Dorrego? The Impressionist painter of the late 19th century? His *Woman in Pearls* just sold at Sothebys for a hefty three point seven million bucks. Old Pascal was married to one lady, but had a scandalously juicy affair with young Mary Dominique van Derayne, another talented but not-quite-as-famous painter of the day, while they were hanging around Paris with all the other Impressionist artists fated to die penniless and leave behind a great deal of rapidly appreciating artwork. Pascal and Mary left behind not only a wealth of art but a son, Pietr van Derayne-Dorrego, Aldo's daddy.

Pietr had built a fairly decent career of his own as a post-Fauvist Abstract painter right before the Nazis overran France. He had just married a widowed Jewish comtessa who happened to be also a grandniece of the composer Moussorgski, and an accomplished concert pianist herself. Just before Paris fell, he and his wife sewed up their money and family jewels in her underwear and fled to America. There aren't all that many paintings left by Pietr Dorrego because he had to leave the bulk of them behind (where they disappeared never to resurface after the Germans looted Paris and the Russians looted Berlin). Once in New York, however, Pietr cashed in a few of the family jewels to set up his wife with her own art gallery while he painted the pictures for her to sell in it. She also sold a good many other artists' works as well, and when Pietr died he left behind a very rich widow and two very, very rich sons.

One son became a famous modern artist. The other ran the art gallery. Guess which one.

This history I eventually got from Aldo, who wasn't narrating it at the time with any degree of pride or boasting. He was, in fact, quite miserable about it all. By then, my tux had been more or less cleaned, Aldo had become more or less my friend, and I was seeing Sarah on a more or less regular basis. I still wasn't painting yet. Instead, I was sitting out in the formal garden of my house, drinking Scotch and getting plastered with Sarah and Aldo as he related his tale of woe.

His brother, the talented and famous modern artist, is also a talented and famous mental patient in one of the most exclusive and prestigious loony bins in Upper State New York. Whenever he's not bouncing off the padded walls in a straitjacket or loaded to the gills on Lithium and Thorazine cocktails, he's churning out paintings like crazy. (Sorry.)

Aldo, on the other hand, while in full possession of all of his marbles, inherited none of his brother's talent. This would have been bad enough, but, while missing out completely on the Talent genes floating around in the family stew, Aldo got all of their Luck genes. Which means that, though Aldo can't draw a straight line with a ruler, he can spot true art within seconds. He has become not only the owner of one of the most sheeky-sheeky art galleries in New York but a formidable art critic as well. If Aldo sez it's art, it's *Art*.

But, sitting in the warm spring sunshine listening to Aldo piss and moan about his talented and famous crazy brother and Sarah commiserating with tales of struggling in the New York art biz, I finally got Inspired. After they had wobbled off in different directions, I opened the door to my second largest room, blew the dust off that four foot by six foot canvas and glared at it.

"You're *mine*, muthafucka," I said to myself in my best Stallone voice, and went to it.

See, while Aldo and Sarah were weeping on each other's shoulders, I'd been ruminating about the summer house Emilie and I built for our fifth anniversary. We'd spent literally hundreds of hours sketching out the design of the house, supervising the blueprints, poring over various elevations and sections and dimensional drawings. We had more fun and more fights, Emilie and I, over that summer house . . . But we both learned a great deal about architecture.

So I sketched out a blueprint outline of our dearly beloved summer house (I sold it a month after Emilie died) in charcoal. Then I painted in wavery lines and blotches of primary colours and squiggles until, unless you knew what you were really looking at, you couldn't tell what the fuck it was supposed to be. I called it *Summer with Emilie*. I rather liked it.

Then I did it again with another blueprint idea. And again. And again. Some of the paintings were very elaborate. Some of them used soft pastel tints instead of primary colours. Once I pasted newsprint and magazine photos in as a collage. When I had painted fifty of them, I stopped.

Neither Sarah nor Aldo had any idea that I was an Aspiring Artist. While waiting for Inspiration, I had figured it was better to keep my mouth shut in case it never showed up and I ended up looking like a jerk. So I kept putting off seeing Sarah and neglected to call Aldo for the two months I painted like a fiend. But the night I'd finished *Nocturne No. 17* I called Aldo before I'd even cleaned the brushes.

"Long time no see, love to, can't come tonight, sorry," he said in a tone of voice that says someone else is listening. "How 'bout tomorrow?"

OK, tomorrow. We made the appointment, and when he arrived I had all fifty of my canvases propped up against the walls for his inspection. You wouldn't believe how proud I was of those paintings. I really thought I'd found my true creative spirit at long last.

Aldo, bless his alcoholic heart, stopped dead in his tracks as he walked into my house and stared at the pictures without a word. I trailed after him like an anxious schoolkid as he silently walked along, looking over each painting carefully, lips pursed, hands clasped behind his broad back. He stopped in front of my debut masterpiece, *Summer with Emilie* and gazed at it for a long time, then glanced at me from the corners of his eyes.

"Well? What do you think, Aldo?"

If Aldo sez it's art, it's Art.

"It's crap," he said quietly. "Interesting, cleverly done crap, but still" — he shrugged apologetically — "crap."

I had a rush of feelings then. Anger, hurt, disappointment, to be sure. But also something very much like relief, as if deep inside I knew I'd been kidding myself. I stood there in the afternoon maximum northern light exposure filtering through the window and listened to Aldo, barely paying attention.

"Look, it's not bad, for what it is," he was saying. "You got a sense of composition and colour, and a couple of these are extremely well done. Y'know, I'll even put you on an exhibition if you want, a small one, mind you, just to give you a little publicity. I can set you up with a couple of guys I know just starting their own gallery. I'm writing a critical piece for the *Times* where I could say just what I'm saying now, it's crap, and there'd still be people buying it up at good prices. Everyone wants to prove Aldo wrong, don't I know it, and you'd end up being a hot fad and have a short-term run of luck."

He sighed, then wriggled his nose, sniffing the air like a rabbit with a cocaine habit. He sighed again. Poor, noble, honest Aldo.

"But in the long run it won't hold up," he finished sadly.

"Why not?" I mumbled, not really caring much.

"Because, while you've got a sense of style in these paintings, they have no real life, no soul, no heart." He smiled remorsefully. "No Genius."

He estimated that, with the right promotion and a little hype, I could make maybe a quarter mill with what I had, and if I could pump out another couple of hundred in a year I could make a small fortune before my value as a trend faded.

See? There it is again. Luck. I knew the right people in the right places at the right time, and could turn my little attempt at art into a tidy profit.

This time, though, I turned Luck down.

"Thanks, Aldo. I really do appreciate your giving me a candid evaluation. Wanna get stinking drunk with me?"

A couple of hours later, down by the lake and swimming in the second bottle of Jack Daniels, I learned that my Luck had gone both ways. See, Aldo couldn't make it the night before because he'd been busy with Sarah. Sarah, as it turned out, was a Real Artist, and Aldo was putting together her first exhibition in his gallery. In his enthusiastic Genius opinion, which I doubted not in the least, Sarah was an Up and Coming, destined to Greatness.

Plus, Aldo was in love. Don't get me wrong, he didn't confess it at the time. Aldo is a drunk, but he's also a very refined gentleman. He knew Sarah and I were a semi-item, that I was still boffing Sarah on a more or less regular basis, and he would never have dreamt of poaching on another man's territory.

But, as we lay on the boatdock getting genteelly snockered, he talked about how lucky it was for him to have spilled my drink all over my tux. If he hadn't, he wouldn't have met me and, through me, Sarah. He enthused over Sarah's talent, her work, her Genius, and it became painfully obvious that Aldo was as much in love with the woman as he was with her art.

I went to Sarah's opening. Aldo was right. Her paintings were wonderful, full of motion and light, evocative and emotionally moving. Abstract forms and shapes that hinted at the spirit moving underneath. Rhythmical lines and colours vibrating with passion. I, like Aldo, could see what I couldn't do. Sarah was (is) a Genius.

"Well?" she said, teasingly, "what do you think of it?"

"It's beautiful." I said. I looked at her, seeing her sparkling eyes, a young Up and Coming face shining with pride and happiness. "You're beautiful."

She glanced at Aldo hovering over her like a nervous father, and I realized that *she* was in love with *Aldo*. Being a beautiful, lovely and honourable woman, she wouldn't have even admitted it to herself, never mind me. I wasn't in love with Sarah, but I felt a sort of loss and relief, the same feeling as when Aldo pronounced my paintings the crap they really were.

I took her home with me after the opening.

Yeah, I know you still think I'm an asshole, but this time you're wrong. I'd kept *Summer with Emilie*, had it nicely framed and hung over the great stone fireplace in my library. The rest I had taken out behind the garage and had a barbecue with. Burning my paintings was somehow in keeping with the meloromantic image of myself as the Great Failed Artist. But I still had all this goddamned equipment left over which I hadn't known what to do with.

I did now.

I gave everything in my second largest room to Sarah — the giant easel, the paints, the brushes, the hundred and fifty blank canvases, everything. Then I gave her a cheque to cover the lease on her atelier in SoHo for a year, which she reluctantly accepted only after I explained I needed the tax write-off, better she got it than the IRS.

We sat in the library and toasted *Summer with Emilie* with a bottle of excellent French champagne, not the saccharine shit the art galleries pour. When she turned and put her arms around my neck, expecting she now had to be grateful in return for my patronage, I kissed her very gently and sent her home. Unscathed.

In my bedroom I have a beautiful abstract painting, a gift. In one corner you can make out the artist's small, neat signature: "S.T. Vignola." But you'd already guessed who it was, hadn't you?

And that is the story of how I didn't find my Genius in Painting, either. Wanna hear the story of how I didn't find my Genius in Theatre? Getting too repetitious for you? OK, the *Reader's Digest* version is I was a lousy actor, but ended up co-producing a small off-Broadway play by an unknown starving playwright which turned into a smash Broadway hit, later a Major Motion Picture Multiple Oscar Award Winner, and I got to boff the leading actress who went from being a total nobody to megastardom making six million bucks a pop for even the smallest of cameo roles in Hollywood.

Only difference this time is that, unlike with Norma and Sarah, we ended up loathing the sight of each other. But the actress, despite her vile temper and unstable personality, was (is) a true Genius. The playwright was (is) a real Genius and is still my friend. Maybe I should have boffed him instead. He certainly was willing enough.

I was still rich, still lucky, and still looking for my Genius. By now, it was pretty obvious to me that I was running out of Arts to find it in as well. I loitered around Hollywood for a year or so, having sublet my East Coast house to a Polish émigré writer who I had no doubt was in the process of writing a bestselling novel guaranteed to win the Pulitzer if not the Nobel, and who was the end result of my not finding my Genius as a novelist, either.

As I was drifting around, one of my former actress lover's sister's friends took me up the coast for a New Age seminar at Eselan, where genuine Geniuses and wannabe geniuses communed. Richard Feynman was lecturing that day, baggy shorts and bare feet. I sat crosslegged in the back, sneering slightly at the wannabes as he patiently explained why Star Trek-ish transcorporeal transmission was as unlikely as antigravity devices. Then I caught the wannabes sneering back at me, which made me uncomfortably aware I likewise was just another wannabe.

I did get to schmooze with Feynman. Only once . . . at a topless bar he frequented with a few friends. He liked to sketch the girls. We all laughed and joked and talked casually about any old thing, like any other group of overaged teenagers out drinking beer and ogling girls. None of them seemed much like Geniuses.

Until I picked up the beer coaster he'd been doodling on the back of and found four and a half lines of cryptic physics notations jotted across the delicate line drawing of a barebreasted dancer. I pocketed it, spending countless hours afterwards either wondering about a mind where a beautiful woman could be equally transposed against the invisible world of physics or despairingly trying to figure out what the hell those four and a half lines *meant*.

They were the reason I was there, in the library with a splitting headache from trudging through yet another musty bound set of science extracts, still trying to decipher those four and a half lines, when I met The Bum. I'd flirted a bit with the librarian, a sure way to induce a willing native guide into the dark and scary depths of paper jungle, and had just popped another Anacin to ward off another of those mojo voodoo curses when she sidled up and whispered in my ear.

Might I do her a favour and do something about that gentleman over in the corner? He was disturbing the other readers, mumbling to himself and, well, he *smelled bad* . . .

Sure. Any legitimate excuse to get out of trying to figure out ultraviolet radiation shifts of gamma-ray pulsars emitting high-density neutron stars spinning cosmic quasar photons and rapidly spiralling and expanding at mindboggling quantum speed through the limits of the universe and my poor aching skull. Something like that.

He was about my age, but looked twice that. One of the hundreds of thousands of homeless, he wore the uniform tattered grey coat in the California heat wave, unravelled knit cap pressed over filthy hair, fingerless gloves over black-nailed grimy hands. He did smell rank, and when I approached, smiling my best social worker smile, he glared up, never faltering in his mumbled soliloquy. Under his greasy palms he held the pages of a book open, pressing it to the table as if it might make the attempt to escape from his rancid grasp.

What if that unknown test examiner hadn't taken the time or interest in young Einstein? What if Fleming had cursed his lousy housekeeping and thrown out that contaminated petri dish? What if Newton had been sitting under a fig tree instead? What if the guy who dreamed of snakes had had insomnia, or that other genius had decided it was a nice day for a walk instead of taking the bus?

What if I had not heard the song of Lady Luck muttered in the harsh melodies of mania, cloaked under the security blanket of anti-social behaviour?

"God damn you," I snapped at The Bum, sitting back and glaring at him. Once again, I'd discovered what I couldn't have in the most unlikely of places. He glared back.

"What the hell do *you* want?" he snarled.

"What you have."

He eyed me up and down, a sneer tugging up one side of his upper lip. "No shit? And what's that?"

"You have Genius."

The Bum's smile widened knowingly and he chuckled, not a pleasant sound. "And *you* have Luck. Big fuckin' deal. Wanna trade?"

At that moment, and I swear it's true, heaven and earth stood still, the infinite cosmos held its collective breath, and all the angels gazed down with bated breath.

"Yes." I barely got it out in a whisper, my heart beating so fast I thought I'd be sick.

He shrugged and thrust out one grimy hand, broken nails long and filthy. "OK. Done." We shook hands, the bargain was sealed. Call it what you will; a fortuitous slip in the fabric of time and space, a metaphysical alchemy of divine transcendence, a moment when cosmic serendipity-doo-dah was in the mood for a practical joke. I *felt* Luck vacate the premises with a sudden ripping in my soul leaving me totally naked for a horrible, terrifying instant, only to have that empty space in my psychic being filled with what I knew — *knew* — to be Genius. I even understood how it had been done, and the sheer simplicity of it left me gaping in awe-struck silence, as if a billion mikes of LSD had suddenly crashlanded in my brain.

Ah-hah, I can hear you snort with disgusted satisfaction. The Bum no doubt is today living in a Fifth Avenue penthouse flat while I've moved in to share a trashcan with Oscar the Grouch and mumble to myself. Well, that's understandable; I suppose that might make for the sort of cheap thematic denouement you'd expect, our grasp of reality Roto-routered by too many movies with their comfortingly trite clichés and banal morality. But you'd be dead wrong.

For the most part, anyway. The Bum *is* living in a Fifth Avenue penthouse flat. Mine. He had a massive stroke of Luck, meeting me, and I've become a Genius enough to see through the murky obstruction of the vast machinations of nature and the universe straight to the core of the mysteries of life.

Of course, it's always possible I only *think* I do and I'm really just as crazy as he is.

The Bum (whose real name is Irving J. Pinkham, by the way) is still an anti-social, reeking, largely incoherent derelict who can't be trusted out on the street on his own. I've had to hire a full-time private R.N. named Trevor, six foot five of no-nonsense black belt body-builder muscle whose only job is to follow Irving around and make sure Luck doesn't smash him flatter than Alabama roadkill.

Because Lady Luck is an unkind mistress. Poor Irving, having bartered away his Genius, is no longer distracted by the siren song of the Lady's twin sister. He stumbles around blinded by chance, unequipped to deal with the deluge of coincidental riches literally falling into his lap, winning lottery tickets found in the pockets of second-hand jeans, the exact millionth person to cross the doors of the Rolls Royce dealership, the ordinary schmuck standing on the corner waiting to cross the street when the President jogs by with his Secret Service workout crew to ask an impulsive opinion. Irving doesn't have a lifetime of hard work and experience with which to harness his Luck. However, he does have *me*. Luckily.

Oh, as for me? Well. Either I have or I have not Genius. Like Balzac, I'm pretty sure I do, but sometimes I don't have a flipping clue. Luck is more than the twin of Genius, it's the opposite side of the coin. It's nearly im- possible to spend one while keeping the other, I've come to realize. Luck has not totally deserted me, nor has Genius completely abandoned Irving. It's only our *perspectives* which have changed.

My famous "horse sense" and "business acumen", at any rate, are defi- nitely gone. I can no longer see the Big Chances, scent the faint winds of change in the fickle sea air of finance. I've put a whoppingly large part of my capital into frumpy, ultra-cautious trusts and money market ac- counts where I'll continue to draw a reasonable but not extravagant in- come for many years to come. Enough to insure I can indulge my Genius and keep Irving's Luck from killing him.

Hey, I may be a Genius but I'm not *stupid*.

I framed that beer coaster I filched from Feynman and I look at it almost every day. And, yes, I do understand those four and a half lines of cryptic physics notations now. More importantly, I understand his sketch of the dancer, the wonder of beauty and the joy of life synonymous with the invisible world inside the skull.

That world where Art is Science, and Science is Art and all is part of a whole and a hole so large it isn't possible to live long enough, alas, to have fun exploring the whole/hole of where, after all, is the only place Genius can exist. Where the prosaic lives in harmony with the celestial, where balding, sweating men who have trouble getting it up have uncanny leaps of logic as they step onto a smog-belching bus, like the breathtaking flights of ethereal ballerinas whom relentless gravity must always bring back down to earth to deal with their bunions and haemorrhoids.

Where the pseudo-swamis would be appalled to know just how close to the Ultimate they really are when they demand Rolls Royces and major household appliances in return for their garbled visions of The Truth. Where answers to half the mysteries of the universe routinely fall out of the mouths of babes unheard by adults grown too wise to hear them. Where shit truly is shinola, for those with the stomach to look and a self-irony healthy enough to put up with the inevitable adolescent scatological jokes. There, buried in the dung of dinosaurs, are the fossilized secrets of evolution. There, in the tidal turds of a thousand years of bat guano in the sea caves of New Guinea, are to be discovered some of the most mysterious and exotic microtic lifeforms ever known. There, in the tiniest traces of fecal enzymes, lurk secrets enough to catch a master killer, given, to unlock them, the forensics Genius who worries about cholesterol and heartburn and mortgages.

So. Have I discovered the answer to life, cured all mankind's diseases, unravelled the mysteries of peace, prosperity and given the world the blossoming of a New Age of Enlightened Humanity? Snort-snicker, you gotta be joking. Einstein's Genius didn't keep him from being a dunce when it came to marital happiness. Feynman's brains couldn't stop cancer. It only took a Roman thug who didn't understand Greek to slaughter poor old geriatric Archimedes for doodling in the sand. It's an instructive cautionary lesson that, when Mozart was my age, he'd been dead over a decade, wiped out by mindless bacteria. Who suffers for Genius? Not me. I live in a wonderful woodframe house I built myself up in Shasta, with two blissfully stupid mongrel dogs and my current girlfriend, Gilda, who has the bronzed body of a California goddess and a mind like the Library of Congress after a Richter nine earthquake. I *am* writing a book — isn't everybody? — where I try my best to Explain Everything which, with a little Luck and decent promotional budget, might become as much a bestseller as Hawking's *A Brief History of Time*, to be bought by millions and read by hundreds, understood by dozens.

Surrounded by all our equally weird, wild and wonderful friends and neighbours, basking in sunshine and drinking homemade Chardonnay, I sometimes still imagine Balzac sobbing away in the soft ample bosom of Mademoiselle Fame, and wonder if he was really as miserable as he made out to be. I doubt it. It might have been important to maintain that image to satisfy *other* people he was a Genius, but I spend most of my time these days too enchanted by the visions dancing like sugar plum fairies through my head to worry whether or not I'm being persecuted and calumniated enough. I haven't time to Suffer for Genius, I'm too busy enjoying myself.

Because I've had the best possible stroke of Luck; I know the secret of Genius, and it's dead simple, and although I know you won't understand, you *refuse* to understand, I'll share it with you anyway:

There's no toy more fun than your brain. Go inside and play.

Joey Ramone Saves the World
Nick Mamatas

It was a day later, 5am Monday, and you were riding down the Long Island Expressway, half-high from diesel fumes and the rumbling of marbles in the engine of your father's sardine-tight Volkswagen Rabbit. The tinny warble of the traffic reporter collapsed into the happy beat of "I Wanna Be Sedated". The female announcer, a bit too happy to be reading the news, explained: "Punk rocker Joey Ramone is dead." You gasped, the first sound you'd made since shuffling into the car an hour before. It was cold for April.

She went on, her sentences poorly punctuated by AM static and crackle. The Ramones started punk. He was born in 1952. His name was Jeffrey Hyman. Bruce Springsteen was a fan and Joey wrote "Hungry Heart" for him. *No, that's wrong,* you thought. *Springsteen wrote it for Joey, but then kept it for himself.* You grumbled audibly.

"What's wrong?" your father said, half-singing, half-gruff.

"He was the same age as Mom."

"What?"

"Joey Ramone was one of my favourites. He was a singer in a punk band." Then, "Sshhhhh," because you wanted to hear the rest of the obituary, and because talking made you gulp down fumes and want to puke. It was still twenty-five minutes till Jersey City. For a moment you forgot you threw your shrew of a girlfriend out of the house three days before, on Good Friday even, because she wouldn't stop dancing around in her panties while you answered an e-mail, the subject of which you couldn't remember any more anyway. You only remembered Joey, and the fact that he saved your world.

#

Or.

#

Jeff was a tall man. From your perch you were able to keep track of his head, or at least his unkempt rat's nest of black hair, for a long while. He was the last of the comrades standing. You did your best to help, kicking a Beaux-Arts bunch of limestone grapes off a cornice and onto a brace of Blue Shirts, and even whipping it out and pissing on the crowd below, but a Libre trios finally cornered Jeff. One, in red and gold, somersaulted off the corner of a rubbish bin and brought him to the ground, then his spangled and sequined partners ran in, grabbed Jeff's legs, and started twisting and cracking. You could almost hear bone crunch under their boots and truncheons. It sounded like the dog back at the squat chewing on a chicken back. Jeff's blood stained their hands and leotards and even their garish sequined masks. But the revolution would win, you knew. Jeff Hyman saved the world.

#

Or.

#

"Whiskey," you said, holding up a shot glass in your right hand. "Gun," you said, hoisting your pistol. It was Thursday night. Revival night. What else would you be doing? "Whiskey," you said with the rest of the room, praising the Lord. "Gun," you said, your voice resonant and deep like His.

You were proud of that. And then the Dee Dee rose, signalling the next act of the liturgy.

"Gabba gabba hey hey / came from heaven," you chanted, and you were hugged by the woman next to you. She smelled of sweat and baby powder. Somewhat like the President when you hugged her last week. There was nothing to fear. Next Thursday you'd be in China with your whiskey and your gun, getting hugs from your brothers and sisters on the other side of the planet. You were one of them. They were one of you. Like the Holy Quartet. And everyone believed. You're all kids of the kingdom now. Joey Ramone had saved the world.

#

"August, 1974," Douglas said. He yawned, to wind himself up. His fish belly poked out from under his T-shirt. "I was so fucking there! I knew it, even fucking then. I was 18 fucking years old and I pissed myself over a man. Joey was so tall. He was fucking wasted. Fucking wasted." An aside, cleverly rehearsed, to himself: "Man, I am so fucking wasted. I am so fucking wasted. If I repeat myself, you know I am fucking wasted."

He waved his hands about like he wanted to hug CBGBs. "Wasn't like this then. Nineteen fucking seventy-four. Who here was even born then?" Doug demanded. He licked his lips. Three girls were listening to him, or at least looking at his stupid salt-and-pepper sideburns. One of them, Melba, biracial, kohl-eyed and sniffling from the feather boa around her neck, was born then. She was two, even. In Connecticut. Now she was in the club she had read about as a kid. She even owned the T-shirt. Melba knew better than to wear it to the club. She wore her Ramones shirt, but one from the *Animal Boy* era when Richie was in the band. She thought that must make her suck somehow. She was frowning about *something*, anyway. Douglas probably thought so too, but you found a way to forgive her.

"This is fucking shit," Douglas said. "This shit is laminated for your protection. There weren't even any fucking lights on back then. Just Joey, holding onto the mike stand like it was his mother's fucking tit. Holding on for dear life! And singing. 'One-two-three-four!' Douglas pumped his fist in the air and shouted, loud enough to make the barback turn around and roll her eyes, "One-two-three-four!" His arm was meaty — like he lifted — and tattooed. Old school. Green bullshit skulls and thorns.

You knew that was bullshit. You knew not to say anything, because Douglas was "so wasted" as he said yet again. Later you told Melba that it was bullshit, that Douglas wasn't there that day because only one person who didn't work at CBs was there and it was a girl, and because Tommy sang at the first gig. Joey was on drums. You read that in *Creem* last year. Melba rolled her eyes, but kissed you anyway, and groped you up against the scooped-out stucco walls of CBGBs. You wished you were in a band. Then you'd have a sticker or a tape to give her. But the kiss was good, like you hoped it would be. She tasted of Red Stripe and Chiclets. Tomorrow was back to high school for you.

#

The invasion was a slow one. Juan Morais was barely known to the public before his troops were on the border. You watched the Sunday afternoon news shows, you read the *Times*, so you knew it was coming. You didn't know the President would fold, and would throw open the borders to let them in. Jeff did know, though, and told you the first time you met him.

"Oh, please, that's a conspiracy theory," you said. You were in line for gas for dad, a pillowcase full of bills in one hand's sweaty grip, a five-gallon can behind you. Wednesday was diesel day. Jeff was hard to believe. He was sniffing a rag, after all.

"Happens all the time, dude" he said between sniffs. "The economy goes to hell, and fascism seems like a good idea to big business. Morais was elected in Brazil! Fucking elected. The Mexicans just surrendered. This ain't like Double-you Double-you Two. Back then building a Navy could end the Depression. But not with gas costing fifteen thousand bucks a gallon."

Make that seventeen thousand bucks a gallon. The greasy monkey hobbled out and flipped the numbers on the sign over the pumps to a chorus of deep-throated boos. Jeff huffed loudly, like he was sneezing into the fucking rag or something. The gas station attendant backed away from the crowd. He undid his jumpsuit a bit, to show that he was carrying. Everyone shut up then, except for Jeff.

"Somebody once said that, when fascism came to America, it would look like patriotism, but I think people are too pissed off for that. They're going to march over us." Another long huff into the rag, one so hard it felt like it was your face was the one going numb. Heat carried the fumes across the tightly packed queue. "But we can stop 'em."

#

You learned the Prophet's False Dilemma as a child. You knew "whiskey" and "gun" before you even learned that you were one of Us. It was a century before you were born and two after The Ramone had died when Old Douglas was faced with his fatal choice. He was an old man, nearly 80, and living on the Lower East Side, close to what you now knew as the Holy Bee. And Old Douglas woke up every morning for no reason, for he had nothing to do, and turned to his end-table. On it was a shot glass, empty except for a ring of sticky old booze, and a bottle of whiskey. Also, a revolver.

And each day he'd wake up, slowly pull one eyelid free of evening eyescum and think.

Whiskey? he'd think. *Or gun.* Sometimes it took as long as five hours to decide. Usually it was the sun crossing the sky to its noon apex that kept him alive. The rays of the sun would come through the window and hit the bottle at just the spot to make the booze sparkle, to make the centre of the liquid shimmer like syrupy gold.

But Morning One was an overcast day. Old Douglas had that snub-nosed revolver pushed hard against his temple, so hard that he might not have even been interested in the bullet's penetrating his skull. He wanted the barrel to do it. And then Douglas was slain, not in the flesh, but in the spirit. He jerked wildly and was thrown back down upon his mattress. The shot glass wobbled against the tabletop, a little *wuddlawuddla* that became the Call of the Ramone: "Gabba gabba. Gabba gabba."

And then He was there, skin white as bone, hair black as night, voice deeper than the oceans, eyes flat and grey like slate. And He spoke to Old Douglas — now the Prophet — and the Prophet transcribed the Word of

Joey on some conveniently located cocktail napkins. He gathered about Him a trio of followers to play guitar, bass and drums, instruments not played live since the Intellectual Property and Creativity Protection Act of 2030, which had banned live instrumentation lest some wayward strumming unwittingly plagiarized an existing chord progression. The True Prophets took to the streets and to the clubs, gathered about them a devoted cult of fans and co-religionists and were eventually gunned down on the streets.

But a century later the God of Abraham was dead and you and he and that guy over there and ol' whatsername were all One Of Us. The nation-state had collapsed in a spasm of three-chord brotherhood. The aesthetics of Ramonism were full of options thumping backbeat upon which nearly anything could be built without rancour, censorship, or vicious iconoclasm. After the final gabba hey of the evening, the gun was flushed down the ritual toilet and the whiskey flowed like sweat in a mosh pit. Some boy was licking it off your belly when you fell to the ground and began speaking in tongues.

#

College was easier than high school. All you had to do was wear the shirt, the one you stole from your uncle. The one that still smelled like pot a hundred washings after you'd stolen it from the drawer of stuff he couldn't wear since getting his job at the insurance company. The Ramones, from the ancient All the Way tour, 1981. Marky on the drums, and his name joining the others around the white-eagle seal, and the rest of the shirt was black, thank God. The kids with the white shirts and black seals had obviously been brainwashed by their parents, who equated wearing black with worshipping the Devil. The black shirt was entrée to the tribe.

A nod in a lecture hall. A well practiced, lopsided smile while walking along the quad. A seat at a table in a campus cafeteria. "Hey," you'd say, or he would.

"Hey," you'd say back, and often say nothing else, until someone turned on the radio and played Debbie Gibson or Erasure. Then you'd snort, and the other members of the tribe would smile.

The banner on the wall over your bed helped too. Not Melba but an-

45

other girl, a white one named Jennifer, as they nearly all seemed to be named those days, lingered by the doorway till your roommate invited her in, but she was interested in talking to you, in dicking around with your CDs. She played with your tie-fighter model. You made love that night to most of *End of the Century*, or at least to the last half of "High Risk Insurance". You jabbed her in the eye with your elbow in the middle of "Danny Says", but it was a slow song so you were able to apologize and be generally soothing. You lost your erection during "The Return of Jackie and Judy", and she gagged on your penis for most of "This Ain't Havana". You giggled at that, stupidly and in time with the "Na na / na na na" of the tune. That made her stop and laugh too. But before the CD ended and went on to repeat your back and belly were soaked with sweat, and her nails tickled your sides.

Now that you think back to it, maybe her name was Jessica.

End of the Century is actually a pretty underrated album.

#

You read Jeff's pamphlet one day after morning exercises down at the plant. The photocopy was fresh and smudged your hands with its ink, but you got the gist. Working-class revolution, fight the "Libre" faction at the point of production. Yadda yadda, easier said than done, right? Right. The union was gone, the shop steward fired, pay had been cut again and there was mandatory calisthenics in the parking lot every morning. Management even dusted off the old *Domino's Sugar Employee Songbook*. "An Ode to The Cane (Sugar, That Is)" was just about your least favourite song ever.

But the pamphlet had something interesting to say: "Revolution — Mafia Style." You don't need to convince everyone to join the revolution, just one special person in the right place, at the right time, ready to monkeywrench. Find a few friends. Do something.

You ate lunch out by the water that day, to watch the military patrol boats criss-cross the East River. Usually you couldn't stomach it out there, especially since the projects of the Lower East Side had been turned into concentration camps. The breeze smelt like badly burnt beef all the time now.

"Good thing the bosses still like their sugar, eh?" he said. You knew the voice, deep but melodic. Every sentence was a song. Jeff and a few of the guys from the plant were on the lip of the pier, dangling their feet over the river and eating sandwiches. Jeff was wearing a wetsuit and sitting in a puddle. He must have swum the river for the meeting. You skootched closer. Douglas, a guy whose neck was about as thick as your thigh and three times as veiny, shot you a withering look, but Jeff just smiled.

"That kid's a friend of mine. Let him in. I'll vouch."

"You're the boss," Douglas said.

"No, dude, we're all the boss, or none of us."

That night Douglas hummed and scatted to himself (God, he was annoying) as you helped him spike fifty tons of granulated sugar with some chemical Jeff had come up with. Tomorrow it would all be in little white packets. Only *los ricos* could still afford morning coffee anyway.

#

And, in a flash, it was revealed. A being, monstrous and beautiful. Cosmic jelly, almost, golden and filling the holes in the inky black sky. You couldn't understand the physics of it all, no more than a dot on a piece of paper would be able to figure out, from its 2-D perspective, what the fingers reaching for it might be. God is infinite and indeed in the details, but nowhere else. God is whiskey, constantly pouring over the rocks of the material world.

You could taste It. It was in you suddenly, hammering away at the specks of chemicals and consciousness that kept you hemmed into a mere I. You expanded, engulfing the planet, and rose ever higher and deeper. Finally, you were huge, with your heart and muscles and bones and brain a flat sheet stretched over the curve of spacetime, and the rest of the universe minding its own business inside you. You turned your perception within, because the face of the space beyond that of the twenty-billion-light-year plane you were covering like a military bedsheet was too horrible to bear.

And You looked within, into the bowels of Yourself and saw Earth. Not one, but billions, little more than *E. coli* peppering the membrane of your colon. And then You knew how right You were. All those Earths were one of You. You had saved them all.

#

A 3.0 would have bagged you two months in Europe and all the fancy-ass crap you could fit in a backpack. You got a 2.8. Grandma promised you'd get a plane ticket anyway, but you'd be back in a week and had better start looking for a job the second you landed back at LaGuardia.

"Two point eight. Jesus Christ, what were you goddam doing in school? Go, go on your trip, then come back ready to be a man. Two point five, grandma would have brought you a one-way ticket!"

You picked Brazil. Pop assumed it was for the tits. Grandma wondered why you didn't want Italy, to see your cousins. Brazil it was, though. São Paulo, which was Italian enough anyway. And in Brazil, The Ramones packed stadiums.

You don't remember the flight. You barely even remember sleeping atop your luggage in the hothouse airport terminal while customs agents and swarthy midget cops pulled apart everyone's bags. The water was hot coming out of the tap in your one-room pension. You were directed to a concrete pillbox with a hole on the floor for you to shit and piss in (Grandma spared pretty much every expense) but didn't care. You'd pee on the streets like the kids did, the kids with those telltale black T-shirts and surly faces. The fans were coming to see them, appearing on corners and near bars like late-night crows looking for early corn. Three days.

Finally, you didn't mind the heat. Sweat shook itself off you, thanks to the roar. The roar you felt before you heard, a mile away from the stadium. The locals, mostly dark or at least olive, fell away as you walked up the cobblestoned streets, and your people replaced them. The fans marched towards it, a bowl of light under the blue-black sky. And that hollow joyous roar became distinct.

"Ah ah ah, Ra-mone-es."

"Ah ah ah, Ra-mone-es."

"AH AH AH."

"RAH."

"MON."

"ES."

You sang the old soccer chant too, instantly adopting the three-syllable version of the name like everyone else did. The local kids.

The pasty and potato-faced German tourists. The other Americans. "Ra-mon-es! Ra-mon-es!" You shouted it in the face of the hard case who checked your ticket, and he didn't even blink. He was probably deaf from being so close to ground zero all day. For another hour you heard nothing more than "Ah ah ah! Ra-mone-es!" and occasional cheers for a roadie or a lighting technician or for a beach ball gone wild bouncing across the crowd.

Then ONE-TWO-THREE-FOUR and the world was torn a new asshole by 50,000 people screaming. Joey grasped the mike stand and leaned on it hard. It was the only thing keeping him from being blown off the stage, through the seats and parking lots, and out into the sea. Johnny and Dee Dee squatted like sumo wrestlers and cradled their instruments. "Blitzkrieg Bop" was over before your brain had even figured out that your ears had heard it. ONE-TWO-THREE-FOUR, then a song. "ONE-TWO-THREE- FOUR," Joey would cry, or Dee Dee would, then another song. No ballads. No slow tunes. No bullshit repartee. Joey didn't even say "SÃO PAULO ROCKS!"

Everyone already knew.

It was dawn by the time they were done, or maybe Joey and the boys had just shattered the black lacquered dome of night and the sun was out by default, never to set again.

You didn't even realize that one of the guys you stepped over as you staggered out of the arena was a half-crushed corpse. A street kid, obviously, in a relief-worker-provided T-shirt and mismatched shoes. He had probably died with that gas-soaked hanky over his face. He had to dull the pain of broken bones somehow.

#

Juan Morais didn't so much escape the shantytowns of Brazil as he picked them up on his shoulders and took them with him all the way to the top. He never even officially joined the Brazilian army; instead he just killed a soldier and took his place. He knew enough about the local drug lords and Communists to make it worth his commander's while to keep him around. He crawled his way up the chain of command on a ladder of corpses.

49

The coup was easy enough, when the time came. He spoke to the people in the language of the streets, in the terms of Mexican *lucha libre* and Portuguese soap operas. There was good and evil in the world, and by God and Virgin he was going to stop evil in the name of good. He wasn't complacent to fan himself in the presidential palace either. Morais did a road tour, filling up stadiums and arenas, sometimes at gunpoint, but often just through force of personality. Brazil was his. He even rearranged regional borders in an attempt to capture his profile in maps.

When Morais moved north, it didn't take a single bullet to march across Central America. Venezuela had turned off the oil spigot at his request and the Middle East had been turned into a glass parking lot a few years previously, so the US was weak and pink, like a fat baby. Morais wanted in. A few hawks in the Air Force wanted to bomb him back to the shit from which he had emerged, but he had already made himself at home in L.A. thanks to arriving with bayonets and bread trucks.

In the end, America wasn't ready to bomb its own West Coast into the Pacific when Morais was just better than they were at what had to be done. No more dissent, no more waste, just discipline and work, with occasional bread and circuses. That's how you ended up at a sugar-processing plant in Brooklyn instead of a cushy office job in midtown. You were drafted. You slept in an abandoned row house nearby.

It was the secret police that got to you. They dressed flamboyantly in spandex, external underwear, and sequined capes, like Mexican wrestlers, and took to the streets in groups of three. Most of them were American, but they all spoke Spanish or Portuguese, just to humiliate the people they were about to beat or kill with incomprehensible demands. It was the masks irked you, worse than the guns. You never even found out how many of Los Trios you killed when you spiked the sugar, or how many died when Lenny directed a charter flight off the runway and into the river. Anyone could be behind the masks. Well, anyone but Jeff, who was too thin and skeletal to ever be obscured by a wrestling getup. That's part of why everyone in the cell trusted him. Mostly it was his charisma, though.

Charisma nearly as strong as Morais's own.

And Jeff's Revolution — Mafia Style meant that he had to sway fewer people. Some bus drivers stalled out on the bridges and tunnels. One or two old school cops looted armouries. It took fewer than a dozen Con Ed workers to shut off the power, but selectively, so the hospitals could keep working. Jeff himself went down to West 18th Street and Twelfth Avenue, in the basement of the old switcher building, and took an axe to the fibre optics.

The street battles were blitzkrieg attacks. Get in, bop a few Blue Shirts or Trios, smash a window, and move on. Depend on the goodwill of the people to feed and hide you. You spent three dark days in the cellar of an old Chinese restaurant, eating nothing but handfuls of MSG. Someone would occasionally drop a leaflet or a zine full of news through the bars of the cellar window. Boston was ours again, Chicago was in flames. The heartland had taken up arms. Mexico re-annexed everything up to Colorado.

On day three you saw a pair of ratty biker boots and frayed black jeans trot by your window. Jeff. You went up to the main floor and clamoured up the fire escapes to the rooftop. It was only a five-storey walk-up (thank God for Chinatown) and you were able to follow Jeff from above. You saw him fall in that alley, but you knew it didn't matter. There were no helicopters in the air. That meant that the junta had lost the sky somehow. And they'd created a martyr in their frustration and rage.

#

Still speaking in tongues, you managed to find your way back to your own earth to at least hear what you had told the congregation. It was simple really, why the Word of Ramone had managed to unify the Earth after 15,000 years of civilized slaughter. Joey Ramone was a finger. A ridiculously small phalange of a great and throbbing cosmic being of near-infinite power and wisdom that scraped across the Earth when it was young, before cooling rock and quivering proteins gave rise to chance and infinite possibility. Joey Ramone was dragged across the planet, every shadow Earth in every quantum possibility, killing and fucking and feeding and inspiring and dying in an opium-induced haze, or of AIDS, or of old age. He slaughtered latter-day Hitlers in the womb or by accident of cosmic bankshots. He sang or sliced meat. He inspired the One True Faith. That's what made it easy. "We truly do have the One

51

True Faith," you said (though you weren't sure whether you said it in English or in the verikilloanguaminesxikienima of glossolalia, but you knew they all understood you). "That's why we succeeded where all the other religions failed."

Joey Ramone saved the worlds. All of them.

#

You only met him once. You were on Third Avenue, on a day sunny enough to make the sidewalks glow. Psycho Rob was prattling in your ear.

"The next Hitler? Milosevic isn't the next fucking Hitler. There isn't one fucking next Hitler." He spat on the side of your face by mistake. Excitable boy. Then he flailed his arms and accidentally smacked you in the chest.

"Rob, fuckin' relax for a minute. You're like the Special Olympics forensics team here," you said.

He turned to you, all blue eyes and ratty blond whiskers and curls. "No man. See, what I mean is this. I think we're ALL the next Hitler. It's just that you need the right ingredients all in place, everything has to go right — well, everything has to go wrong for the next Hitler to really be the next Hitler." He spun on the heel of his tennis shoe and pointed.

"That old lady," he said, nodding and jabbing his finger. "She's the next Hitler." It was an old, probably Chinese, woman in a floral blouse. She was standing on a traffic island, waiting to pull her granny cart across the street.

"That is an old lady. She has a hump. She can barely move. She is not Hitler."

"Hitler," Rob said, defiant. "All it takes is a little of this and a little of that. That old lady could lead a rally in Chinatown and have 100,000 people ready to die for her tomorrow. If she wasn't a hunchback, maybe her charisma would be enough to split the world down the middle. Osteoporosis may have saved us all!" He turned and looked over his shoulder at you, then shut his eyes dramatically. "Anyone!" he shouted, "can be a Hitler!" And, eyes still closed, he spun again with his arm and forefinger outstretched, and pointed.

At Joey Ramone. Joey had just turned the corner and was nursing a big

McDonalds cola. His hair was shorter in that it was all piled at the top of his head, and didn't flow down his back. Black streaked with a thread or two of silver. Purple Lennon glasses, and a nerdy shirt with horizontal stripes and a crooked collar. He had a paunch but that was it — four pipe cleaners sticking out of a ball of clay. The world stopped for a moment, like it does when non-New Yorkers see celebrities. You had rolled your eyes at Sandra Bernhardt buying deli flowers at midnight, and didn't even recognize Leonard Cohen when he bought the *Times* at the newsstand. The girl you were with just turned the corner and left after you admitted that.

But Joey you just stared at. His shadow was half a block long. "Hi guys," he said, and he walked past you and Rob both to cross the street. You just smiled back. The old lady eyed him warily, then smiled a wide toothless smile.

An Open Door
David V. Barrett

The summons came when Paul and Ainne were still in bed; they had made love, and were resting in each other's arms, for the moment exhausted, but strong in the strength of their love.

"My lady, Madame Guiche is below; she wishes to speak with you," the servant said, through the door Ainne had opened part way.

"Tell her I have just awoken," Ainne said, "and that I must complete my toilette. She may wait in the garden. And, Sybille, would you have some jugs of hot water sent up straight away?"

She closed the door and turned back to Paul.

"I'm sorry, my love," she said. Paul had begun to stroke her breasts again just before the servant had knocked on the door; they would certainly have made love a third time.

He reached for her, but she moved away.

"I'm sorry," she said again. "I must prepare myself." She went into the bathroom the Count had recently had installed for her and poured two large jugs of cold water into the tub.

Paul followed, stood behind her; still almost erect, his prick brushed against her thigh.

"My love . . . "

Ainne turned. "No," she said, and the firmness of her tone caused him to step back; his own firmness faded with the word.

She saw his face. "I am sorry, but I must do this."

There was another knock on the door.

"Behind the curtain," she said, pointing to her clothes alcove. Paul obeyed; Ainne picked up her robe from the floor by her bed and wrapped it around her before calling: "Enter." Three servants came in, each carrying two large steaming jugs.

After they had gone, Paul emerged from the alcove and followed Ainne once more into her bathroom. She was sitting in the bath, soaping her breasts.

"May I?" he asked, reaching to take the soap from her.

"Not this time, my love."

"May I join you?"

"No." Again he stepped back at the tone of her voice. This time she didn't apologize.

"Paul, I have to prepare myself. This water is not just to clean my body." She put the soap down and slid down the bath until her head was completely under the water. When she surfaced, Paul saw her lips moving. She stood, and touched her forehead, each breast, and her belly.

Paul stood back as she stepped out of the bath, and she smiled approvingly at him.

"Tonight, I promise. I'll come to your room for an hour; two, three if we want. We'll love then, I promise, darling. All right?" She searched his eyes until he nodded.

She dressed with care, touching each piece of clothing before she chose or rejected it.

"Can I help?" Paul asked.

"Something of yours, close to me; that will help a great deal." She thought for a moment. "May I wear your cravat as a neck scarf?"

"Of course." He handed it to her, and began to dress himself.

She lifted her pendant to her neck just as he picked up his ring from her bedside table, and paused. They had bought them together, six months ago; they bore the same design, of a cross with a tiny rose at its centre.

"And I would like you to wear something of mine, for a link between us." She kissed the pendant, held it to his lips for him to do the same, then placed it around his neck.

He wanted but did not try to kiss her.

"I have the protection of water; you still have the burning of fire in your loins. Outside there will be earth beneath me, and air around me. Most of all, the Lady is of water, and she will be with me."

"And I?"

"Stay within the manor; I may need your strength. Keep away from the garden; the knowledge of your presence would distract me. The court-yard. Sit and read, play with the dog, flirt with the servant girls — No, not that, not today; I need your heart pure for me. Touch your ring; touch my pendant. Be there for strength if I need to call upon you."

As Ainne opened the door, Paul called softly, "If you do need me, reach out and take. I'll be open for you."

She smiled her thanks, and left her room. Paul listened to her soft footsteps fading down the corridor.

Gods, but he loved her. For a moment he wished that Madame Guiche might rot in hell, then he pulled back the thought; that decision was not his to make.

He had known Madame Guiche for three or four years; she was a pow-erful force in the district. On her word people were included or excluded. She chose who was acceptable in society, and who was no longer so, for whatever reason. Her late husband had been a rich and powerful mer-chant, though it was her power he had wielded through his business. Since his death five years ago, the business had been in the name of his son; but everyone knew who made the important decisions, and trades-men and craftsmen had gone out of business, no longer able to get their supplies, or to sell their goods — because, perhaps, of some imagined slight in church. And in this age of at least some tolerance, after centuries of persecution, she was turning people's hearts against the Jews once more.

The abbé, also, was in her hands. A small and weak man in himself, his power was in his position — and she controlled its direction. She used the Church, as she used everyone and everything, to strengthen her own power.

But who knew where that power came from? There was talk . . . and he had seen people make warding signs.

Yet her power was growing. And it was against her that Ainne was now standing.

#

Paul always found the courtyard restful. Even in the height of summer it was cool; the walls of the manor caught the sunshine, but the small stone fountain in the centre freshened the air. This was where he had first met Ainne, when her husband the Count had brought him through from his dark study to show him some figurines in the outdoor light.

She had been sitting on the plainer of the two benches, just here; she was dressed in a simple blue gown, with a wide-brimmed straw hat on her long corn-yellow hair shielding her face from the sun and from Paul's gaze. Her fingers were busy on her embroidery; she didn't notice the two men approach until the Count introduced Paul.

She looked up, smiled at him, and Paul fell in love.

So, over the next few months, did she. It was not until Midnight Mass that Christmas Eve that she was able to tell him so. The Count, having to be in Paris for a meeting with a marquis, or a merchant, or more likely a mistress, had asked Paul to accompany his household to the Mass. Moments after taking the Host on her tongue, Ainne appeared to stumble by the ancient Black Madonna near the chancel steps. Paul stopped to give her his arm for support, and she leaned into him for a moment. Any of the congregation who noticed would have assumed she murmured a word of thanks; instead, her breath on his ear formed words which nearly caused Paul to stumble himself: "Je t'adore." Her hand gripped his arm a little tighter and for a moment longer than was needful.

By conducting their romance in public they were able to avoid any hint of scandal. He was seen often at the manor, and at events, formal and informal, in the town; sometimes with other members of the household, or with both the Count and the Countess, or with her alone. He took on the role of advisor, tutor, companion and, in some of the Count's trading deals, partner.

It was nearly a year after they first met before Ainne took Paul to her bed; but thereafter they made love whenever it was safe for them to do so.

Safe meant not only when the Count was away, which was often, and the servants were out of the way, which was seldom, but also only on certain days each month. Ainne could not be sure that she was barren, though in six years she had not borne the Count the child he demanded. She would not risk having Paul's child; her body was hers to give, she said, though the Count must never know, but her child would belong to her husband. That was her duty.

Before Paul, Ainne had slept with none but her husband who, though never brutal towards her, performed the act with brief efficiency; she did not know that lovemaking was pleasurable. Paul had been told by other women in the past that he was considerate but uninspired; for him, making love for a few minutes before falling asleep in a woman's arms was enjoyable. But with each other, they discovered a natural fire spreading from their loins throughout their bodies; their passion was not dulled even after three or four hours of loving.

Paul ached with unspent longing for her. He sat on the bench where he had first seen her, and took out a book of poetry. He read little of it. He could not guess how her conversation with Madame Guiche was progressing. However civilized it would undoubtedly appear on the surface, beneath that it would be a battle between two strong women. And for Madame Guiche, strength and power were all.

She did not yet control the Count, but it was clear to Ainne, and thus to Paul, that she desired to. The Count was not a cruel master; he was efficient in the control of his lands, and firm with his people, but the people knew that he was fair. Paul might not like him much as a person, but he had some respect for him, and was happy to work with him or for him.

But Madame Guiche saw the Count's fairness as weakness, and had been heard to criticize him for it. She believed in a strong, unbending rule; if she were to trap him, seduce him, enslave him, as she had the abbé and so many others, then the common people would suffer.

Would she supplant Ainne, have the Count put her away for her barrenness, by divorce or death? Or would she take more pleasure by watching Ainne suffer too, as she saw her husband controlled by another woman?

Madame Guiche was strong, and who knew what other powers she could draw on to strengthen her own? Ainne had asked the Lady's help and protection, but how safe was she? Paul touched his ring, and her pendant around his neck, and opened himself up to her, so that she might draw whatever strength she needed from him.

#

The sun had dropped below the top of the west wall of the courtyard when Ainne returned to him. She looked tired, but the taut awareness she had carried from her room some three hours earlier was gone.

"Did you win?" he asked, reaching for her.

"No one won," she said. "It wasn't that sort of battle. But, more importantly, no one lost."

"I don't underst — "

"I need something to refresh me," she interrupted. "And something for energy. A herb drink: the vervain mixture. And honey. No, put the honey in the drink; I'll have a slice of beef and some bread. Sybille! Sybille! Oh, blast the girl, can you go and find her, Paul? And tell her to be quick. There are people coming for dinner this evening — you will stay to help, won't you? — and I must be ready for them. Sybille! Oh, go and look for her, Paul."

He went. He found her. He returned with the food and drink himself, to find that Ainne had gone in to the dining room to supervise the table. He followed her about, but she was busy, organising the cook and the butler and her maid and the other servants. He began to get a headache.

He tried, three times when they were momentarily alone, to find out what had happened during the afternoon, but each time a servant came in, or she remembered something else that needed arranging.

His headache became worse.

Eventually, when he found himself getting in her way for what seemed the fifteenth time, and she ordered him to move this from here to there in the same voice she used to the servants, he had had enough.

"I'm sorry, my lady" — there were servants in the room — "but I have a bad headache. I think I need to lie down for a while."

"The guests will be here in an hour, and there's still so much to do."

He put a hand to his forehead; it was getting worse, and he was beginning to feel faint.

59

"Oh, very well. But be ready for dinner; I need you to help entertain everyone."

Paul retired to the small guest room which was now kept for him. He lay down on the bed but the sun, streaming through the window, was too bright; he rose to close the shutters, then lay down again. His head was burning; he got up once more to soak a cloth in the basin of water on the washstand and hold it against the back of his neck; then he soaked it again, wrung it out, put it to his forehead, and lay down on his back in the darkened room.

Now that he had stopped moving, he started to shiver. He was burning up, but he was so cold. He began to unfasten his boots, his head pounding and his fingers shaking as he tried to unlace them and pull them off; giving up the struggle, he wrapped himself in the bedcovers. The washcloth had dried out and fallen off. He curled up, his knees almost to his chest, his arms hugging himself, and lay shivering on his bed.

The sounds of laughter and loud conversation from downstairs roused him some time later. He untangled himself from the covers and groaned, raised himself from the bed and swayed. He stumbled in the dark as he crossed the room, and stubbed a toe against the washstand; he must somehow have managed to remove one of his boots. He opened the shutters and winced, though the low evening light was not as bright as it had been even an hour before.

He washed his face and neck; his mouth tasted foul, so he rinsed it out, spitting the water back in the basin. Drying himself off, he realized that the pain in his head had faded to a dull ache, and that he had finally stopped shivering.

He looked in the glass, and saw an unkempt mess: his eyes looked red and tired, the black waves of his hair were tangled, his clothes were creased. He managed to brush some order into his hair, then started to dress for dinner. As he fastened the only cravat he could find, not one he had ever liked though it looked smart enough, he remembered letting Ainne wrap his favourite cravat around her neck; it seemed many, many hours ago.

Merde, but he hated that Guiche woman for ruining their afternoon of love; such afternoons were rare enough as it was.

He still knew nothing of what had happened between her and Ainne, and there would be no opportunity to find out tonight. Damn all women for their inconstancy!

Checking his appearance in the glass again, he wondered for the hundredth, the thousandth time, why Ainne loved him, why any of his lovers in the past had loved him. He had little money or position, and his looks were nothing special. But who could fathom the ways of women?

#

The evening lasted for ever.

The dinner itself was, as always, excellent; the Count had coaxed his cook away from a lord whose fortunes were fading, and had managed to keep him by both paying him regularly and letting him choose the kitchenmaids.

The food gave back to Paul some measure of strength.

But he was seated between a simpering woman with a lisp and appalling breath and another with a large bosom, too much powder, and a loud laugh. One of them kept breaking wind throughout the meal.

After dinner he was at last able to escape from them as they looked for new targets for their attention. As the brandy followed the wine, however, and the volume of the conversation increased, his headache came back worse than ever. It was impossible to excuse himself and leave; he was a house-guest, and the insult to his hostess could not be contemplated.

He was never fully comfortable in the formality of such social gatherings anyway; as a scholar and the son of a merchant, he was not born to it, as Ainne was. She had lowered her station in marrying the Count, but the duc d'Anjou had needed to seal an alliance. Parties like this were as nothing to her, who had been raised to dine and dance and dally with dukes and princes.

Now, with bright spots high on her cheeks, Ainne was radiant with energy, flitting from group to group, giggling conspiratorially with one, laughing aloud with another, hooting uncontrollably at something his over-powdered dinner companion said. Paul tried to catch her attention, to be included in some of the conversations she was a part of, but she barely noticed him, except twice: once to ask him to get the butler to bring another bottle, and once to ask the maid to fetch her wrap from her room.

At last people began to leave, and Paul breathed a sigh of relief; the noise and confusion of so many people would be gone, and he would have Ainne to himself for a while before they retired for the night.

It was not to be. One of the dinner guests was an old friend of the Count's, had not seen him for years, and was disappointed to find him not here.

"But he will be back in a few days," Ainne said. "You must stay until then; I insist. Paul!" she called without even looking to see where he was, "Could you get the servants to prepare a room for Marcel? The blue room, I think. Oh," she said to Marcel, whom Paul saw was tall and blond, with craggy good looks, "it's so good to meet new friends, and be able to share one's home with them."

The last of the guests, apart from Marcel, departed, and Paul wandered around, pointlessly supervising the servants as they cleared away the glasses and other detritus of the evening. As he went from room to room he would keep catching sight of Ainne and Marcel talking animatedly, her hand resting on his arm as she showed him a painting or, in one case, a particularly fine statuette that Paul had acquired for the Count. His name was not mentioned; he might not have been there.

Eventually he could take no more. He found them in Ainne's salon, she stretched out on the chaise longue, he seated on a padded stool at her side, talking quietly.

"If you will excuse me, my lady, I think I shall retire," he said formally. "I am still feeling unwell."

She glanced up. "Oh, good night, then," she said, and turned back to the man at her side.

#

His bedroom was cold; he had left the shutters open, and the maid — busy, no doubt, with the evening's dinner party — had neglected to close them. His bed was as he had left it, a rumpled mess.

He lit a lamp, closed the shutters, and undressed.

He knew he would not be able to sleep yet; he felt tightly wound, tense, fed up, irritable. He tried to read some poetry, but the words made little sense.

How could she? Oh, he knew he had no rights, he was her lover, not her husband, but to turn from him like that, to ignore him all evening, to drape herself so seductively in front of the handsome Marcel . . . How could she? He had lost her now, lost her to some new man, some flight of fancy who had walked in unknown tonight and who would rest his head on her pillow before the night was through.

But would she then come back to him, after Marcel was gone? Would she expect him to be waiting for her, to welcome her to his bed, to whisper again to her the things he had whispered only this afternoon? No, he would not, he could not. If she could throw him aside so easily, so carelessly, he wanted nothing more of her. He would pack the clothes and books he had in this room, and take them back to his own house tomorrow, before she even woke, so that he would not have to see her again.

Having decided that, he tried once more to read, but could not. He blew the lamp out and settled down to try to sleep, though he knew it was beyond his reach. His thoughts and feelings were too roiled, too intense, too bitter; they spiralled round and around, dragging him lower and lower into their tight coils. But if he lay here long enough, sleep might catch him unawares, might sneak up and take him before he realized it. With this hope, he turned over and stretched himself out, then curled up, trying to find a position in which he might be comfortable while he waited for sleep to claim him, if it would.

It was pointless. The same thoughts, over and over, round and round, down and down, deeper and deeper into the mire of doubt and self-pity — oh, yes, he knew that, but knowing it did not lessen it — and of hatred of Ainne and hatred of Marcel and hatred of himself, of the fickleness and perfidy of Ainne especially, and of his own worthlessness. From a distance he watched himself, watched as he wound the rope that bound his soul tighter and tighter until he could hardly breathe, watched and remarked to himself, *I always despised self-pity*, and so despised himself the more; and from a farther distance still, observed himself observing, and saw it all as part of the same inwound self-destructive pattern.

He heard the door open, and hope leapt, to be dragged down and brutally trampled on by his despair and hatred. He kept his breathing soft, steady, slow.

DAVID V. BARRETT

He heard her footsteps cross the floor, saw through closed lids the glow of her candle as she placed it on his nightstand, and felt her sit on the bed. She must not realize he was awake still. He kept his breathing steady, slow, soft.

Her hand touched his shoulder through the covers, and he suppressed the movements his body yearned to make, either to fling himself into her arms or to fling her across the room. Slow, soft, steady.

She stroked his hair, her palm touching gently against his cheek. He sobbed, suddenly, and turned his face away.

"Paul, Paul, what's wrong?"

He would not answer. Her hands, both her hands, were on his face now, coaxing, firmly turning him so that his face was towards her.

"Paul, what is it, my love?"

He tried to turn his face away, but she was too strong, or he was too weak. She bent down to him, then sat up again with him in her arms, holding him so that his face was on her breast, rocking him as tears poured scalding down his cheeks, and more tears for the shame of it.

She held him for a long time, held him tightly against her so that she shook with his shaking, until the sobs quietened down, and his body was more still. And then she held him a little longer, one hand stroking his hair as if he were a child upset.

"Paul?"

He said nothing, did not move.

"Paul, listen to me. I love you, my silly darling, I love you."

"Then why . . . ?" He lifted his head to speak, and she stopped his mouth with hers, holding the kiss even when he struggled to be free.

When she did release him, she spoke first.

"Paul, whatever you think, I love you. I don't know what's wrong, I don't know what I've done, but I love you. Do you believe me?"

She waited. Then:

"Do you believe me?"

Eventually, he said, "Yes."

"Then tell me what's wrong, and I'll try to make it right."

He began, slowly at first, then the words poured out as his tears had, chasing each other in their effort to say everything, to miss out none of his misery. Their interrupted lovemaking; her turning away from him as

64

she washed her body so carefully, removing all traces of him, his semen, their mingled sweat, their love, in preparation for her confrontation with Madame Guiche; the three hours waiting, not knowing what was happening, unable to help, except being open for her to draw strength from him if she needed it . . .

"Paul, did you . . . ?"

He continued, over-riding her interruption. When she came into the courtyard, he had been expecting her to tell him everything that had happened, but instead she had started organizing tonight's dinner party; all the preparations for that, and his pounding headache, and shivering; he told her about his going to bed, and his shaking and trembling; then the dinner itself, and all the jolly conversation afterwards, and how he was excluded from all of it, and from all of her; and then, on top of all that, Marcel, and the way that she had held him, and talked to him, and looked at him; and how all of this had built up together into the inevitable conclusion that it was all over between them, which he could somehow have borne if she'd told him, but not like this, not like this, it all hurt too much . . .

He talked himself out, and she waited, this time, until he'd finished, and then kissed the tears away from his eyes. She let go of him, and all his doubts flooded back again; and then she slipped in beside him.

"Oh Paul, I'm sorry, I'm truly sorry."

He started to caress her, but she took his hand and held it still.

"Paul, listen to me."

He kissed her mouth, and her cheek, and when she turned her head, the corner of her jaw.

"Paul, this is important." The tone of her voice stopped him.

"You opened yourself up to let me draw strength from you."

"Yes, in case you needed — "

"Did you close yourself again?"

"What?"

"Like opening a door. Did you close it again?"

He thought for a moment. "No," he said. "But I thought you might need to draw strength from me."

"I did, and I did. Oh, Paul, I should have known, I should have thought, I should have realized that you'd left the door open. I'm sorry,

I've hurt you so badly. I didn't mean to, but it's my fault."

"But if you're not drawing anything out of me — "

"Don't you see why you've been so drained all evening, so physically and emotionally exhausted? And why I was so full of energy, so over-excited? You left the door open. I drew on your strength, your power, this afternoon, and it's been draining from you into me ever since. Close the door, Paul. Close it now."

"How?"

"How did you open it?"

"I just . . . willed it, that my strength was there if you needed it, the fire you said was in me, and if you needed it you could draw on it, and it would flow from me to you. You wouldn't even have to ask; if you needed it, it would be there."

She moved her face back from him a little way, to see him better in the candle-glow.

"Paul, you have to close that door, now. Picture it however you want, however it makes sense to you, but close it, quickly. Shut off the flow, before it's too late. Do it."

He closed his eyes. With some difficulty he imagined a door: broad and solid oak, with iron studs, and strong iron hinges, and heavy bolts. The door was open towards him, and beyond its edge he saw a long tunnel, winding away from him, and the light from the hearth-fire on this side of the door was shining down the tunnel. He could see the flow of the light in the dust-motes as it swirled, as it poured down the tunnel. And where normally a light shines without diminishing its source, he could see that, as the light flowed away down the tunnel, the fire on his own side was becoming weaker, less bright.

He tried to picture the door closed, rather than open, but it stayed as it was; and the light continued to flow through the doorway.

He ordered the door to close, but nothing happened, except that the hearth-light on this side grew even dimmer.

With a last effort of his mind he reached out as if with his hands, and grabbed hold of the door, and slammed it shut, and shoved the bolts home. The movement caused the light to flicker, like a candle flame in a draught, and then he saw it brighten a little, and stay brighter.

He looked at his own hearth-fire, and felt its warmth flow into every part of him.

He opened his eyes again.

"I've done it. It's closed."

Ainne let her breath out. "I could see. Thank you for letting me." She opened her eyes as well, and looked into his as she stroked his cheek.

"I had too much energy all evening; I couldn't understand it, why I was feeling so strong when I should have been so tired after this afternoon. I was just leeching it out of you, as if I were a succubus."

"You can stop now."

"I don't have the choice. You've closed the door; you've cut off the supply." She paused, then said, "I didn't realize you were so powerful, Paul."

"I'm not."

"Oh, you are. Spiritual fire."

He shrugged. "I didn't know."

"Then know this. Tomorrow — not now; now is for healing you, and us — tomorrow we must put your power and mine together. I'm a water person; you're fire. Together we might be strong enough."

"For what?"

"Our fight against Madame Guiche."

"How will we do it?"

"I said tomorrow, my love. Tonight is for our love; that too will strengthen us."

He pulled back — "If that's the only reason . . . " — but she could see that this time he did not mean it.

"Paul, love me. Take my body. Consume me, and be healed."

#

Tomorrow became next week, and then the week after. Heavy rains began to fall, turning the hot, dry summer into a chill, muddy autumn in days. The Count sent word that his return would be delayed; his business in Paris required his presence for a little longer.

Paul thought it more likely that the Count preferred the warmth of his mistress's bed to the cold and wet unpleasantness of the journey south. Marcel, the Count's old friend, stayed on at the manor; Ainne devoted time to him each day, as a hostess should; but at night, when she could, she came to Paul's bed, or took him to hers, and proved to him that he need not be jealous of her attention to others. Marcel, in any case, soon discovered the charms of Ghislaine, one of the serving maids; and although Ainne had to speak sharply to the girl on several occasions about her lack of attention to her work, at least the liaison kept Marcel occupied much of the time.

No one ventured far outside, unless they had to. Paul, sitting warm and dry in his own room, or in the library, or in the Count's own study working on his accounts, would see through the window the servants trudging back from the market with food, or from the forest with wood for the fires which kept the damp and cold outside the manor's walls. He spoke to Ainne, and found that she had already instructed the servants to light fires in their own quarters. When he visited the kitchens he found that the smell of damp wool from the servants' cloaks drying in front of the stoves overlaid the usual scents of tomatoes and onions and herbs and roasting meat.

On the third Sunday after Ainne's meeting with Madame Guiche in the garden of the manor, they met again at Mass. Ainne was accompanied by Paul and Marcel, and by two of her servants; Madame Guiche was standing outside the church with a tall, slender young woman whose mass of black hair almost escaped her bonnet.

"Madeleine," Ainne whispered to Paul. "The midwife." *La sage-femme.* "But you should look to her deeper nature rather than her outward profession."

She watched the two as they talked quietly and entered the church together.

"I would not have thought her a natural ally to la Guiche," Ainne said softly as she and Paul took their places near the front of the church.

The abbé preached of authority and obedience, the authority of God and the obedience of man — and the authority also of those whom God had appointed to serve him, his representatives on earth, the Holy Father and his cardinals and bishops and priests; and the obedience owed to Holy Mother Church by the lay people.

After the service Paul saw Madame Guiche speaking to the abbé; one gloved hand rested lightly on his arm, and she was smiling. He looked small and insignificant beside her.

"She is tightening her strands around him," Ainne said that night, when they were in Paul's bed. "He will preach again on obedience to God, and to the Church, and to himself, and the day will come soon when he will use his pulpit to pass on her message to his flock, be it a command or a condemnation. 'Shun those merchants who trade openly with the Jews, who consort with the Christ-killers and the child-murderers' — I can hear it now. The people will obey; they have been told they must. And so more money and more power will flow to her."

"They forget that the Christ was a Jew himself," said Paul, his hand stroking the curve of her breast.

"They don't forget, but they will not allow us to remember. I have heard that on the earliest crucifixes the Christ was naked, as he would surely have been. His loincloth now is not to avoid blasphemy, nor even for modesty, but to hide his circumcised prick."

Her hand closed gently on Paul's own prick, and he groaned with pleasure.

"If they allow him to have one at all," she added. "After all, in their theology he'd have used it for naught but pissing. Such a waste."

She squeezed him again, and Paul found himself hardening for the third time. He took one of her nipples between tongue and teeth, and felt it stiffen also.

Ainne stroked his head where it lay on her breast. Paul freed his mouth for a moment.

"If he was fully man as well as god, then he had to know the joys of lust and love to be complete," he said.

"And to bring those joys to the Magdalen," Ainne said, then gasped as Paul's fingers slipped from her belly to the wetness between her thighs. "I hope for her sake that he was . . . as skilful . . . as . . . aaah . . ." — and said no more for a time.

#

A messenger stood dripping and shivering in the entrance hall the next morning when Ainne came down the stairs.

"My lady."

"Have the servants not let you warm yourself?"

69

He indicated his muddy boots and the pool of dirty water on the tiles where he stood.

"Oh, la! It is only honest soil. Sybille!"

Her maid appeared at the top of the stairs, Ainne's half-folded night-clothes in her arms.

"Leave those for now. Take this boy down to the kitchen, dry him off and put some broth in him, and, when he's warm, bring him to me in my salon. Borrow clothes for him if his do not dry in time. I shall eat break-fast first."

Paul rose as she entered the dining room.

"Lady," he said, as if she had not been in his arms four hours past. He waited until she sat before resuming his own seat.

"Did I hear your voice . . . ?"

"A messenger, from my husband no doubt."

"Saying?"

"Saying that he is cold and wet, and that my servants are too busy warming their own arses in front of the fire to see to him, and whatever else he has to say can wait for an hour."

She poured a little wine into a glass, and added water until the colour was almost gone. She took a sip, then reached for the plates of cheese and sliced meats.

"I'm sorry, Paul. I'm not snapping at you. It's the thoughtlessness of my servants; I thought I'd trained them better."

"Maybe Ghislaine answered the door. She forgot the bread rolls; I had to ask her three times before she heard me."

"Well, Marcel will not be with us forever. Where is he now, by the way?"

"From the look of the girl, lying exhausted in bed with a smile on his face." He grinned. "As I should be," he added softly.

"Hush." There were no servants in the room, but who knew who might be outside the door? Their affair had been kept secret for so long partly because they never exchanged words which could be revealing to passing ears.

They discussed instead the matters of the estate, the business matters which they ran while the Count was away. There had been trouble with some suppliers: some of the meal had been mouldy, and maggots had

AN OPEN DOOR

been found in a carcass of mutton.

"It's not their fault," Paul said. "I've spoken to them, and they know their goods are not up to standard. But it has been made clear to them that they must not borrow from the moneylenders, and without capital they cannot afford the good meat and corn. And so they buy the cheaper stuff, and have to sell it at lower prices, and so make less profit, and have still less capital."

"La Guiche."

"She is tightening her grip."

"And, with the abbé on her side, she will strangle us all," Ainne said. "We must find a way to stop her. Perhaps I shall talk with Madeleine."

They left the table and went through to the salon. The messenger stood near the fire, visibly warmer and drier than before.

"My lady," he said, bowing, and moving away from the fire to let them near it.

"Have you eaten now?"

"Thank you, my lady, your cook was most kind."

"So what is your news?"

He drew himself up.

"Your husband the Count is staying with his majesty the King at the royal château of Fontainebleau," he said. "There is a large hunting party in the forest. The Count may be there for some weeks to come, and wishes that you should join him for a few days."

"Myself alone?"

The messenger turned to Paul.

"You are invited also, sir, and whatever servants and other companions you may both require."

"Marcel?" Ainne said to Paul.

"If not, and you take Ghislaine with you, he may remember at last that he has business elsewhere."

"But he would like to meet my husband. No, he can come with us."

She turned back to the messenger.

"When does the Count wish me to join him?"

"As soon as it is possible, my lady. But . . . "

"Go on."

"The weather is much better farther north. I did not know the roads

71

would be so bad down here. A horse can get through the mud, but your carriage would not be able to."

"How is the road from Orléans to Fontainebleau?" asked Paul.

"Those roads are clear, sir. It was only after I left Orléans for Tours that I had difficulty. After Tours it becomes even worse, and they say that by Saumur it is quite impassable. The Loire has overflowed in many places where its banks are low, and the rain has washed the road into the river. I could hardly tell one from the other at times."

"So we take a boat up the Loire as far as Orléans, and there hire a carriage," said Paul. "Will that be acceptable, my Lady?"

"That will be fine. Would you arrange the details while I organize my household? We shall leave tomorrow."

#

The Count's own barge had been holed recently, and had not yet been repaired. Paul had planned to borrow the corn merchant's good barge, but that had suffered a similar fate. Others were unsuitable or unusable for a variety of reasons. It was mid-afternoon before he accepted what he had known for most of the day: the only barge in the district which was both suitable and available belonged to Madame Guiche.

"But certainly, Monsieur. I was planning to go to Orléans myself tomorrow, on business. I shall be delighted to take you there, Monsieur . . . " — her voice dropped — "but I may call you Paul, surely," she said, laying gloved fingers on his arm as she had with the abbé. Paul resisted a strong desire to pull his arm away, and managed to suppress the shudder which threatened to run through him. This was the woman who was snaring the whole community in her web; this was the woman whom Ainne was fighting, and the aftermath of the opening battle had nearly driven him away from Ainne.

"Do come and have a glass of Chinon with me — or would you prefer something more delicate, the Borgueil rosé, perhaps? We have been too formal with each other, I think. I should like to get to know you a little better. Would you not like that?"

She leaned towards him, offering him a view of her wide décolletage and a strong whiff of musk and roses.

As subtle as a barracks whore, Paul thought.

And yet . . .

The sweet muskiness of her scent drew him towards her. He imagined holding her heavy breasts, burying his face between them; he could almost feel their soft weight in his hands. In his mind he could see clearly her rounded belly, and the hairy mound between her plump thighs. His prick pulsed, and he felt it begin to thicken. It was a long time since he had made love with a well-built woman; Ainne was slender, almost . . .

Ainne.

He slammed the doors in his mind, closing off the effects of the woman's scent and her half-covered breasts, shutting out the lust; he felt his erection fade. His hands, half-risen towards her, fell back to his side.

Just for a moment, to his eyes, she was older; he saw wrinkles beneath the paint on her face; the skin of her breasts was withered. He blinked, and she was lush and voluptuous again.

He stepped back and forced a formal smile.

"Thank you, but no. I have much to organize before tomorrow. We shall meet you by the river at nine."

He bowed, turned and left, conscious of the sudden hardness of her face, the fury that she had barely kept from her eyes.

And now I have made an enemy, he thought.

As he undressed Ainne that night, he let his hands cup her breasts; they were small, but they were firm, and they were beautiful, and they belonged to Ainne, whom he loved.

Their first lovemaking, as always, was eager, urgent in their desire for each other. As they gained their breath before their second, more gentle union, Paul told Ainne of his meeting with Madame Guiche; that afternoon, with servants around them, he had only told her about the barge.

"I'm proud of you," Ainne said, hugging him close to her. "There is no temptation stronger than lust; it calls you through all your senses, and draws you on every level of body and mind. To shut it off like that was magnificent. You are learning how to use your magic."

"That wasn't magic; it was simply a tremendous effort of will."

"And what do you think magic often is? The Holy Word doesn't say you can move mountains by snapping your fingers and muttering a formula; it says you must have faith, and that means believing and wanting something so much that you make it come to happen. Magic of that sort is hard, Paul; if it were not, everyone would use it."

"But casting a spell of seduction is so easy. At least, it was for her."

"She is well practised, my love. And I fear she calls on powers that you and I would shun to strengthen her siren call. I'll wager she has had the abbé between her thighs in these last weeks. He has not your strength of will, and by gaining his body she gains his mind also."

"And how many else?" Paul said. "Who else has lain between her legs, I wonder?"

Ainne sighed. "As many as she wishes to control. This is her evil, that she uses her magic for power, not for healing. She is dangerous, Paul."

"She's a cunt," said Paul, then finished the saying: "*Sauf qu'elle n'avait ni la beauté ni le profondeur.*"

"Oh, but she has, Paul. She is very deep, very intelligent, and this makes her the more dangerous — and it is her beauty which draws men to her, like bees to a honeypot. She has that luscious beauty which men cannot resist. Except you, my love."

"I wonder . . . No, that's stupid."

"What's that?"

"Do you happen to know how old she is?"

Ainne shrugged.

"I don't know. Thirty, thirty-two maybe. Mature, but still good-looking."

"She is beautiful, yes: that full, lush, earthy beauty, like a peach that is almost over-ripe. At least, that's how she looks. But just for a fleeting moment I thought I saw something else." He described how she had looked, the wrinkled face, the stringy grey hair, the collapsing mouth, the withered skin on the sagging breasts.

"And then I blinked, and she was back to normal. It was for less than a second. I must have imagined it, in my disgust at how easily I'd nearly fallen under her . . . What's the matter, love?"

Ainne had sat up straight in the bed, one hand to her open mouth, the other held out before her, as if to ward something off.

"Ainne, what's wrong?" Paul took hold of her arms; she was utterly rigid.

She shivered visibly, right through her body, and then relaxed, but

Paul could see the effort of will that it took for her to do so.

"That would explain . . . Of course, it's so obvious."

"What?"

"Her beauty. It's a glamour. It's a spell in itself, a spell of visual deception. Everyone always sees her as beautiful, because that's the bait she can use best. But when you slammed out of her spell of seduction you broke her glamour for a moment and saw her as she really is — an evil old woman."

"So her beauty is a mask? But how can she do it?"

Ainne shook her head for a moment.

"It's something all women can do, to some extent, if they want a man. Have you never noticed how the most ordinary-looking woman can become attractive when she smiles at you in that special way? The smile that says, 'I'm interested in you, I think I might like you to come to my bed.' It's not just her mouth that smiles; her whole face softens, gentles; her eyes widen; her hair shines. She's casting a glamour, usually without even knowing she's doing it. She's aiming it at you, but other men in the room will notice it as well. She becomes attractive because she wants to attract you. And if you don't respond the spell fades quite quickly and she becomes ordinary again."

"So that's how they do it."

"So it has happened to you."

"Once or twice," he said reluctantly, and clearly meaning a lot more often than that.

"Oh, Paul." She nestled against him, one hand between them, stroking his chest. He stroked the curve of her breast, and bent and kissed her.

It was half an hour later, as they rested a second time, that they worked out what they might do.

#

Madame Guiche was sweetness itself as she welcomed them onto her barge. Ainne had brought Sybille and Ghislaine, and two of the manservants; with Paul and Marcel, their party was seven, a holy number. The previous day Ainne had offered to take the King's messenger, with or without his horse, but he had thought it better that he ride back straight-

way to give word of their imminent arrival, so that rooms could be prepared for them.

The rain had stopped, mercifully, and the Loire's flow was not as
strong as it had been for the last few days; there was also enough wind for
Madame Guiche's men to use the sail to carry the barge up-river.

She and her retinue totalled six, Paul noted: the number of Earth.
Ainne had quizzed Madeleine on the pretext of working out the best
omens for the journey. The *sage-femme* had kept her professional confi-
dences, as was right, but had allowed Ainne to discover that Madame
Guiche was under the sign of the Goat, an Earth sign, and was ruled by
Saturn. Early that morning Ainne had spread the cards, and had found
herself opposed by the Queen of Coins, the Earth suit. The characteris-
tics of the stars and the cards together were an exact image of Madame
Guiche.

Ainne was Cancer, the Crab, a Water sign, and her horoscope was governed by the Moon; the cards which usually represented her were the
Queen of Cups — Water again — and amongst the Major cards the Moon
itself, or the Papess — spiritual mystery and hidden knowledge — or
sometimes Temperance, the Healer.

Paul's own card was the King of Wands, the communicator and medi-
ator: Fire, with some aspects of Air. And there was Fire also in his star
sign, Sagittarius.

"Between us, we might be able to overcome la Guiche today," Ainne
had whispered as they had left the manor. She was wearing his cravat
again, beneath her cloak; he was wearing her pendant.

Madame Guiche gave no sign of her brief struggle with Paul the day
before. She bustled about the boat as they set off, making sure that everyone was comfortable on the benches, offering to have extra rugs fetched
for anyone who was cold. At noon she brought out a hamper of food and
wine, but Ainne produced her own, and the two parties ate separately.

Ainne and Paul made sure that they drank sparingly; a little wine was
good for relaxation, as well as for the stomach, as the apostle had said; but
too much would weaken and befuddle, and they needed their strength
and their wits.

Madame Guiche took no such care; by three in the afternoon she was
roaring with laughter at her own bad jokes.

The wine weakened her, and befuddled her, and made her careless in her boldness.

Paul went to stand in the bow; the wind felt stronger when he stood, but moving, he was warmer. After a few minutes he heard Madame Guiche come up beside him.

"It's a fine day, after all that rain." Her voice was slurred.

"A good day for travelling," he agreed. "Thank you again for giving us the use of your boat."

"I'm glad to, glad to, for someone as beautiful as you."

She leaned forward to kiss him, but Paul managed to step sideways as if he had begun his movement before hers, and avoided her lips.

"She will suck you in if she can," Ainne had warned him. "With the power of her glamour, her lips will entrap you whether you will it or not."

He glanced back along the boat, and saw that Ainne was watching them; she touched his cravat at her throat.

"Madame . . . " he began, and felt the woman lay her hand on his arm, as she had the day before.

And he felt more: the fierce, hungry worm of her consciousness boring into him. He had thought she was acquisitive; now he knew she was engulfing. The tendrils of her soul wound through his body, up his limbs, around his groin and his stomach and his heart; he could feel the heavy cloying stickiness of her within him, like honey spilt inside a cuff. He could smell the sweetness of her, yeasty like a thick barley wine. And he could taste her corruption, foul as cat shit.

She was at the doors of his being, now, pulling at their handles, pushing at their solidity, all his doors at once, all around him, deep within him. His doors were tightly closed, locked, bolted, sealed around symbolically with the love juices he had shared with Ainne last night.

The invading woman caught the trace of Ainne in his mind, and stiffened.

"Be rid of her, Paul. She is young and pretty, but she is weak. I am strong and mature and beautiful. Look at my beauty, Paul, look at it!"

He could hear her thoughts as clearly as if she had shouted them into his face.

He felt her incorporeal touch at his groin, like a warm hand enclosing him, fondling him, holding him close.

"I can give you so much more than she. Pleasure such as you never dreamt of, unbounded power over weak beings like her, like all the petty weaklings who surround us: pleasure, and power, and wealth. Do you want wealth, Paul? Gold coins and jewels aplenty, more than you can hold, more than you can ever spend in a lifetime of indulgence? You want what I can give you, don't you, Paul?"

Her words, her promises were nearly smothering him. They—she!— battered around the very centre of his being. He could feel the soft padded weight of her breasts, her hips and thighs and belly, inside him, inside his head and his heart, but not inside his soul, his self. His doors were still sealed tight.

"Paul, I want you. I want all of you. I want to open you up and come inside you. I want to take every part of you inside me. You and me together, Paul, you and me, your new young strength and my experience, my maturity. Together, Paul, together. Open yourself up, Paul. Merge yourself with me. Let me take you inside me, all your youth, all your strength, all your power. Let me have you, Paul, let me have you now!"

It was a command.

It was the right moment.

She was pulling, pulling at him — and Paul flung open his doors, every one of them wide open to her, and let everything that was in him pour down the channels she had created between them into the very heart of her.

He was fire, and fire burns earth. He was fire floating wild on water, and she was earth with no earth beneath her to ground her to her elemental might. He was fire, unfettered, and she had invited him, called him, pulled him into the centre of her being. And the water beneath him, and Ainne's spiritual water surrounding him like a bubble, protected him from the explosion that tore through her, that burnt through every part of her soul, that burnt her evil into ash, then burnt so fiercely that even the ash was consumed.

The explosion within her was himself; but it was she who had dragged him into her.

There was a splash of water, and the flames went out.

#

Paul felt the wet cloth on his forehead, and opened his eyes. He was lying on a bench in the middle of the barge, and Ainne was sitting beside him.

"Welcome back," she said.

He tried to sit up, but she held him down easily.

"In a minute," she said. "I've asked Sybille to warm some soup; there's a small stove in the stern. That will give you a little strength. Lie still till then."

"Is . . . ? Is . . . ?" He couldn't focus his mind to form words.

"All is well."

He saw her face, upside-down as he lay; she smiled, and he had never seen anything so beautiful.

He closed his eyes until the soup came, and then Ainne helped him to sit up, and fed it to him as to a child.

When he had finished it he looked around the boat. The rest of their own party were together at the back of the boat; he could hear Ghislaine's giggle as Marcel fondled her. There were a few other people, Madame Guiche's servants tending the boat. And there was a small, very wrinkled, very old woman, toothless and half bald, sitting on one of the benches; a servant sat with her.

"Is that . . . ?"

"Yes."

"But . . . Don't they think it strange . . . ?"

Ainne shrugged.

"That is her natural form. Her glamour has vanished away. They see her as she is, as she has always been. Already they have forgotten the mask she wore; it was never real anyway. She was never as people saw her. The glamour worked in their minds, to change their perception. Now it has gone . . . "

"And her power — is that gone too?"

"You were there . . . No, you were too close. I saw, I felt. The power that you let go, I . . . I could hardly believe it."

Paul hung his head.

"I could have killed her."

"No. No, Paul! Had she died, it would not have been your doing. She demanded your power, she sucked out your essence in her greed, and it

DAVID V. BARRETT

consumed her. It was her doing. You just opened the door, allowed her to do it. She destroyed herself. And, anyway, she did not die."

He wrapped his arms around himself and shivered. She picked up a blanket and draped it around him.

"You're exhausted, my love."

"Without you I couldn't have done it. You . . . "

He stopped, and sat up straight.

"She might have died. She would have died. You threw a bucket of water over us. You put the fire out."

She smiled.

"That's partly why you're so drained. I doused your fire as well."

"Thank you. And thank you for saving her life. It was not for me to take it from her."

She put her hand on his.

"Paul, you are blessed. You are learning the ways of magic, and wisdom, hand in hand. That is as it should be, and almost never is. When we return, I shall introduce you to Madeleine. We can study together."

"Study? With the midwife?"

"I told you: look to her deeper nature, not her job. Madeleine is a follower of the true way, a daughter of the Magdalen. With three of us, working together, we can undo the harm done by la Guiche. And maybe look for others to join us."

Together they watched as the walls of Orléans approached.

The Art of Self-Abuse
Keith Brooke

Where do I end and you begin? We are each an island of consciousness, a self-aware node in the social matrix. Fuzzy boundaries between us, that is all.

It is a question for the philosophers, perhaps. Am I a philosopher, then? Can someone who is incomplete also be a philosopher? I ask too many questions. As with any design flaw, this can easily be put right.

I sit alone, my elbows resting on a Formica table-top, its surface filigreed with fine cracks — too fine for you to see, I would hazard. Before me: a moulded white polystyrene container, three-quarters filled with dark "coffee". I use the term advisedly, with caution — just as I sip, occasionally, at the beverage. With caution. It is hot, at least.

I chose my table for its view. The street is busy, grimy, the people confrontational and hostile. The mores of the age: in an overcrowded world on the brink of collapse, personal space acquires disproportionate significance. You have far worse to concern you, if only you knew.

I sit and stare at the people and the slowly crawling traffic. I know not what I am looking for, but I have every confidence that I will recognize it.

I pick up the cup, my grip carefully controlled. I am powerful. I must be careful.

Fibre optics run from the biode hub in my left forearm to the siliconeural net interwoven into the substance of my brain. It is the best that money will be able to buy. When I am home, my memories — every thought, every experience and sensation, every fear and emotion — are automatically offloaded into the community's archives. I've been re-loaded seven times, as a result of biological breakdown or accident.

I have eyes, of course: two, just like you. Only better than yours, enhanced for a wider spectrum. I can kick up the sensitivity at night, partially opaque my corneas in bright sunlight. I can pick up the signals from proxies wherever I go — get a bird's eye view of myself walking down the high street, see round corners before I get there. I could see through *your* eyes, if I wanted, if you wanted to let me.

That remote camera — over there, on the edge of that building: you probably see it only as a bird — is it part of me, then? That mechanical eye that I can access with a brief mental impulse? No? Are the two eyes sitting in sockets at the front of my reinforced skull a part of me? Naturally, you would say yes. But you don't know that these are the second (left) and third (right) replacements. Vat-grown, vision boosted by a biode seeded into the retina of each.

You might have gathered by now that I am suffering quite a severe case of existential angst. I'm down. Blue (I could be, quite literally, if I chose). The year is 1984. I don't belong here.

#

It happens a short time later, out in the street.

I walk with my head up. Perhaps it is my manner that unsettles those around me, the smile on my face as I revel in the physicality of this age.

So many people, each with a purpose! So busy, so self-important. As if your day-to-day concerns have the slightest significance.

People bump into me repeatedly as I refuse to partake of the intercourse of the street, the impregnability of personal space. Perhaps you see that I am enjoying myself, perhaps that is why I disturb you.

But then you — *you* — pass by in an open-topped car and everything changes.

You look so comfortable, leaning back in the passenger seat, the breeze pushing collar-length chestnut hair away from your face. At one with your world. At peace. The girl who drives your car clearly adores you — I can taste it on the air, the pheromones, the sex. I hope you enjoy her. She could almost have been made to be enjoyed, I think.

It is you, I realize. You who gives my existence purpose.

There is a sheet draped across the back of the car. Big letters daubed in black paint on the white. You are publicising something then. That explains the noise of your car, the nasal honking sound it makes that is over and above the normal sound of its engine: your young assistant is making extra noise — some kind of horn — to draw attention to you, to make people read the banner draped across your car.

I stare at the letters. Writing. I have practised your script — I am nothing if not well prepared — but at this angle, on a moving vehicle, it all looks strange.

Why should "miners" wish to "strike" the "universe"? It puzzles me.

You are gone. I am left with the memory from which to piece together meaning. It is all I have.

#

The posters explain all. You were not intending to strike the universe, after all. The Socialist Workers' Students' Society is holding a rally at the university to support the striking miners.

The terms puzzle me. A miner is some kind of manual labourer but I do not know what is striking about them and why there should be either a meeting or a race to support them.

Language acquisition is a continuous process for me, even now. I had thought I was doing so well.

I learnt the basics of your language quite easily. The meat-silicon fuck of a brain I have is good for such things. It processes sound and visual information, identifying patterns, constructing the native grammar, analysing the cues and rhythms of speech. At first I faltered, but soon I picked up enough from common terms, gestures and context to fumble my way along. Now, I can process new terms and constructions in real time so that those around me will not spot anything abnormal in my communicative abilities.

My makers made me well. And, when I was broken, they made me even better.

They made me with a purpose, of course.

I want you. So badly do I want you.

#

It seems that you are greatly in demand at the moment. Here at the university it appears that you are something of a figurehead.

I should have expected that, of course. If there is trouble you will be at its centre.

I made my way here on foot, a walk of some twenty-five minutes, the route memorised from a two-dimensional map in the city centre. I could have used a bus, a two-tiered vehicle with promotional images on its outer skin that belches smut into the air and provides transport for the poorer sections of your society.

But I would use such a contraption only if I could operate it myself, and the driver objected when I broached this possibility. I spared him, despite his invective. I have no wish to draw undue attention to myself, just yet.

Walking is better, in any case. I am strong, I am in control.

And so, too, are you.

They adore you, just as the girl who drove your car adored you. There is a crowd exceeding 200 in number at the rally, waiting to hear you speak, each with an intensity that is almost sexual in nature. Is this rally to be some kind of orgy, perhaps? I have known such things, I think.

As we wait, there is chanting from some parts of the crowd — mainly those carrying placards bearing the white on red masthead of the Socialist Workers.

The favourites are, "The workers united, will never be defeated" — sadly lacking in scansion — and the more heartfelt, "Maggie Maggie Maggie, out out out." After a time, I join in with these chants, sensing the bonding effect of the communal singing.

And now a man with a megaphone talks above the noise, telling us of unity and solidarity, of jackbooted fascist filth, of working-class values and capitalist plots. He is a miner, I gather. The rally is for this man and his kind. He seems rather angry. I do not understand.

But you, you are different.

You take the megaphone from the angry miner and you do nothing. Your silence says more than the previous speaker's words. You play it like a musical instrument, stretch the moment so that it feels right, then begins to get uncomfortable, and finally you speak.

"My friends," you say. I like that. Friends. From anyone else it would have sounded cheap. I do not believe that these people are your friends. You probably do not even know a lot of them.

"We are privileged," you continue. "We are spoilt. We can stay here in our ivory towers " — I see neither ivory nor towers — "and forget that the world outside exists. Or we can make use of our position of privilege to fight for a society that is equal and fair.

"Friends." Again, that word, that intimacy! "Here in the coalfields we are at the heart of a class war. I put it to you that, if you are not a part of the solution, then you are a part of the problem. The time has come to choose sides, to stand shoulder to shoulder with our comrades and fight the fascist oppressors!"

I understand little of what you say, but I feel the power of your words. You want to fight, cause trouble. I should have known.

Afterwards, an unwashed woman rattles a bucket at me. "Support the miners," she says. The bucket is full of coins.

I stare at her. "I want to fight," I say.

She steps back, smiles awkwardly. "The vans are that-a-way," she says before moving on, rattling her bucket.

#

Squeezed into a mini-van, so tightly packed someone has to force the doors to close from the outside. Here there is no such thing as personal space. I breathe the odour of your kind, analyse the chemicals. Tobacco, alcohol and other contaminants are mixed in with the smells of stale sweat and shit.

I had hoped to share transport with you. We could have gone in your open-topped car. I would have worked out how to drive the thing quite quickly, I am sure.

Not to worry. I will locate you later. We are all heading to the battleground, I have been assured of that.

The fascist filth stop us at the point where a lane from our road tries to feed onto a larger road that is divided into two opposing streams of traffic.

Our driver argues with them through his open window, but I can see that they are not amenable to persuasion. We are not to be allowed onto the large road. These men, with their car marked POLICE, do not want us to join the battle.

"Do we have weapons?" I ask of the man squashed intimately between me and the window.

He laughs. "Too fucking right," he says. "We should take them right here, eh?"

We find an alternative route, through narrow lanes flanked by untidy stone walls. After a time we stop, abandon the van and walk across the fields.

One of my friends carries a petrol can and another carries a rucksack full of clanking bottles. We could make those into crude firebombs, I think, but that has probably occurred to them already.

Before long I can hear the chanting, the roaring of the crowd, the continual blare of sirens. I walk faster, leaving my new friends behind.

I scramble down a heather-matted bank, the battlefield spread out before me. There is some kind of industrial installation there: towers, buildings and lorries huddled together between heaps of black rubble. The installation is surrounded by high chainlink fence. This site is valuable, I suspect. This must be what they fight over.

Its entrance is shielded by white vans, marked with the same POLICE insignia as the car that blocked our way earlier. Fanned out around the entrance and the vans is a double line of dark-uniformed men, cowering behind transparent shields.

Gathered nearby are more vans, more policemen, some even on horses. It is like a scene from a medieval battle. Why do they not appear to have any guns, I wonder?

A short way up the main road to the installation there is an angry crowd, the source of most of the noise. They shout and chant, gesturing at the gathered fascist filth, occasionally throwing stones at them.

I feel vaguely disappointed. I had expected far better of you. I think you need some help. And that would allow me to get close to you.

#

It is easy to forget yourself down here. The crowd surges around me, angry voices clamouring in my ears, rattling around my skull. I am repeatedly pushed and jostled. It is exciting.

Recognizing my state of increasing arousal, I block some of my neurochemical pathways, damp down the adrenalin rush.

I stand solid. Those who jostle me now rebound as if from a tree, a statue. I do not yield to these creatures. They have no significance. It is good to be calm.

I look around, calibrating my vision both for breadth of field and pattern recognition. You are the pattern I seek, my friend: the boyish contours of your face, the flowing chestnut hair. I know you are here, you see: I can taste you on the air. Your olfactory signature is written across the smell of the crowd, faint but unique.

I see you. Twenty metres away, no more. You are with the other man who spoke at the rally, the miner. Heads together, trying to hear each other against the din. Hands gesture, point. You are plotting, planning your campaign.

I move towards you, ducking my head as a red-faced man hurls a stone at the ranked shields of the fascist filth. I hesitate, eyeing the man, weighing up cost and benefit. He turns away, hasn't noticed that his missile had passed within centimetres of my impact-resistant skull. I let it pass. Cost and benefit.

I can feel the excitement growing as I approach you. A surge too powerful to resist.

You are still unaware, only metres from me.

The crowd dynamic is changing, the noise more frenzied, the surges and flows redirected. Something is happening, then. I look around again, and in that moment I see that the filth are advancing now and that you have slipped away into the crowd with your miner friend.

The oppressors, behind their plastic shields, are hollering and whooping at us, trying to intimidate, trying to bolster their own spirits. They must be very scared.

More stones are being directed at them now. A fencepost hurled like a javelin flies over my head and strikes a shield, knocking one of the uniformed men off balance.

Firebombs. Someone has filled the bottles with petrol, stuffed the necks with rags and ignited them. They fly through the air almost apologetically, but when they strike the ground they erupt in liquid flame, spreading under the shields, up their plastic surfaces.

There is a concrete post in the ground nearby. A man is pulling at it but it won't shift. I knock him aside with the back of my hand, seize the post and pull. It breaks at ground level — I am very strong indeed, have I mentioned that? — and I raise it above my head.

I am getting excited again.

The filth are close now. I am confused. I see your face, even though you are no longer here. I need to break something. Inflict pain. I raise the post high and swing it down.

These shields may deflect stones and firebombs, but against more serious weaponry they are useless. One blow knocks it out of your — no, his — hands. The second blow . . . well, the second time he has nothing to protect him, does he?

#

It was a mistake. Stupid. I forgot my purpose, why I am here. I became too excited. Such flaws should have been designed out of me long ago.

I allowed them to beat me when they got me to a cell. I deserved it for my stupidity. I still deserve it, for their beating did not hurt — I simply ignored the pain. My body repairs itself as I fill endless hours in my cell, sometimes alone, sometimes shared with other combatants who have been captured by the fascist filth.

The man in the interview room introduces himself as a doctor. "I have been asked to talk to you, so that I can make a report to the Magistrates' Court," he says. "I need to know a little more about you, Mr Magee." That is the name I have given them: Mr Out Magee. It amuses me, if not them. They think I must be from another country.

I tell him about myself. That entertains me, too. I have nothing to lose, after all.

"I am a killing machine, a vampire come from the far future. I am a genetic hunter-gatherer, exploiting the resources of the pasts to satisfy the genetic famine of my future. We need variety. Adaptability. We need the diversity that is so abundant in the primitive depths of our various pasts."

He humours me. "Do you have no guilt?" he asks. "No sense of responsibility?"

"No," I tell him. "That was left out at some stage. I am blank, without a conscience. It would be surplus to requirements, after all."

And it is meaningless, too. Responsibility for — to — what?

He looks at me attentively. He feels superior.

"You are not even my predecessors," I continue, enjoying myself, I think. "You are not my ancestors. In your own pathetic understanding, you are aware of the future as a multiplicity of alternatives, of options, choices to be made. But the arrow of time works in both directions. Just as timelines diverge towards the future — each branch governed by dichotomy, decision upon decision upon decision — so they diverge as you look into the past. Our own timeline is there, our own ancestry, written in the histories. But each line heading back into the past is another dichotomy, another branch. There is a chaotic flowering of alternative pasts, a fractal history.

"The past is a foreign country. Many foreign countries. I am visiting one now."

Still, he looks attentive, sympathetic. Violence is tempting, but would be counter-productive, I suspect.

"You mean nothing to me," I explain to him instead. "You are irrelevant. You are just meat, raw materials for a greater age." I smile now. "I," I tell him, "I am a miner."

"And how long have you felt this way?"

He thinks I am deluded, but I can prove that I am not. If I choose to.

#

They treat me like a fool, albeit a dangerous fool. It is their mistake that they do not believe me.

There is to be some kind of hearing, a court. For this to happen they must transport me in a van. I have told them that I am strong — really, very strong — but they merely humour me. They do not believe that I broke that concrete post with my bare hands, for instance. They should know better.

I sit in the back of the van, my wrists bound together by a metal brace-let device. A policeman sits across from me, eyes never leaving my face. He is one of the ones who beat me upon my arrival.

He looks surprised when I wrench the bracelets apart, the chain between them fracturing with a sharp crack. He probably hasn't seen any-one do that before. I feel no compunction about knocking him unconscious with a back-handed blow.

I brace myself against the side of the van and kick the back door open.

The van is going faster than I had anticipated, and I hit the ground in a spinning, flailing heap. Immediately, brakes squeal as the van skids to a halt.

They will blame faulty workmanship, I suspect, for both the bracelets and the door.

I catch myself, clamber to my feet, and run.

#

I do not have much time here, I suspect. I have hurt two of the fascist filth, perhaps quite badly. Such things do not matter, but they are of concern to the filth themselves. They probably think I am deranged, that I am a danger to the public. They are right, I suppose, although my derangement is a consequence of my nature and I am only a danger if you obstruct me.

Every one of my actions is defensible, when seen in those terms.

The university is the obvious place to go. You spoke at a rally there, you might be a student or a teacher.

It is growing dark when I get there. The square where you spoke to the crowd is deserted. I should find someone, ask questions. I am familiar enough with this setting not to arouse suspicion.

But there is a reluctance within me, another design flaw, perhaps. I long for my barren future, for a time when something might actually matter to me.

I linger in the shadows, watching as people walk by, sometimes alone,

90

sometimes in boisterous groups. I walk the paths bordered with shrub-
bery and trees, leading between concrete buildings, some lit, others in
darkness.

You have betrayed yourself. You have written your scent signature on
the night air. You have been here recently, must still be nearby.

I am close, my friend, my target, my prey. So close.

A row of lavishly lit windows, smoky within. Music and voices belch
into the night with every opening and closing of the doors. Inside, people
sit around tables, or stand at counters drinking brown liquid from glass
receptacles. Some lean over green-topped tables, striking balls with
sticks. Others thrust at brightly lit machines, slapping at them and pulling levers, turning away to exclaim or laugh. They appear to be enjoying
themselves. It must be a participatory thing, its meaning and value lost to
mere spectators.

You are in there, my friend.

I stand in the darkness and look in, scanning the faces until I see you,
standing at a long counter where they sell the drinks. You are laughing
and talking. You must be enjoying yourself, too.

I may be short of time, but I know when to be patient. I wait.

I understand now that I've come here to kill you, for whatever reason.
I am your nemesis. I will extinguish your life and then be snatched back
to my future by those who watch. You do not have long now.

Eventually, you leave, accompanied by two of your companions.

I follow. Your body heat shines strongly in the darkness, a beacon to
guide me.

You three head into one of the buildings and I follow. Up a flight of
stairs and then along a corridor lined with red doors. This must be some
kind of dormitory building for students, I think.

I follow your trail at a distance.

There is a number on the door. 134. Your signature is all over it. Your
companions have gone on along this corridor, but, even though I did not
see, I know that you have stopped here, that 134 is your room.

I touch the handle, still marginally warmed by your touch.

I enjoy this part.

I ease the handle and it turns. You haven't locked it yet, so soon after
your return.

I push it gently before me and walk in to the room.

The gun is unexpected.

I have not seen its like before. It has a compact stock with a long, fat muzzle. That's a silencing device, I realise: fitted to deaden the noise. The gauge of the muzzle is about seven millimetres.

I will probably not feel a thing.

I look from the gun to your face. Your expression is unreadable.

"You've been here before," you tell me.

I stretch my perception of time to its extreme, slow everything down so that I can react as quickly as possible. But there is a limit: my body relies on the firing of neurones, the passing of signals from eye to brain to motor system. Electricity and biochemistry are the fundamentals of my being, as they are of yours.

I see the muscles twitch in your hand, the tightening of your trigger finger. The flight of your bullet is too fast, even for my heightened reactions.

I was right. I did not have much time left in this place.

#

I walk the streets, trying to orient myself. It always throws me, I think, the shock of the new. Or rather, the shock of the old.

I let myself be jostled by the crowd, smiling in reply to their curses. I should watch where I am going, they tell me. The physicality of this bustling age is invigorating.

I do not know how long I have been walking through these streets. I have been learning your social syntax, letting the rules of your world soak into my consciousness.

I am looking for something, I know. I have been sent here with a purpose.

It will become apparent. Eventually my reason for being will find me.

I walk. And learn how to be normal.

The year is 1984. I do not belong here.

#

Information is everything here, in a world at this level of development. They usually call the stage that you are entering the Information Age.

It nearly always comes before the Crash.

I know who you are, now. I have information about you. The name you use is Gary Cromwell and you are the Vice-President of the local Students' Union. Nice touch that: you can abuse the power and spend the Union's funds without any of the responsibility of the presidency. You are a troublemaker, you stir things up. You are a thrill-seeker. You are, in the vernacular, one selfish sonofabitch.

I want you, Gary. You are mine.

Or you will be soon.

#

You like to drink. You make regular use of the Students' Union Bar.

I watch you there, Gary. It's easy to stand outside and look in. I have the measure of you, my friend. I know you as if you were my own brother.

#

I follow you to your room. Number 134. Your scent signature is all over this corridor, focused on the door.

I rest my hand on the doorknob — still warm from your touch. I twist but it does not yield. A little more pressure and the lock pops. I blame the workmanship.

The gun . . . the gun is unexpected.

Its single black pupil stares at me. You are using a silencer. You are well prepared.

I will probably not feel a thing.

I look from the gun to your face. Is that compassion in your eyes?

"You've been here before," you tell me.

I stretch my perception of time to its limit, slow everything down so that I can react as quickly as possible.

I see the muscles twitch in your hand, the tightening of your trigger finger. There is a faint puff of smoke from the silenced muzzle, a flash of metal as the bullet emerges.

I am very strong — have I mentioned that? I am fast, too.

My right hand swings across, swats the bullet from the air. In the same movement I knock the pistol from your hand.

That is not compassion on your face now. It is fear.

I smile. "You should be proud," I tell him. "Honoured by our attentions. You have been chosen, Gary. You are valuable to us. You will be making a contribution to my future. You are the one person from this age who has any significance."

Your attitude puzzles me. That is a flaw, I suspect. One that should have been designed out. The fear was only transient. Now you are angry, defiant.

"That's what you think, is it, my friend?"

I like that: fighting for your life and you still call me "friend".

"It is the truth."

"It's your understanding," you say. "It's what they've written into your head."

You handle this situation well. With those few words you reveal that you are not an innocent target, that you actually have some understanding of the situation. With your words you undermine me, make me question my purpose. Sometimes the less obvious weapons are the more powerful.

I step closer to you. Your scent is so strong to my heightened senses. I am getting excited.

"And what is your understanding, friend Gary?"

"You're a toy, an entertainment." Your words disappoint me: I had hoped for more subtlety, a better fight. But . . . your attitude. Your tone is apologetic. You pity me. You are full of surprises, my friend.

"You've been here before," you tell me again.

I have already suspected as much. I remain silent.

"Twice. Both times I killed you. But you came back. You don't have to do it, though. You could stay here like me. Break out of the system."

"Why would I do that?"

"They're in your head," you say. "Riding in your mind, feeding on your experiences. They have a name for it here. Snuff movies. They want to watch you killing me. You're a living, historical snuff movie, my friend."

That's all you are."

"No," I say. "That's not true. You have been chosen. I come from a future where diversity has been squandered. You and your kind will replenish our stock."

"My kind?" you ask. "I'm just like you, except I saw through it all, decided I didn't want to be used any more. I'm your predecessor, an early version of you. I know the hunger you have for meaning: there is meaning here, in this age, when we can make a difference. I know what it's like, my friend: you are me, we're kin. We are each other."

"I don't believe you."

In your eyes the pity has hardened, become contempt.

"In this age I matter," you say. "You . . . you're just a tool. You have no significance."

That does it. I *am* important.

I reach for your neck, a fast, direct movement.

But you, too, are fast. Your right arm swings, deflects my strike.

Surprised, I stagger under my own momentum. You push and I smash into the wall, *through* the wall. A man screeches, leaping from his bed. I choke on the plaster dust, roll over.

You have gone, of course.

#

Outside it has started to rain and the dust runs in rivulets down my face.

I hear the sirens, but it is just one more alien noise to me. They have no significance. The flashing blue lights mean nothing to me, either, although I should sense the danger.

I resist when they seize me, but I have been weakened, I realize. It is not just rain and wet plaster dust running down my face; it is blood, too.

#

They are scared of me. They keep me locked up alone in a cell. Whenever I emerge I wear thick metal bracelets around my wrists and ankles that even I cannot break. They call me Mr Out Magee, for some reason.

It is easy to lose track of time here. They have moved me around: I have been in four prisons already. They are trying to disorient me, I think. Or they do not know how to handle me.

I have spoken to doctors, and in front of public hearings where my supposed crimes have been discussed. They say I have attacked policemen. I argue in my defence that I have scarcely had the opportunity, but given the chance . . . That amuses me, at least.

I do not think they will let me out of this place — or places like it — for some time. They think I am dangerous. The opportunity will arise, I am sure, but they are being very careful.

I wonder about you, Gary, my friend. About your words. You clearly believed them.

Perhaps it is true that I have been misled. Perhaps I was sent to punish you, Gary.

Your strength and speed of reaction surprised me, you see. It makes me think that perhaps there is an element of truth in your words: that you, too, are not of this time, this place. Are you one of us, Gary? Are you some kind of renegade? Are you, as you claim, a rogue version of me? Is that why I must kill you?

That changes nothing. If what you say is true, I am a killing machine, tracking down one of my kind gone rogue. Does that knowledge change me in any way? I think not: my mission is within me, it is central to my being. I do not possess the design flaw that would allow me to deviate: I have been made too well this time.

#

You couldn't resist, could you, Gary? You had to come and make sure that I have been secured.

Have you come merely to gloat? Or, perhaps, have you come to kill me again, fearful that I might still escape and track you down?

Foolish of you, Gary, my friend, my brother.

I was expecting another doctor, another investigator of psychopathy.

We are in the special interview room. I am bound up in a wire-reinforced straitjacket, tied by tethers to the padded bench where I have been forced to sit.

You stand across the room from me and study my features. Is that pity again in your eyes, or contempt?

"You'll be here a long, long time, my friend," you tell me. "No more stalking innocent people. No more beating policemen with concrete blocks. You could help yourself by talking about it. Let us inside your mind."

I have been preparing for this moment. I am strong, you see. Very strong.

They know that, of course. Hence the reinforced straitjacket, the constraints.

You think that I am being sullen, refusing to talk.

But no, if you observe closely, you will see the workings of the muscles in my jaw. I have to swallow the blood so that you do not guess my plan.

I watch you, as you pace the room. I gauge the distances, the angles, the required trajectory. I will get only one chance.

I curl my tongue, forming a rough cylinder. I position the tooth carefully and take a deep breath.

I spit.

I am very strong — did I mention that?

You are looking right at me and my aim is good. The tooth hits you in the right eye. There is a popping sound, a spurt of clear liquid. Then a duller crack as the tooth emerges from the back of your head and embeds itself in the wall.

You weren't expecting that.

#

I do not think they will let me out of this place — or places like it — for some time. They know how dangerous I am, even if they do not truly understand my nature.

I think that I have been abandoned here, in this age. In vain, I wait for them to snatch me back to my future but the summons never comes. I think I must have broken the rules somehow.

I must resign myself to my fate. I will die here of old age.

#

It is 2012 and I have finally come to realize that I belong here as much as I will ever belong anywhere.

Which is ironic, as I do not have long left. Your Information Age was not a long one. Your Crash will probably not take long, either. Your world is warming and your seas are dying and you were too selfish and short-sighted to do anything about it. You deserve your fate.

A fate I share: soon I will die from the disease of your age. I have cancer. A primary in the oesophagus, with secondaries in the liver, lymphatic system and large bowel.

It will be a messy way to die.

I do not have long now.

#

It always throws me, I think, the shock of the new. Or, rather, the shock of the old.

I am walking through some kind of shanty town, an endless sprawl of lean-tos and shacks protected from an angry ocean by a barrier of bulldozed earth. Dogs bark and children cry, and I tip my face up to the violent sky, let the invigorating rain run down my features. I feel released and I don't know why.

I do not know how long I have been walking like this. I have been learning the rules of your world, acclimatizing.

I am looking for something, I know. I have been sent here with a purpose.

It will become apparent. Eventually my reason for being will find me.

I walk. And learn how to be normal.

The year is 2024. I do not belong here.

Crowd Control
Lou Anders

"Touch me like that again, and I'll blow your brains out," I said.

Of course, the threat didn't carry very much weight. Dan gave me a wicked grin and then he started to reach for my tit again.

"Tell you what," I said, revising my statement, "touch me like that again, and I'll blow my own brains out."

This time he frowned. My contract wasn't as good as Dan's, so he'd have to wait the full twenty-four hours to have me up and running. He was sick, but not so sick that he'd fuck me without a head.

"Wouldn't want to touch you anyway," he said pouting, and turned to flick the holowall to the Disney Soft Porn channel. Then he dropped onto the couch with his hairy back to me like I wasn't even there. I slid the little gun back into my purse, but kept my distance nonetheless. I still had three hours left on my timeslot in Real and damned if I was going to spend it under him.

"I'm going out into the Mall," I said. Already absorbed into whatever he was watching, Dan grunted some sort of response.

I keyed in my exit request and stood at the doorway waiting for it to unbolt. The display above the lock showed that some two hundred fifty people were currently engaged in using the hallway. I was third in line to get out, so I watched as the display jumped down to two hundred and forty-nine and back up twice before the pneumatic lock slid aside with a hiss of air. As the door opened up, a tall, skinny kid tumbled a few paces into my room, then righted himself and pressed back into the wall of bodies. I didn't say "Clumsy" and he didn't apologize. These things happen. Sucking in my chest, I pressed into the throng of people without a word to anyone, my face automatically assuming the same blank stare we all shared as we worked our way slowly down the hallway. Despite the sweat smell and armpit odour and, yes, even the farts, the rules were clear out here. Each of us was alone, withdrawn into our own isolated worlds. Eyes downcast and arms at sides, we slowly pushed and shuffled forward, winning space step by step.

This crowd was making good time and within a half-hour I'd reached the end of the hallway, where it joined the larger promenade. Pushing out into it, I was swallowed up by a thousand people, bodies as far as the eye could see. This was the Mall proper. Shops lined the eastern walls, restaurants the west. Hallways intersected every five businesses. West-east promenades every kilometre. I had no idea how big the Mall really was. I'd never been more than a few kilometres in my whole life. There wasn't any point to it. After ten blocks all the stores and restaurants started to repeat. I've heard of people getting lost and not caring, just settling right in wherever they wound up. At least one good thing comes out of it, nobody ever runs away. When the landscape anywhere you go is exactly the same as home, what would be the point?

A teenager on the level above me was threatening to jump. All his friends were gathered around, and he was anxious to show off his new contract. I'm not sure, but I think they were laying bets on how long it would take to put him together again. I could upgrade my own contract, but the one time I was dead was the only real release I'd ever gotten, and, although I didn't plan to make getting myself killed a regular habit, it was nice to think that that little interlude of nirvana was available for me should the occasion arise.

Moving on, it took me twenty minutes to make it three shops down, then five minutes waiting in line for the store to drop below capacity so that I could enter. I had three purchasing coupons that were going to expire this week, and I thought I'd get some accessories for my wardrobe while they were still good.

If I have to have an outfit, chances are it's black, so my purchases tend to reflect that. First order of business: a purse. I wanted one with clean lines. Nothing frilly or girlish. Something to hold in your hand, not on your shoulder. I settled on one almost immediately. The design was guaranteed to be limited to fifty per square kilometre, which statistically speaking meant in an area this dense I'd never have to worry about bumping into someone with the same one. Then I spied some earrings, diamond-studded. I know, but that's what I wear. Other girls might like to buy some different earrings. Of course, once I'd gotten both items off their respective racks, it was a good fifteen minutes making my way to the register, and another thirty before I could pay.

I noticed that, mercifully, there wasn't a line at the exit, so I slipped up fast and keyed in my request. As I stood in line waiting for the counter to drop enough to let me back out onto the Promenade, I thought maybe I should buy some shoes as well. The shoe store was just two down from this, so with an hour thirty-five minutes left I could just about make it.

Half an hour later found me torn between a pair of black funky shoes and a pair that was more classically conservative and stylish. I decided to forgo both and instead spent my last purchasing coupon on a pair of heels with square toes. They were available in two hundred per square kilometre, but I liked their more masculine design, so I didn't mind. Besides, these petty choices, between Product A and Product B, were the only illusions of real freedom any of us had.

That left me with just over an hour to make it the three store-lengths back to my hallway and then down to my apartment. Since it had taken me thirty to get out of the hall to begin with, and another to go from the last store to this, I thought I could just about do it, but it was definitely going to be close. These were the kind of mental gymnastics you had to go through in Real, but it was only fair for the other couples who were waiting on me to return so they could enjoy their block of freedom.

When I made it back to the apartment, Dan was already nude and just getting ready to leave Real. I slid my purchases into my assigned closet without looking his way, then took off my own clothes and slipped them in as well.

"You're late," he said irritably. He didn't say anything more and I didn't argue. I just turned and tapped the wall console, which slid our two cubicle doors open, as well as the two doors for Marjorie and Jeff. We waited for them to fully extract themselves, then lent a hand as they stepped blinking out into the middle of the room.

"Oh, thank god," said Marjorie, tumbling out into the room on uncertain legs. She breathed a deep sigh of relief, grateful for this temporary physical liberation.

"Seems like it gets shorter and shorter." Jeff scowled at no one in particular. He was a fat prick, but I didn't begrudge him his attitude. Each of us came out screaming for Real when it was our turn. "I still say we should take turns offing ourselves. The time one of us spends getting rebuilt could buy the rest of us a little more in our block of Real."

"We could maybe draw lots for it," Marjorie suggested. I couldn't tell how serious she was.

Dan nodded in my direction. "Get her to do it. She was threatening to do as much this morning."

Jeff moved up into my face.

"That so? You want to go jump off a ledge, buy me a little more time in Real?"

I told him what he could do with it. Not that I wasn't tempted, of course, but I wouldn't be goaded into anything. Jeff backed down, and we got on with the exchange. Of the five pair bonds that shared this apartment, Dan and I only ever saw these two and the two on the other side of our rotation. We didn't even know who the other two couples were. It was sort of strange, knowing they occupied this same space that we lived in while we were closed up inside the wall. I wondered about them sometimes, about all the people who lived right alongside of me, separated only by ticks of the clock.

For convenience, the day was divided up into twenty-five one-hour segments. That gave each couple a block of five hours out. The remaining twenty hours were spent on the inside. It didn't matter that it didn't match up with the sun. Who'd ever seen the sun anyway?

"See you inside?" said Dan, leaning out from his hole in the wall.

"Hell, no," I replied, keying the command to slam shut my cubicle door.

Dan and I might have liked each other once, but if we had it was so long ago that neither of us remembered. Until we qualified for a separa-

CROWD CONTROL

tion and re-pair bonding we were stuck together, so we just coexisted as best we could. It was a bit like life out in the hallway outside, complete with the occasional groping.

As the door slid down into place, closing me inside, I felt the sensofoam, like warm skin, molding itself to my contours. It smoothed itself up around my body, closing over my eyes and mouth, pushing up around and between my legs in an almost sensual embrace. The sensofoam not only relayed information back and forth from every square millimetre of my skin, it also took care of such necessities as perspiration and waste extraction. And, of course, it was also totally oxygen permeable. As the last of it engulfed me, I gave over and slipped out of Real entirely.

Inside my Virtual, there were no hallways, there were no doors, there were rarely any people. I'd configured it so it was just space, space, space. This time, I configured the scape so it was a vast, green lawn that stretched off in all directions without meeting any horizon. Even so, I couldn't quite manage to vanquish the ever-present feeling of claustrophobia. It crouched in the back of my mind, a tiny, nagging reminder that, despite appearances to the contrary, in actuality I was squeezed into a cramped, coffin-shaped box.

A request icon popped up in my field of vision, Dan signalling me that he wanted to come across. I marked it "ignore", then flagged his user name and made certain that no subsequent intrusions from that sender were to be accepted. I took some time just walking across the plain, relishing the sensation of moving without being bumped or jostled.

Then I decided I'd go visit Mom. I called up the simulation, and the graveyard slowly rose up around me. It was always strange seeing the clusters of craggy headstones rising out of the ground. They grew into place like plants, until I was in a veritable forest of the dead. How many others were visiting their lost loved ones in this same simulation I didn't know, since I kept the program from revealing anyone else's avatar to me, and vice versa. So, as the only person in sight, I strolled between the tombs looking for my mother's grave. I could have scrolled Mom's resting place directly over, but I enjoyed the illusion of a walk.

A raven landed on a nearby headstone and cocked its head at me. I didn't remember birds being programmed into this scape, but the program

103

was sophisticated and often improvised on its own. The raven flitted from stone to stone, then paused a few metres away when I came to the one I was looking for.

Mom had been one of the lucky ones who died of natural causes before the bioengineers and the nanotechnicians ensured that none of the rest of us ever would. Nor were we very likely to stay dead from any other cause very long. Everyone had an insurance contract that saw them put back together anywhere from five minutes to three days after any accidents occurred. To top it off, the current administration had ethical problems with suicide, an attitude that had existed for as long as I could remember and was likely to continue unabated for even longer.

The whole situation was ludicrous from any but a corporate perspective, and, of course, it resulted in the overcrowded and environmentally exhausted planet we all shared. Space probes had long ago told us that there wasn't anywhere else we could live, and it was too expensive to send us anyway. But, of course, there were still the rumours. Some people claimed that we were the ones who had been left behind, that there really were beautiful, paradise planets where you could have acres and acres to yourself, and that they weren't that far away. Then there were the really paranoid rumours. The current favourite was that we were all still in Virtual, even when we were in Real. Everything was just a simulation housed in some gigantic computer someplace. How would you know, huh? Either way, life was nothing more than one very long malaise. We were human sardines, packed in a world-sized can with no variation and no end.

Of course, Mom hadn't been all that lucky when you think about it. Her real grave had been dug up and paved over long ago, along with everyone else's in the cemetery, and all she had was this virtual simulation for a remembrance.

Something caught my attention in the shadow of my mother's tombstone. At first I thought it was a defect in the program, a problem with the algorithms that created the grass. I peered closer, and saw what looked to be like a little round rabbit hole.

"I can get you out," said a still, small voice. I looked around. The raven was still behind me. Nobody else was around. I wondered if some weirdo had hacked into my scape.

104

"Dan, is that you?" I said.

"Just step inside," said the voice again. "I'll explain everything."

I'd never heard of anyone being injured in Virtual, and being functionally immortal tends to relieve most fears (fear of boredom excepted), so I decided to go along. I stepped over the hole.

I didn't fall immediately, not according to any real rules of gravity or physics. Rather, I stayed suspended over the hole like a cartoon character, then dropped suddenly (but without any sense of motion) straight down into darkness. A paintbrush appeared and painted me into a bright blue-and-white dress, which ballooned out around me, as if in a rush of air, and slowed my fall. Before too long, a lit square of floor appeared below, and I was deposited gracefully in the middle of it.

The surroundings were pretty sparse. There were no walls, just uninterrupted blackness beyond the immediate square of the floor. At one perimeter, a tiny round door was set against the darkness. Near to it, there was a wooden chair with a jewelled bottle placed on its plush, red seat cushion. A note tied around the neck of the bottle said exactly what I'd expected it would: "Drink me."

"Fond of Lewis Carroll, are we?" I hollered into the void.

"His real name was Reverend Charles Lutwidge Dodgson," replied the still, small voice, "but yes, very much so."

"So what happens now?" I asked.

"Well," said the voice with a giggle, "there is only one way out of here."

I looked at the bottle and at the little door. "Nothing to lose" was practically my mantra.

It was in the tall grasses beyond the door that I met up with the caterpillar. Now that we were roughly the same size, his voice didn't sound so still and small. He sat on his mushroom. He smoked his hookah. He repeated his offer.

"I can get you out."

"Out of where? Here? I've got at least nineteen hours to go."

"Out of it all," said the caterpillar, stretching out with his multiple arms in a gesture that encompassed the space around him. "Out of everywhere. Out of their control."

"Who are you?" I demanded.

"No one. Anyone. Someone." He rolled the words off his tongue in a leisurely manner, as if the virtual hookah came with its own virtual buzz. Then he fixed several pairs of little black insect eyes on me. "Let's just say that I represent a growing concern, a belief that the status quo has robbed the human race of its dignity. By removing the uncertainty of death, they have robbed us of the preciousness of life. We can give you back that uncertainty, for just a little while."

"Are you asking me to kill myself?" I said, not understanding.

"Not at all," he replied. "We're asking you to live a little while in a span of time where that is an option. We'll free you from their manacles, remove the programming that preserves and rebuilds you whenever an injury occurs. You'll be truly free for the first time ever, able to go on living or take your own life. Whether you choose to end your existence or return to it is up to you."

"Why me?"

"It was thought that someone who spends as much time dressing in black and brooding in graveyards as you do might be sympathetic to our cause."

He had me there. So, instead of pointlessly pretending that my circumstances were other than what they were, I asked him to explain just how this miracle of choice was supposed to be provided.

"By means of a very special virus. It travels back with you as information, but once in Real it will seek out and corrupt the nanoprogramming in your cells. Once they've been disabled, all the king's horses and all the king's men won't have a fucking prayer of putting you back together again."

There didn't seem to be but one thing left to say.

"How do I sign up?" I asked.

"You already have. We loaded the virus into your avatar the moment you came through the door. Once you go back to Real, you'll have about ten hours before their nanoprogramming begins to reassert itself. What you do with it . . . is entirely in your hands. The door back out is that way."

He pointed over his shoulder, where a path ran into the tall grasses. I lingered a moment, then started down it.

"Oh, one more thing," he called back to me. "Don't eat or drink anything in Real. All food is infested. If you take anything, it will readmit their coding into your body."

106

Winding through grasses, I thought I caught a glimpse of the raven flying low through the underbrush, just a sleek black bullet flanking my steps. Then the vegetation parted and I stood in a little clearing before an ornate doorframe. A clock hung in the air above it, similar to the ones we all use in here to keep track of our turns. If it could be trusted, then my term in Virtual was up and it was time to return to Real. It didn't feel like enough time had passed, but the caterpillar's voodoo had probably screwed with my perception. So I stepped through the archway, keying in my request to be awakened as I did so.

Returning to the other side, I experienced a momentary sense of euphoria, a giddiness that was both elation and fear, as I felt the sensofoam sucked away from my body for the last time. The partition slid away and I stepped out into the room, naked as the first time I was born. But then I had been a statistic, a lemming, one pawn among billions in a game without winners or losers, in which the only rule was that you never left the table. Now I was a new creation, a singularity, a unicorn in the herds of horses, the one player who had a choice to roll the dice or walk away.

I did my best to keep my composure while Jon and Tom (the couple on this side of our rotation) shook hands and vacated our mutual space for their cubicles. Dan was taking his time getting dressed, and that was always a trouble sign. He scowled and averted his eyes when I looked at him. I was sure he was just pissed that I'd ignored his requests inside, so I didn't give it any more thought. In fact, I think I was positively glowing.

"Looks like you got something good going on inside, huh, girlfriend," said Tom, grinning and rolling his eyes knowingly. I gave him a wink, then punched his cubicle closed for him. Jon smirked and disappeared in the wall as well. When I turned around, Dan was staring at me.

I started to walk towards my closet to get my clothes back out, and he moved to block my path.

"Outta my way," I said. For once, I was anxious to get out into the crowd. I wanted to wade among them and know that I was different.

"You're not going anywhere," he said with a snarl.

"Like hell!" I tried to push past him, but he caught me and twisted me around. I tried to struggle free, but he shook me.

"I know what you did in there," he said. I stared into his angry brown eyes and the penny dropped.

"You prick! You were the raven!" I wasn't fighting him now. I knew he had me. He'd hacked into my scape, followed me around using the raven as an avatar. He'd seen everything I'd said and done with the caterpillar. Which was about as serious a situation as I could imagine. Dan and I hadn't been anything remotely resembling friendly in years and, as I said before, the current administration didn't look kindly on suicide. I straightened up and tried to look cool.

"Well, now that you know, what are you going to do?" I asked him. "Going to turn me in?"

"I could turn you in," he said. "If I did, you'd be in it deep. They might stick you in a box and run you through a Virtual cell for a hundred years or more. Not a cheerful prospect, is it?"

It wasn't. And he was right. I'd be lucky to get a box. Tampering with the nanoprogramming was just about the worst infraction left in the book.

"I figure I got you in my pocket right now," he said. He let me go then, and stepped back. "But you're a pain in the ass, and it's not like we've enjoyed each other in a while. If you offed yourself at least I wouldn't have to sit around here watching porno and waiting for our Pair Bond Dissolve Request to come through."

"You're going to let me go?"

"Maybe. Yeah, I will. If you do something for me first." He cocked his head over at the wall where the bed unit folded out.

That wouldn't be too bad. Even in his younger days, Dan was never too good on stamina. If a few minutes under him would buy me back my recent sense of freedom, well, it was a small price to pay. I let him lead me over to the wall, push me down when the bedding gel swelled out of the wall to form a mattress. He was easy with me now. I could see the little boy in him, anxious and eager and even grateful to be allowed back into me after all this time.

"Get something," I said, nodding at a drawer.

"Nah, what's the point?" he replied, his voice getting all throaty as he swelled. "If you're so keen to die afterwards, what do you care about protection?"

Point taken. So I let it slide. He pushed on top of me, and I didn't resist.

Frankly, knowing that the reins were about to be handed back put me in too good a mood not to enjoy myself, so I started rocking under him, and in a minute we had a nice rhythm going. This was to be my last fuck, and so, despite Dan, or maybe even because of him, I put my reservations aside and gave over to the moment. We oscillated between greedy embraces and tender ones, and somewhere in our coupling I think maybe we recaptured a tiny ember of the spark that used to be between us. When it was over, Dan held me for a little while. Then I moved his hand away and stood up. He watched me in silence when I dressed and didn't speak 'til I was in front of the door and the display said it was almost my turn to go out.

"I'll miss you," he said. I nodded and even smiled as I stepped out.

Smashed in amid the sluggish flow of human bodies, I simply allowed myself to be carried along while I drifted internally in a sea of private exuberance. "I'm free of all of you," I wanted to call out. I even broke with protocol and smiled at one or two people. They didn't smile back, of course, but I didn't care.

My part of the pack was moving to one of the upper levels, where I'd seen the teenager joking around the last time out. I laughed now, thinking of the lost bets if anyone tried to take odds on the speed of my new contract. Fifty says she'll stay dead forever. If they only knew.

It might have been five minutes, and it might have been three hours, but I was on the uppermost level. I clung to the balcony rail so the throng wouldn't drag me along with it. Gazing down, I worried briefly about who I might land on below, but it didn't matter. Anyone I squashed would be up and running again within a day. It was only I who'd be taking the plunge one way. I put a shoe up on the first rung of the rail and took a deep breath. If I was to get away with it, I'd have to be quick.

I slung myself over and dove before anyone could react. Time slowed down to an infinitesimal crawl as I hung in the air. It seemed that I turned slowly, graceful as the raven had been in its flight, then picked up speed as I swooped down to the multitude below. Free as a bird. It was the final moment of my life, and it was the most beautiful.

#

When I awoke in the hospital, I didn't understand what had happened at first. They had to sedate me, I was so emotional. Afterwards, I managed to piece things together without giving anything away. The doctors didn't know anything about the caterpillar and his pirate codes. They hadn't found anything unusual in my biochemistry when they stitched me back together. As for my suicide attempt, Dan had actually covered for me when the hospital had grilled him. He'd lied to the administration, told them that he'd been there with me and that I'd somehow tripped. I wasn't in any trouble at all. They released me that afternoon, smiling and telling me I was free to rejoin the crowd.

The caterpillar had warned me that food was infested. He'd told me that if I ate or drank anything, nanomachines would get back into my body and rewrite his renegade virus. I should have been able to see it. I should have insisted Dan use protection. His spilt semen readmitted the codes, planting more in me than it was ever meant to. Through his sperm, the administration's programming re-entered my body, turning me back into another immortal member of the populace, destroying my one and only chance at self-determination. The dream was over.

Things are pretty much like they always were now, except that I keep giving over more and more of my time in Real to the other couples. They are grateful enough for it that they don't question why anyone would want to spend so much time inside. Dan leaves me pretty much to myself. I think he feels guilty for having fouled things up. I don't know. We don't talk much at all. I keep looking for the rabbit hole, but, so far, it's never appeared again.

Reflections
Fay Sampson

In the gulf westward of Az lies the mages' island.

Let us call it Phalaroop.

What do you mean: "Isn't that its real name?"

On the finest of days the seas around it are the colour of amethysts. The outer islands rise in the humid haze like green verdigris. The skies are strange. Clouds hang, as if they were the base of a vast copper cauldron, and in their glinting surface scenes appear distinct for a while till the wind distorts them, then tear, reform elsewhere. A shifting mirror, or mirage?

The mainland is lonely. Few have found and farmed it yet. Small coracles creep along the coast, their occupants more shy and wary than the dolphins. No great ships ply the waves.

Thus, at the dawn of the era, even Phalaroop, at the mouth of the Dum River, seemed dangerously remote from land, a sanctuary only to be reached with difficulty and daring.

Here Lil, the mother, and Mada, the father, came and set up the standing stones. And, yes, they are too heavy for human hands to lift. Four young men and two women one of them young, the other a mature student, formed the first intake of their Sorcerers' Seminary.

But if the land was almost empty, the sea was not.

The Water Elementals had created mermaids.

The who? . . . Ssh. Elementals are not as accessible as Directory Inquiries. Be patient. Read on. Then turn the next page very quietly and try not to stare.

As I was saying . . .

Mermaids are born nowadays the size of human babies, for obvious reasons. Towards the end of their very long lives they become, briefly, gaunt and grizzled, but because of their wonderful bone-structure still terribly impressive. For the rest of the time they are fifteen-year-olds. That is how the Elementals first made them, probably because the female Elementals felt they had missed out themselves on the pleasures of teenage girls.

So had the males.

There were, at the time we are speaking of, no mermen. Neither sort of Water Elemental felt that to be desirable. The female kind are rather prim about some things. The males just didn't fancy the competition.

So the mermaids sat on rocks combing their butter-yellow hair and gazing in mirrors and singing with piercing sweetness, as mermaids have always done, and as the few who survive today still do. The female Elementals smiled, when no one else was looking, with what might have been mistaken for nostalgia if they themselves had ever been young. The males stirred the sea like a summer storm.

The singing was clearly audible at the Sorcerers' Seminary on Phalaroop. It caused Father Mada to make some regrettable mistakes in his lectures and the four pupil sorcerers to confuse their notes and skip their homework in their eagerness to scramble out over the rocks in search of a sighting. I am afraid the consequences have been far-reaching. The library of the Sorcerers' Seminary is a repository of great wisdom, but also, on some subjects, alas, a source of significant error. The mermaids were also the reason for the very early invention of the telescope. But not yet.

It is time to focus on three of them, perched quite close to the Island of Phalaroop. Above the waist they are almost indistinguishable one from another. Their individuality begins at the hips. Shushulushi's tail is ivory-white, each scale edged with gold. Pliplip's is jade-green shot with crimson. Angharoom's scales are iridescent.

They are almost the mirror-image of their maternal creators, but not quite. In her female manifestation a Water Elemental looks relentless, penetrating, chill. She usually is.

The male Elemental is more . . . well . . . elementary.

Look. There's one of them. An indigo suffusion under the surface of the amethyst water, like an excited inkblot. Racing this way against the wind. With shrieks of nervous laughter the mermaids hauled themselves higher up the rocks and flicked their tails out of reach of the oncoming waves.

The shadow swirled around the rocks and a hollow groan boomed in the gulleys. Shushulushi giggled.

"Holy jellyfish! I wish he wouldn't do that."

"Go on. You don't really mind, do you?"

"Well . . . "

"They're not supposed to harass us," said Angharoom. "Tseawish wouldn't like it."

"Tseawish's just an old . . . "

"Ssh!"

Since this first generation of mermaids could hardly have been born in the normal way, the Elemental Tseawish was the nearest they had to a mother. She was *very* penetrating and *very* chill, in public, anyway.

Fortunately, male Elementals have a short attention span.

"Has he gone?" asked Pliplip.

"I think so." Shushulushi was cautiously lowering herself into the cool water. It is important for a mermaid not to allow her tail to dry out. "No! Look out!"

Between the shore and the reef swirled another disturbance, clouded gold, as though the sea-bed had been stirred up. The mermaids quickly retreated higher, still clutching their mirrors. It is not easy to climb rocks when you have no legs. Already the mermaids had developed powerful arm-muscles. Shushulushi raised herself on her stomach and peered down. A wave more golden than the rest slapped the stone beneath her. She leaned further out.

"I wonder what it would be *like*," she whispered to the others.

"Oh, Shush!"

Angharoom played a fingernail over the teeth of her chalcedony

113

comb. "I suppose one day, one of us . . . "

"One of us?"

"You mean, one of *us*?"

Shushulushi and Pliplip stared back at her. All three of them were round-eyed, breathless, frightened, curious, ignorant and bursting with unexpressed excitement.

"Tseawish wouldn't let us . . . would she?"

"She taught us to say no."

This time the formless golden shadow did not go away. He sighed around the reef, slithering through the seaweed. The mermaids sighed too, and picked up their combs and mirrors and began to do as they had been trained to do in moments of stress. They held the mirrors in front of their lovely faces, and combed their yellow hair and sang their exquisite wordless song.

You have probably been given the impression that mermaids gaze in mirrors and endlessly comb their tresses because they are vain, and that they sing siren songs with the express intention of luring sailormen to their death. This is not the case. It is true that they are very fair, as well as blonde, and their songs have an unsettling effect upon the males of related species. But since they are all of them fair, and so alike that their faces are almost indistinguishable one from another, vanity would be pointless. Where is the competition? Errors in coastal navigation and the walking into water out of their depth by fully clothed men, however regrettable, are merely unfortunate side-effects. That was not the original purpose of the exercise.

The mermaids are simply practising their devotions. The mirror and the comb are sacred objects, their song is a hymn, and the combing of the hair a ritual act.

Whom do they worship? What do they hope to find reflected in the mirror? Who can say? Their religion has never been verbalized. Their only teaching is by imitation. They have no holy book. The music is never given words. Tseawish, Mistress of Mermaids, did not explain. As each new-formed mermaid woke into consciousness, Tseawish put a comb and mirror into her hands and the other Elementals sang the song over her as they combed their own hair.

The practice is universal among mermaids. It spread to the women of the coast. At dawn and dusk they stripped naked and sat waist-deep in the water, hiding their pale ungainly legs. Each had her own comb and mirror. They did their best to imitate the mermaids' song. You can still find their gravestones carved with the mirror and the comb. Prosaic archaeologists will tell you this simply denotes that a woman is buried there, which is like saying that a grave marked with a cross means the deceased was a joiner.

A more careful observation will reveal that there are gradations of mirrors. Some are polished stone, which gives a blurred, opaque reflection. Some bronze, with marvellously patterned backs. A few are beaten gold. A doctoral thesis awaits someone speculating whether this difference relates to the economic status of the woman, her age and standing in the cult, or the measure of her personal devotion.

Shushulushi's mirror was of nautilus shell, Pliplip's of scroll-edged silver, Angharoom's a seal-bone frame, skilfully carved, holding a disc of polished opal that showed her face in swirls of jade and rose and turquoise. Three faces, almost identical. Three different reflections.

When the song was finished they looked round apprehensively. The water seemed amethyst and untroubled again. Fortunately, there were a great many mermaids and far fewer Elementals, so the latter spent a great deal of time and energy chasing from rock to rock. The three mermaids dived into the sea, down and down to touch the shell-strewn floor, then streaked away to race each other for the outer isles.

But the clouded golden Elemental Conchor proved more single-minded than most. Again and again he lapped the rocks of Phalaroop.

"That superblob of gloop is getting to be a nuisance," said Shushulushi. "I've spent so much time out of the water my scales are beginning to suffer from split ends."

"Dirty old polyp," shuddered Pliplip. She trailed her hand in the clear water. A golden commotion surged beneath the next six waves. Pliplip leaped back at the last moment, shrieking with laughter. The waves sobbed against the rock.

Angharoom leaned over the edge. She could no longer see the bottom. She bent her head lower and lower, searching the bubbles for what might be eyes. The tips of her yellow hair trailed in the liquid gold. She felt the slightest tug. When she peered closer she could no longer see where the

Elemental ended and she began. A delicate shiver ran through her to the tip of her rose-pink tail.

"Excuse me, sir," she gasped. "Would you mind if I had my hair back?"

"Anghar*room!*" hissed Pliplip.

"For Lyv's sake, don't encourage him," said Shushulushi, stroking the calcined edge of her pearly mirror. "I'll tell Tseawish."

"Just a minute," said Angharoom, bringing her face almost down to the water's edge. "I'm trying to see what shape he really is."

"Ugh! I don't think I want to know."

The tug came harder. Angharoom felt herself slipping on the rock. She gave a little gulp and sat up straight, flicking back her wet hair in a shower of spray. Her face was as pink as her tail. She grabbed her comb and began to pull it through her hair very fast. The hymn wobbled breathlessly for the first few bars.

"Serves you right," said Shushulushi. "Sex-kipper!"

#

That night the mermaids woke with a hundred others in their sea-cave dormitory to hear a deep voice booming through the reef:

A... A... A... A... A... A... A... A... A... A...
N... N... N... N... N... N... N... N... N... N...
G... G... G... G... G... G... G... G... G... G...
H... H... H... H... H... H... H... H... H... H...
A... A... A... A... A... A... A... A... A... A...
R... R... R... R... R... R... R... R... R... R...
O... O... O... O... O... O... O... O... O... O...
O... O... O... O... O... O... O... O... O... O...
M... M... M... M... M... M... M... M... M... M...
!... !... !... !... !... !... !... !... !... !...

Electric eel striplights shocked the cavern with blue-white illumination. Ninety-nine pairs of emerald, sapphire, amber eyes glistened in Angharoom's direction. She retreated deeper into her blanket of kelp. Tseawish, Mistress of Mermaids, was standing over her.

"Have you been talking to a Lord of the Elementals?"

"I only asked him to let go of my hair."

"You allowed yourself to be *touched* by him!"

Angharoom hid her eyes. Tseawish's voice swished over her.

"Contact with Elemental Lords is strictly forbidden. We all know what *that* could lead to. At least, your Elemental Mothers do. You girls, I trust, do not. It was decided at the drawing-board stage that procreation by mermaids would be unnecessary and undesirable. With Lyv's cooperation, the Ladies of this Element created sufficient mermaids to populate the entire oceans of the planet to the required density. Any addition to the number would be quite superfluous. We gave you the necessary . . . er . . . configuration for purely aesthetic reasons. We do not want any of *that*. It was extremely hard work to create so many of you, let me tell you. Lyv himself only produced two prototype humans to people the land. Though, now I come to think of it, if he had concentrated more of his energies on mass-production of the economy model, this planet might have had fewer denizens of the more bizarre kind instead. But can you point to anything a male Elemental has created?"

Tseawish's lips set more primly than before.

Angharoom shook her head. A pearly tear slipped from between her fingers.

"I'm sorry, ma'am. It won't happen again."

When she woke next morning her gleaming opaline mirror had gone. In its place lay a plain pewter one. Grey, heavy, dull. Her chalcedony comb was missing too, replaced by common herringbone. Angharoom was in disgrace.

It may have been her imagination, but she fancied that Shushulushi and Pliplip started to spend rather more time than they usually did at their devotions, and that they held their elegant mirrors up more ostentatiously, twisting them this way and that to catch the sun.

Angharoom hunched herself on a sandstone shelf with barely her shoulders out of the water. She turned her head away. Her hymn was hardly more than a whisper. She looked in the mirror, which was dull enough anyway, with eyes blurred with tears. The first time she pulled the herringbone comb through her hair, two teeth broke off.

When they had finished singing she looked round to find Shushulushi and Pliplip watching her.

"I . . . um . . . see you've got a new mirror," said Shushulushi unnecessarily.

"It's . . . er . . . smaller, isn't it?" said Pliplip, who may have meant it kindly. "Well, I mean to say . . . easier to hold."

"It's heavier," snapped Angharoom.

"No need to bite our heads off! We didn't tell you to fraternize with that oversized amoeba."

Angharoom thrust herself off the ledge and swam away. She felt very miserable. Even the Elementals had vanished, as if they were no longer interested in her. It *had* been rather nice to feel the power in her beautiful voice, even though that is not what the hymns were intended for. And the face that looked back from the opal mirror had been exceedingly fair, even if that may not have been the vision you were meant to see. As for the comb . . .

The trouble with being a mermaid is that, while Tseawish may have been right about the aesthetic effect of bare human breasts coupled with iridescent fishtails, the result is inconveniently lacking in pockets. It is necessary to hang one's mirror and comb in a pouch of shimmering seaweed from a thong across one shoulder. The hateful pewter mirror and the brittle herringbone comb bumped against her as she swam through the water. She snatched them out and did a bad-tempered backstroke, hitting the water with each object in turn. For a rebellious moment she wondered what would happen if she let go of them, just allowed them to drift to the bottom of the ocean while she swam on without looking back. She stopped swimming and sat up suddenly in the water. Her heart was racing fast. Could she do that? Could a mermaid live without a mirror? Would she die, and go to Hel?

With a dismal sigh she laid her face in the water and settled to a weary sidestroke, the silly comb stuffed back in the pouch and the pewter mirror pushed out in front of her where she couldn't see it. She did not know where she was going. It did not seem to matter. Perhaps she would just swim on and on, farther than anyone had ever ventured before, too far to turn back. That night Tseawish would miss her in the dormitory. All the mermaids and the Elementals would scour the coasts for her in vain. They would never find her. Then they would all be sorry. That Elemental

Conchor, who had got her into trouble, the old sea-cow Tseawish, and especially Shushulushi and Pliplip.

No mermaid had ever died yet. It was not that they were intended to be immortal. It was just that they had not been created very long. She wondered what they would do for her funeral service. Humans died. She had swum under the sea-cliffs of Az and seen their funeral pyres on the heights, heard the women keening, and the solemn roll of drums. When a mortal woman of the mirror-cult died the mermaids all came out in the moonlight and raised their wordless hymn.

Of course, for a mermaid, cremation was not a practical option.

And they wouldn't find her body, would they?

She almost turned back.

Just then she saw, black against the topaz sky of dusk, a square forbidding island. Powerful muscles or not, she felt excessively tired. She swam in under its cold shadow. Her tail brushed shallow beds of bladderwrack. There was a narrow cave. To reach it, she had to haul herself over a raised bar of shingle. Then she slid down over gritty sand into a deep pool roofed with rock. It was almost dark. She shivered with cold and loneliness. What sea-monsters lived out here, so far from land? Could the Elementals find her, unprotected now by Tseawish, Mistress of Mermaids, a single hissing word from whom had been enough to clear the bay outside the dormitory of lascivious Sea-Lords in one shake of a sprat's tail? And what if one did find her alone, crouched in her cave? She was *very* lonely.

She lifted her comb and mirror as she had been taught to do every night. But the pewter was very heavy and the arm that raised the comb ached with effort. She let them drop. Without uttering a single note of music she fell asleep.

Nothing happened. When Angharoom woke next morning she found the misty sun already forty degrees above the horizon and the water relaxingly warm even in her subterranean cave, but everything else as before. Angharoom did not know whether she felt relieved or disappointed.

She had swum a very long way. She could see nothing but waves no matter which way she looked. And the island was too steep and high for a mermaid to climb to get a better view.

The clouds hung lower than ever, more bronze than gold today. They had that burnished underside that makes the whole sky look like a gigantic mirror. The sun glinted teasingly and lit up strange scenes. Reality? Magic?

Angharoom swam round to where the shore was sandier and the filtered sunshine warmed a shallow bay. She felt lazy and self-indulgent now. It was time somebody was nice to her, anyway, even if it was only herself. Still, habits die hard. She had a brief look in the mirror, made a few perfunctory passes at her hair with the useless comb, and trilled hurriedly through the shortest hymn. Duty done, she put down the mirror and comb, and lay on her back in the yielding sand with wavelets lapping over her scales to keep them nicely wetted. Her hair, rather more tangled than usual, fanned out across the beach behind her, drying slowly from buttercup gold to primrose yellow. Her open eyes, dark blue as the shells of mussels, roamed lazily over the shifting scenes reflected in the sky above her.

Was there a world beyond the waters where such things were happening? She watched amazed as Giant Sand Slugs dragged their viscous bulk over an undulating landscape of desert dunes that rippled in the wind, only to crumple into compacted hollows as the monsters passed.

Marsh gibbons jibbered. Marsh jibbons . . . Large hairy anthropoids kept up an incessant nervous communication in the mandrake swamps.

On the Sorcerers' Seminary of Phalaroop two pupil mages appeared to be paddling in the cove with their skirts hitched up round their knees, ogling a pair of giggling mermaids who looked irritatingly like Pliplip and Shushulushi.

"Squid-faces!" hissed Angharoom and sat up in annoyance and grabbed her mirror.

A... A... A... A... A... A... A... A... A... A...
H... H... H... H... H... H... H... H... H... H...
!... !... !... !... !... !... !... !... !... !...

A deep tremor rocked the bay.

"No!" cried Angharoom, looking round wildly. The cave was on the other side of the island. The cliffs were behind her. There was no escape.

She skipped her tail clear of the surf and clawed her way hastily up the beach. A wave, higher than all the rest, ran sinuously over the sand to stroke her tail. It was a deep soft gold.

"Don't!" gasped Angharoom. "You mustn't."

"WHAT ARE YOU DOING ALL BY YOURSELF?"

"N-nothing. Sunbathing. Watching the sky. Twitching?"

"YOU ARE A LONG WAY FROM HOME."

"I'm a good swimmer."

"TSEAWISH IS SEARCHING FOR YOU."

"Good."

"DID YOU COME HERE BECAUSE OF ME?"

"Yes. No! Don't flatter yourself. I felt like a holiday."

"I CAME TO APOLOGIZE. I HEARD SHUSHULUSHI AND PLIPLIP TALKING. I FEAR MY OVERZEALOUS ADMIRATION MAY HAVE CAUSED YOU A SIGNIFICANT LOSS OF FACE."

"Come again?"

"YOUR MIRROR WAS CHANGED."

"Oh, that!" She picked it up. It was very heavy and very grey and very dull.

"I SHOULD LIKE TO OFFER A SMALL COMPENSATION AS A TOKEN OF MY PROFOUND ESTEEM AND RESPECT."

"You what?"

Something broke the surface of the water that was now almost entirely filled with gold. A mirror rose, mystic, wonderful.

"Oh, I couldn't," said Angharoom. "We're not allowed to accept presents from Sea-Lords."

Another wave washed closer and deposited the mirror at her tail-fin. Angharoom tried not to stare. It was one of the most beautiful mirrors she had ever seen, small and delicate, fashioned from rose-pink quartz that had been polished till it caught the light like crystal. Beside it lay a comb, with curved teeth cut from dragon's claws.

Angharoom swallowed hard.

"No, really, I shouldn't."

With a reluctant finger she pushed the gifts back to the edge of the water. Then she grasped the pewter mirror that Tseawish had left her, and the fishbone comb. With a frightened earnestness she began the ritual combing.

121

D... D... D... D... D... D... D... D... D... D...
R... R... R... R... R... R... R... R... R... R...
A... A... A... A... A... A... A... A... A... A...
T... T... T... T... T... T... T... T... T... T...
!... !... !... !... !... !... !... !... !... !...

With a heavy sigh the undertow swallowed the quartz mirror and the dragon's-claw comb. The bay rocked and the waves settled to violet normality. Angharoom felt a sorrowing pang of loss for . . . She was not sure which.

Next day, she was crunching the last of her breakfast shrimps when the bay seemed suddenly flooded with sunshine. Angharoom smiled, and then leaped back like a flying fish. It was not the sun that had turned the waves from lavender to gold.

"Oh! It's you again."

Y... Y... Y... Y... Y... Y... Y... Y... Y... Y...
E... E... E... E... E... E... E... E... E... E...
S... S... S... S... S... S... S... S... S... S...
!... !... !... !... !... !... !... !... !... !...

"The answer's no," said Angharoom quickly.

"YOU ARE NO COMMON MERMAID. FOR YOU, NO COMMON GIFT. I HAVE BROUGHT YOU A MIRROR OF STARDUST THAT WILL SHOW YOU YOUR FACE AT THE DEAD OF NIGHT AND A COMB OF THE SEVEN BRISTLES FROM A RED WHALE'S SPINE. WHEN YOU DRAW THEM THROUGH YOUR HAIR YOU WILL HEAR THE SINGING OF THE GREAT CETACEANS FROM AROUND THE PLANET."

"Oh!" breathed Angharoom. Then, "What would I have to do in return?"

P... P... P... P... P... P... P... P... P... P...
L... L... L... L... L... L... L... L... L... L...
E... E... E... E... E... E... E... E... E... E...
A... A... A... A... A... A... A... A... A... A...

S... S... S... S... S... S... S... S... S... S...
E... E... E... E... E... E... E... E... E... E...
!... !... !... !... !... !... !... !... !... !...

"I'm sorry. I just thought . . . Tseawish warned us . . . "
But the gold was gone.
Angharoom let the shimmering mirror and the scarlet comb lie on the sand. At times she put out a tentative finger to touch them, then drew it back. Often she lifted her face to scan the ocean. Amethyst waves tossed snowy crests in every direction. She returned to her cave, leaving the Elemental Lord's gifts lying on the beach. When morning dawned again the tide had taken them.

A... A... A... A... A... A... A... A... A... A...
S... S... S... S... S... S... S... S... S... S...
K... K... K... K... K... K... K... K... K... K...
!... !... !... !... !... !... !... !... !... !...

Angharoom jumped. Her heart started thumping fast, even though she had been waiting for this.
"IS THERE NOTHING YOU REALLY WANT?"
The mermaid lay back on her stomach and let the sand trickle lazily through her fingers.
"Well . . . I dunno really . . . "
In fact, she had been thinking about this for the last thirty-three hours. She rolled over on her back and let her eyes roam over the coppery clouds suspended above her.
"Perhaps if . . . "

Y... Y... Y... Y... Y... Y... Y... Y... Y... Y...
E... E... E... E... E... E... E... E... E... E...
S... S... S... S... S... S... S... S... S... S...
?... ?... ?... ?... ?... ?... ?... ?... ?... ?...

"No. It's nothing. You couldn't really."

T... T... T... T... T... T... T... T... T... T...
R... R... R... R... R... R... R... R... R... R...
Y... Y... Y... Y... Y... Y... Y... Y... Y... Y...
!... !... !... !... !... !... !... !... !... !...

"I thought . . . I mean, I don't know what Elementals can manage, and all that. I know Tseawish's lot made us mermaids. But you males . . . Well, she said you never were no good at making things."

The bay shook and a spray of amber foam arched threateningly over the rocks.

"I'm sorry, sir! Nothing personal. I'm sure you could, if you put your mind to it . . . "

W... W... W... W... W... W... W... W... W... W...
H... H... H... H... H... H... H... H... H... H...
A... A... A... A... A... A... A... A... A... A...
T... T... T... T... T... T... T... T... T... T...
?... ?... ?... ?... ?... ?... ?... ?... ?... ?...

The breakers had settled themselves into a sandy swell. But waves still slapped alarmingly on the sides of the bay. Angharoom edged further towards the cliffs.

"It's just . . . I've been lying here looking up at the sky. And it's like a giant mirror. I can see all sorts of things. Houses. Not like the fisherfolk's little cottages, but huge tall ones with towers like rock-stacks. And miles and miles of great branching trees, like coral reefs, only all out of the water. And . . . and . . . people, and dragons and rats as big as whales and elephants the size of prawns and . . . and . . . stuff like that. And I was wondering . . . well, if it was true? Are there places and things like that? I can't just swim up on to the shore and start walking, can I?"

H... H... H... H... H... H... H... H... H... H...
M... M... M... M... M... M... M... M... M... M...
M... M... M... M... M... M... M... M... M... M...
!... !... !... !... !... !... !... !... !... !...

Angharoom lowered her eyes from the clouds to the amethyst sea. A trail of gold was wandering away from the island just underwater, as if Conchor the Elemental Lord had too much on his mind to pay attention to where he was going.

#

A week passed. And another day broke. The sun, a luminous fuzz through the coppery clouds, climbed towards its zenith. Angharoom sighed. She was beginning to wonder if she had been away from home long enough. Surely if she came swimming in past Phalaroop now, very slowly and languidly, as though she were almost at the end of her strength after terrible experiences, she would be surrounded by love and concern and not by stern reprimands? Even Tseawish could occasionally be maternal when a mermaid fell ill.

Somewhat reluctantly she picked up the pewter mirror and the herring-bone comb. Did she really have to take them? Would Tseawish ever restore that more flattering opal one?

A wave reared on the skyline. At first it seemed as dark as cuttlefish ink. Then the dim sunlight turned it to gold. Another cresting breaker, and light flashed as clear as diamonds. Angharoom hoisted herself onto a rock to see better. Something very large was coming her way. It was breaking the surface now. Really, it was very big. And the shape was like nothing she had ever seen in the sea before. It was more like . . . Well, it reminded her of the rectangular doors the fishermen hung in the entrances of their cottages. Only this couldn't be a door, could it? It flashed with light, clear as a fish-eye. It seemed to gather colour from all around it. The tawny gold of Conchor, the slaty green of the rocks, the periwinkle wavelets of the cove.

"It's a . . ."

M... M... M... M... M... M... M... M... M... M...
I... I... I... I... I... I... I... I... I... I...
R... R... R... R... R... R... R... R... R... R...
R... R... R... R... R... R... R... R... R... R...
O... O... O... O... O... O... O... O... O... O...
R... R... R... R... R... R... R... R... R... R...

Conchor gasped with satisfaction as he saw her face.

"For me? *That* big?"

It was huge, bigger than Angharoom herself. The rectangular frame was plaited with mother-of-pearl and gold and from each corner slanted a gigantic shark's tooth. Common enough. What made it truly remarkable, besides its size, was the quality of its surface. No sea at evening calm was ever more smooth and shining. No starlit rock-pool gleamed with such flawless clarity. No iceberg in sunshine gave back such brilliance. She saw herself in it like a twin sister, as clear as she had seen Pliplip and Shushulushi, from the crown of her daffodil-yellow hair all down her iridescent tail to the tip of her rose-pink fin.

"I'm . . . It's beautiful! What is it made of? Where did you get it?"

G... G... G... G... G... G... G... G... G... G...
L... L... L... L... L... L... L... L... L... L...
A... A... A... A... A... A... A... A... A... A...
S... S... S... S... S... S... S... S... S... S...
S... S... S... S... S... S... S... S... S... S...
!... !... !... !... !... !... !... !... !... !...

Conchor's pride of achievement made the water of the cove dance.

"I INVENTED IT. SILICATES OF POTASH, SODA, LIME, MAGNESIA, LEAD AND A TOUCH OF ALUMINA. THEN I HAD TO FUSE THEM. YOU'LL NEVER BELIEVE THE TROUBLE I HAD WITH THOSE FIRE ELEMENTALS. FORMS TO FILL IN IN OCTUPLICATE. AND JUST FOR A LOAN OF THEIR FURNACE I HAD TO PAY FOR PLANNING PERMISSION, CHANGE OF USE AND UNIFORM BUSINESS RATE. TO SAY NOTHING OF BREAKING ALL THE HEALTH AND SAFETY REGULATIONS. I CAME DANGEROUSLY NEAR TO TERMINAL DEHYDRATION OVERSEEING IT. BUT IT'S GOOD, ISN'T IT?"

"It's lovely. Does it . . . well, you know what I mean . . . work?"

"TRY IT."

Angharoom bent cautiously closer. Her hair brushed the glass. She felt the faintest tug. As her face approached, her dark eyes grew huge, till her own breath steamed them over. The mirror touched her breasts coldly and then grew warm. The scales of her tail slithered against it. For a moment Conchor saw two Angharooms merging like Siamese twins. She disappeared.

"THERE'S A COMB, TOO," called Conchor. "I'VE INVENTED STAINLESS STEEL."

#

She was gone a long time.

For a month Conchor hung about the cave like a tawny scum that had eddied into a backwater. As the nights went by he darkened from a gold ebullience into a brown study. By daylight he watched the mirror which showed only empty rocks and sea. It did not occur to him to scan the burnished clouds for happenings in distant Phalaroop or Az. If he had, he might have witnessed some startling scenes.

Supposing, that is, that the sky *did* reflect the earth.

Then, just as suddenly, she was back, bulging her way through the mirror-glass into separate identity, like the fry emerging from a salmon's egg.

A... A... A... A... A... A... A... A... A... A...
N... N... N... N... N... N... N... N... N... N...
G... G... G... G... G... G... G... G... G...
H... H... H... H... H... H... H... H... H... H...
A... A... A... A... A... A... A... A... A... A...
R... R... R... R... R... R... R... R... R...
O... O... O... O... O... O... O... O... O... O...
O... O... O... O... O... O... O... O... O... O...
M... M... M... M... M... M... M... M... M... M...
!... !... !... !... !... !... !... !... !... !...

"Oh! Hello!"

Her hair was dishevelled and she was breathing very fast. She picked up the stainless-steel comb and tidied herself, humming happily.

"HOW WAS IT?"

"Brilliant."

FAY SAMPSON

"YOU'RE SURE?"

"Yes, thanks."

"THAT WAS YOUR HEART'S DESIRE?"

"Oh, yes!"

More beautiful than ever now, glowing with rosy warmth, she slid herself down into the warm water.

"Mmm. Perfect!" she sighed, as the shallows closed over her and she let herself sink beneath the gold of Conchor onto a bed of soft dark kelp.

It was three days later that she was sighted off Phalaroop, towing the mirror wearily like a water-logged raft and clutching the comb.

"Where have you *been*?"

"We thought you were *dead*."

"What's *that*?"

"A mirror."

"It's a bit . . . er . . . large, isn't it? It's bigger than you are."

"It had to be."

With considerable care and difficulty Angharoom manoeuvred the Elemental's mirror onto the rock. The others watched in jealous silence. Nobody else had a mirror that big. Nobody else had a glass one.

"Bit . . . *flashy* . . . isn't it?" said Shushulushi.

Pliplip reached out to feel its surface.

"Don't!" cried Angharoom. "I mean, I wouldn't get too close if I were you. It's not an ordinary mirror."

"Snooty! I suppose you think you're not an ordinary mermaid now." Pliplip tossed her hair.

Angharoom lowered the mirror back into the water out of danger. It was quite impracticable to carry it around with her as she swam. She found a reef inhabited only by cormorants and left the mirror there. If you were a cormorant you wouldn't have much interest in looking in mirrors, either. At the hours of prayer, she climbed up out of the water and sang to her own glittering reflection while the steel comb played in her hair. Sometimes she found herself starting to lean closer. Then she laughed softly and sat upright again.

The hardest thing was facing Tseawish. But it was obvious that her story of self-imposed exile must be true. She could not have been getting into mischief on the mainland coast without being intercepted by search-parties of mermaids and Elemental Ladies, could she? It is true, she was not admitted to the next Council of the Sea, and Lord Conchor was conspicuously absent from the vicinity of Phalaroop for a long while after it. But that was hardly her fault, was it?

After a while, Shushulushi said with a self-righteous air, "You're letting your figure go a bit, aren't you?"

Angharoom's face softened into a slow smile, and her hands stroked her curving shape.

When the time came, Tseawish sent for Mother Lil, who rowed out from the Sorcerers' Seminary with her two female pupils, Panthea and Rheon, who needed more course-work for their Level Three midwifery.

Being not only her first child but the primogenital baby of the species, it was rather slow in coming. Mermaids give birth best on the move, like dolphins. It was an exhausting labour for everybody, keeping pace with her.

"Push!" commanded Lil, for the hundred and nineteenth time.

"I am!"

And a dark-green blob of jelly shot into the deep and drifted away from her.

"Catch it!" snapped Tseawish.

Panthea, the girl pupil, grabbed for it, but it slithered through her hands.

"It's got its father's . . . er . . . " she tried, politely.

"Ectoplasm?" suggested the mature student, Rheon.

"Can I stop now?" panted Angharoom.

"No!" ordered Lil. "There's still the afterbirth. Come on, there's a good girl."

"Here it comes!" cried Rheon.

But what emerged more slowly into the purple water was something quite different. Golden curls, creamy shoulders, a slate-blue fish-tail.

"Twins?" said Lil and Tseawish together.

"This is more like her, isn't it?" smiled Panthea, cradling him.

Tseawish studied the boy's tail, which was decidedly forked.

"Hmm!" she said.

"Hmm!" said Mother Lil, examining the lad's face, and finding herself inexplicably reminded of one of the application forms for last year's

Summer School at the Enchanted University, Rockdrop, two hundred marches inland.

#

They called the Semi-elemental Dylan and the merman Waterstone. The children thrived and grew. Dylan appeared nearly as pervasive as his father, but somewhat better defined. There was a suggestion of tentacles flowing out behind him and a solidification that might almost have been called a head. Likewise, Waterstone was very like his mother, though you could almost imagine a slight surgical adjustment to his forked tail might have separated it into two legs.

Tides came and went. The planet turned. Centuries passed. At last Angharoom declined into a swift but elegant old age and died. They laid her to rest on the sea-bed in a forest of coral. She was not the first mermaid to die. It had become the custom to lay them out on their backs with their faces to the light and their mirrors and combs on their breasts with their hands clasped over them.

In Angharoom's case, of course, this was not a good idea; she would have been flattened. Dylan wafted the steel comb into her hands. Waterstone propped the great mirror against a branching pillar of coral beside her. The mermaids laid patterns of cowrie shells at her head and feet. Then they all rose to the surface in a circle, singing over her and combing their hair. Conchor sobbed.

When the mermaids and the Elementals had gone away, only the two brothers were left. The mirror was tilted towards the light. Waterstone admired himself in it, while Dylan hovered behind him like a dark-green spillage.

"Odd," said Waterstone smugly, "that we look so different, when you're my twin brother."

H... H... H... H... H... H... H... H... H... H...
A... A... A... A... A... A... A... A... A... A...
L... L... L... L... L... L... L... L... L... L...
F... F... F... F... F... F... F... F... F... F...

brother!" sniggered Dylan and whisked away in a cloud of cockle-shells and soggy fish and chip papers.

Waterstone stared after him. Then he turned back to the coral grave. His mother's face smiled wordlessly. The mirror winked at the daylight. Slowly he swam away in the opposite direction to Dylan, thinking.

#

For hundreds of years the mirror stood there, above the smiling skull of the mermaid, amid the crumbling coral. Its clear, bright surface reflected scenes in the shifting clouds above, that might or might not have been images of far-off mountains, where scattered huts were carved out of rock ledges and young scholars dreamed over scrolls. Crabs scuttled past the mirror, glancing nervously sideways at it with eyes on stalks. Sometimes a curious devilfish nosed too close and was not seen again for a considerable time.

Some never came back.

The Pier
Sarah Singleton

The sea glitters in the distance, out of reach, beyond fields of mud. Close at hand, two little boys dig up the beach. In a bus shelter, a fat, sweltering woman in a halterneck sells fish salads from tupperware boxes. On the pier, in cubicles, boys peddle bags of shrimp-pink candyfloss. Amongst the plastic paraphernalia, inflatable sharks and aliens, sticks of rock are piled in chromatic ranks. I pick up half a dozen. Julienne. Her name circumscribes the top, in perfect pink letters stretching down, down, through the body of the sugar rod. Her face stares from the grainy, monochrome photo on the label.

#

I betrayed her compulsively, right from the start. I don't think she knew. I trawled through the nightclubs, in the city, looking for the decorated girls in black. They were very easy, and very young, seventeen or eighteen maybe. I would watch them, exchange glances, sidle up, engage them with a kind of distant, yearning homage, staring into their unformed souls. I made them, briefly, in the image of my own fantastic desire, in curls of cigarette smoke and glinting silver. Obliterating myself before their own fledgling sense of self, asking, and asking, building them up, embroidering a fragile persona for them to take up and wear. They unfolded their dreams, and vanities. I never took them home. Instead, they led me to their own student rooms, bedsits, or shabby shared houses where I fucked them, under posters of Bela Lugosi or Marilyn Manson, the pale little girls in a lustful palpitation for the self they saw reflected in my eyes. The curious narcissism of desire. But the spell was always shortlived. Afterwards, loosened up, they started to chatter about college, or family, or how they made a living. The mundane reasserted itself. So I slipped away quickly, calling a taxi, unable, even, to stay the night. And every infidelity, each chance I took to prove how unattached I was, made the opposite more painfully obvious. Always, always, I went back to her.

Until, that is, she tired of me.

"Shall we go to Weston?" she suggested. It was May, the last time we went. Outside, the rain fell in fits. The colours of the cityscape faded, beneath the clouds.

"Why Weston? It's an awful place."

"I know. It's so hideous, it almost has charm. A grotesque charm. It's a horrible day. I can't think of anything else to do."

Julienne was bored. We had woken late. We lay in bed for an hour or more. I wanted her, and wanted her, but, dozing, Julienne turned her back to me, pushed my hand away from her breasts, her lips pressed shut when I kissed her. In the beginning, we had spent entire days making love. And my appetite had grown, instead of fading.

"No, don't," she said. "I'm not in the mood."

"You're never in the mood," I said. "You don't want me any more."

"Don't say that. Don't." She stepped out of bed. In the subdued light, her body was paper-white. Her hair was very long, the softest, glossiest black, though the hair at her groin was pale brown. When I had first met her, two years before, she was only seventeen, though she looked older. She was sitting, alone, at a wine bar, wearing a metallic mesh vest. Her mouth, and her nipples, were painted purple. She had looked bored then.

"What shall we do?" Now she stretched, pushing up her thin arms, standing on tiptoe. Then she folded herself in half, pressing her face against her knees.

"What shall we do?" she repeated. She didn't look at me, but away, through the window. Her boredom infected me, with a weight like lead. My head ached.

"I'll take you to Weston if you like," I said. I didn't want to go. The day stretched away, yawning emptily.

"OK, we'll go." She sighed, picking up clothes from the floor. She rubbed her face, ran her fingers through her hair.

I drove down the motorway. Julienne stared out, at the fields and hedges.

To reach the sea front, we had to drive around the edge of the town, skirting retail parks and housing estates. We left the car in a painted bay by the pavement. A surly youth in a yellow plastic tunic which flapped in the wind took four pounds from me, in exchange for a parking ticket. We walked along the front, above the beach.

The sea was far away. In a clump, by a rack of hay, a dozen donkeys dozed. Julienne stepped into the sand, and wandered over. She patted the scrawny neck of the nearest donkey, dappled grey and brown. She stroked its broad, passive face. On the browband, the name "Elvis" was spelled out in metal staples.

"You want a ride?" A short, dour man stepped forward, a buckled money pouch at his waist. The wind snatched the words from his mouth. His face, habitually crumpled against weather and sand, was seamed like the leather on the donkey's back.

"What?" Julienne said. She lifted her hand to shade her eyes. Her hair blew about her face in ribbons. A few desultory raindrops fell upon the beach.

"A ride. D'you want a ride? A pound a time."

Julienne smiled.

"I don't think so," she said. Then she laughed. The donkey nuzzled her arm. I liked the picture we made — Julienne in her velvet dress, while I stood at a distance, tall and thin, in my frock coat and long boots. The other donkeys shifted, gathering about Julienne, pushing against her with their soft noses.

"Come on you lot, come on." The donkey drover grabbed Elvis's reins, and jerked, so the beast threw up its head, and lumbered heavily away. The others followed, returning to their long, indifferent drowse.

We walked along the beach. Three empty trampolines waited for bouncing children. In shelters of ornate Edwardian ironwork, up on the pavement, warped, white-haired pensioners stared out at the plains of mud, and the distant promise of the sea. Posters on litter bins heralded the arrival of aged variety performers and a circus. On the road, traffic roared past.

The pier rose before us. I grasped her hand, but Julienne's fingers were limp in mine and she soon pulled away. At low tide, the pier's elaborate insect legs were entirely exposed. In the forest of rusty metalwork, a man and a dog played with a stick.

"Shall we? Shall we go up?"

Julianne shrugged. I led the way, through the ice cream parlour portals, along the length of the pier. She sat upon a bench, under shelter. It wasn't quite warm enough to be comfortable, but at least we had relief from the wind. I bought her a cup of tea.

"I love you, Julienne. I really do."

But she frowned, and didn't answer.

"Did you hear me? I said I love you. Don't you love me too? Don't you love me any more?"

"OK, I love you. I love you. I've said it. Will you leave me alone now?"

But I wasn't satisfied. I could feel her drawing away, and away. She wanted to be rid of me. The fear of losing her ate into me, like a disease.

"Julienne, do you really? Do you really love me?" I craved reassurance. Every time I asked, she seemed farther away, but I kept on asking.

"But you don't love me like you used to, do you? You seem . . . bored with me. Haven't I given you enough? Haven't I given you everything? Relationships are like this. They have ups and downs. Is something on your mind? D'you want to talk about it? Is it us? Do you want to be free?"

I could feel myself becoming smaller and smaller. She was shrugging me off.

"What is it? What have I done wrong? What do you want?"

People strolled past, and the little train laden with those too inactive to make it from one end of the pier to the other. Everyone looked so very ugly. Bloated, or misshapen, a freak show. A bearded lady. A family with pig faces. A trio of girls with pasty rings of fat around their thighs.

"If you want to finish with me, tell me. Tell me. Stop bloody tormenting me."

Julienne shook her head. Tears squeezed from her eyes.

"Shut up, will you? Shut up," she said, and then she did start to cry, hiccuping with tiny sobs. The passers-by glanced at us, then away again. A little girl with a huge bobble of yellow candyfloss stared and stared 'til she was walking with her head twisted over her shoulder.

"Come here," I whispered. I put my arm around Julienne's shoulders, and she rested her head upon me, still weeping.

"Talk to me," I said. "Tell me what you're feeling." But she didn't talk. She pressed her face against my arm.

I gazed out, from the pier, to the curve of the town along the coast. Houses and hotels rose from the sea front, piled up one behind the other to the top of the hill. Further along the beach, children were sailing boats in a murky tank of water. And I remembered in a blaze the first months of our relationship, when she had wanted me.

She never went to clubs. She didn't like them. She was finishing A-levels before moving on to a textile design course in Bristol. Already, she created the most alluring outfits, fashioned from silk and mesh and gauze. On our first outing, I took her to the theatre in Bath, to see an exotic modern ballet, *The Emerald Venus.* I splashed out on a box, beside the dress circle, and we were seated like royalty on soft red chairs right above the front of the stage. She loved the theatre, the swags of velvet, the gilded cherubs and scrolls, the fringed pelmet above the box. She wore a dress of black tulle, like a flower, a tight bodice, the skirt springing out like petals from her waist. Her neck was thin, and very bare. Beneath her eyes were shadows of the softest, palest mauve. She watched the ballet intently, but I watched her. The wonderful, fragile quiver of her face. I wanted to eat her up.

After the ballet, I had a table booked in a tiny restaurant, high up on the top floor of a huge Georgian house. The light was subdued, the diners very quiet. Huge vases of red and white roses perched on the great mantelpiece above our heads. Later, at my house, I covered her face with a scarf of soft black silk and gently removed the fuchsia-shaped dress. But I didn't touch her. I stood and stared at the narrow white body, the shallow breasts, and I told her, very steadily, what I would like to do. I could see tiny beads of perspiration breaking upon the skin below her neck. Her pulse throbbed in her body. I swear I could see the blood thundering in her veins, like a torrent.

#

And now I remembered how that very morning her flesh had seemed to contract and shrink away from my hand. Her body shivered me off. A seagull alighted upon the overpainted metalwork of the shelter. "It's not you," she sniffed. "It's me, don't you see?"

"What d'you mean?"

"I've changed. I've grown. I need something different."

"So you do want to finish it." My voice broke. Julienne collapsed into another spasm of sobs. I stroked her face.

"There," I said softly. "It isn't so bad." But I had the peculiar physical sensation of wounding, as though, inside, my bodily organs shrivelled, my bones losing marrow. Worst of all, like a stabbing, an excruciation, was the image springing up of Julienne finding someone else. The very idea of another man having her.

"What the hell am I doing?" I cried. "Here am I comforting you because you're having such a hard time ditching me. For Christ's sake!"

The eddy of my emotional outburst seemed to swirl out and founder the pedestrians moving continually down the pier. An old lady stopped and looked at me; her mouth opened and closed again.

Julienne stopped crying abruptly.

"I've given you everything," I said. "Everything I have, everything I am, and you tell me it's not enough? For fuck's sake. All the money I've spent on you."

As soon as the final words were spoken, I regretted them. Was she a prostitute I had bought? Stupid, stupid. "I didn't mean that. I'm sorry. It was my choice. I wanted to."

Julienne regarded me coolly. But at least she engaged with me.

"Don't you see? That's the point, isn't it? I'm like a helpless baby bird with its beak open in a nest, and you're the big parent coming back with more juicy grubs to stuff into my face. You're like some comforting pillow to rest my head upon. I don't want it any more. That's why I said it was *me*. I've changed. I'm sorry." She turned her head, so her face was half away from me.

137

"Perhaps you should find someone else. Someone nearer your own age. Who wants to make the next step."

Her voice was very soft, but it was a treacherous blow.

"I'm too old for you? After all this time, you can say that? You've had all you wanted, and now you want to fuck off and find someone younger? You're telling me to find a girlfriend my own age?" Anger threatened to swallow me up. At that moment I wanted to slip my hands around her white neck and squeeze the life out of her. I wanted to hit her.

A month before, she had asked to meet my friends. I had kept her to myself so much. I was reluctant. Eventually I gave way, and I took her to Tim's house.

Tim lived in a modern house on the edge of Bath. He had two little kids, and his wife had given up her job to care for them. The house was strewn with toys, and large framed photos of the brats adorned the living room wall, as if they were the household gods.

Julienne looked about her, taking in the careless mess, the heaps of picture books and the laundry drying by the radiator. She went to the kitchen with Marie, leaving me to chat to Tim, while she asked politely the ages of the children and, later, read them bedtime stories.

"How old is she?" Tim asked me.

"Nineteen. Nearly twenty."

"Yeah? She's beautiful."

I smiled, in a moment of pride.

When at last we sat down to eat, Julienne began to question Tim about our friendship.

"So how long've you known each other?"

"Since the sixth form. Nearly twenty years, isn't it?"

"Eighteen, actually," Marie said pointedly. "So you're at college? How did you two meet?"

"Oh, it's a bit of a cliché, I'm afraid. Paryss chatted me up in a wine bar."

"Paryss? You call him Paryss?" Marie and Tim exchanged glances. Marie stifled a smirk. I hated her, in that moment. And all women, at that age. The sense of smug superiority that went along with the subtle visual markers of a fading complexion. A personality settled and set, a self-acceptance I found so fatally unattractive.

Is that why Julienne had never lost her flavour for me? She shifted and altered. I was never sure of her, of what she was thinking. I couldn't quite make out what she might do. Even after two years, she evaded me.

After the dinner, Julienne exuded a quiet air of triumph, as though she had won some kind of victory. And in a sense I felt I had lost something vital. She was making me ordinary, to shrug me off some more. And I held on tighter.

#

In the first months, I was a giant. I took her to galleries and exhibitions. I held her shoulders and thrust her in front of paintings, stuffing her with my own sense of wonder.

"Too much, you're too much for me," she cried. She held onto me, laughing, and we stood in the Bristol museum wrapped in a tense embrace before the works of the Pre-Raphaelites, while the more sedate appreciators of art filed past in silence. That afternoon, in my bedroom, she took off her clothes and crawled to me, wrapping herself about my legs and telling me she had no wish but the one, to obliterate herself in the service of my desire. So I tied her wrists behind her back and fucked her for an hour or more, till the air itself was saturated with the scent of sex and her Poison perfume.

#

The tide was drawing in. Now, at last, I could see the white flash of waves breaking beyond the end of the pier.

"Shall we buy some chips?" she asked, brightening.

"I couldn't eat," I said. My throat felt choked and constricted, but we walked to a booth at the entrance of the funfair and I bought her some in a cardboard cone. She cheered up then, munching, though the smell of the frying fat made me feel sick. The tears dried on her cheeks. We embarked on a curiously unreal conversation about the qualities of an ideal next partner. She laughed. I wondered if anything really meant much to her. Her feelings rippled, one after another, glittering but superficial. Was that my mistake? Had I mistaken shallowness for something more

139

enigmatic? Then the image rose again, of Julienne having somebody else. The blade twisted in my guts. This was the worst of all. Though I might survive without her, I could not endure the prospect of Julienne finding another partner. But she was mine first, I comforted myself. No one could take that away from me. It was fixed, fatally, that Julienne had given herself to me. Anyone else would be second, now she had a history.

Maybe that was what I found so unappealing about older women. I didn't want to be compared to previous lovers. I couldn't bear the thought of a comparison, that my partner still wanted or wished for the past. Experience polluted and corrupted. I wanted a blank page. A tabula rasa.

When she'd finished eating, Julienne crumpled the cone and tossed it into a bin.

"You know what?" I said bitterly. "The prospect of losing you hurts so much I wish I had never met you. I would rather never have set eyes on you than have to endure this, your leaving me."

Julienne looked at me incredulously. Then she turned on the tears again.

"How can you say that? How can you say it? You'd miss out on all the wonderful times we've shared together?"

"Yes! To avoid what I'm feeling now. My god, I wish I'd never met you. I've never loved anyone like I love you, and you're dumping me."

Although she wept still, I caught a flash of triumph in her face. She had me in the palm of her hand. The puppet had broken free, and now tugged the strings of the puppet master. She put her arms around me. For an odd moment, the distance between us was overcome. A moment of intimacy, kindled by the process of going through a crisis together. Even the crisis of breaking up. Maybe, maybe she would change her mind.

"I'd still like us to be friends," she murmured, her face against my chest, dashing my painful delusion. I broke away. Reality was too much to bear.

"You're not leaving me," I said. She looked up at me. Her lips parted. She didn't know quite what to say.

"I'm sorry," she said. "It's for the best, don't you see?"

"For the best? Who for? Not for me it isn't."

"You've got to move on, Paryss. It's been lovely, but it's over."

THE PIER

"You bitch. You're not leaving me. You're not. I won't let you. I'm leaving you."

She looked puzzled. She turned away, to the railings. The wind lifted her hair. The seagulls screeched, fighting over the scraps in the rubbish bin.

"I am leaving you," I repeated. "I'm leaving you here, on the pier. You can stay here."

She stared out, at the encroaching waves, the ugly flats of mud slowly, slowly surrendering to the incoming tide. Her face was still now, passive and resigned, like the donkey with Elvis on his browband.

"I leaving you here, you understand? You're staying here."

"OK," she said quietly. "If that's what you want. I'll stay here." The seagulls hopped, hugely white, dancing about a scatter of fallen chips. The little train rumbled past again, laden with passengers. Two boys skipped by, faces splodged with ice-cream.

I backed away, slowly, keeping my eyes fixed on Julienne. I half ran, still looking behind me, seeing her fixed in position by the railing. I hurried off the pier, and along the sea front, to the car.

#

High season. Weston is teeming. I replace the rock, where Julienne's face is repeated, over and over, upon the labels. I step into the funfair, a vaulted hall at the end of the pier, where two pink mechanical horses stand at the door. A migrainous assault of noise hits me, from arcade games, shooting ranges and slot machines. A monstrous shoot-'em-up unspools on a screen, a vista of zombies in a haunted house waiting for despatch. Upon the invitation of a string of text, I slide in fifty pence and take up position. A skeletal soldier and a grinning, walking corpse are gunned to pieces. Then, from a door to the left, a girl in a black dress emerges, turning to me a white pixellated face. She crosses the room, falling away in the fierce video perspective. The gun drops. I cannot shoot her.

I pass numerous machines with sliding shelves covered in coins. A corral of mini-dodgems. A carousel of gaudy horses. In the House of Fun, Julienne moves behind the distorting mirrors. Upon the fortune-telling machine her face surfaces briefly, when a young man presses his hot hand upon the designated space. She prophesies loss, and remembrance.

At the far end, mounted upon the balconies of the Castle of Doom, lurex monsters move slowly on pistons. A head dripping red plastic entrails is lifted and lowered, in jerks, by a shiny gorilla. I pay my fare and take my place upon the ghost train, weaving back and forth inside the guts of the hardboard castle. Pitch blackness, interspersed now and then by bursts of noise, wails and clanks, and bright illumination falling upon dismembered ghouls and twitching body parts in glass cases. I fail to be startled. The train lurches, and I am uneasy, instead, because light steals dimly through the chinks in the planks flooring the pier and I can make out the grey sea moving a long way beneath me.

She waits, as she always does, in an upright coffin at the end of the ride. The train slows. The spotlight flashes on, and she lifts a pale hand. When the piston stops, her arm bounces a little, her face turns, and her mouth opens. The coated plastic glistens. I hear a hiss, but it might be the sea. Then the light shuts down, the train heaves into motion, and bursts through the door, back into the light of the funfair.

I walk back, along the pier, among, apparently, exactly the same people. A bearded lady. The pig-face family. Three fat girls. A parade of perfect grotesques. I found a single grey hair at my temple this morning. And I have developed the modest beginnings of a paunch.

I see Julienne standing in her place by the railings, and I walk past, unable to quell the stab of pain her image still provokes.

She can stay on the pier. I am still not ready to let her go.

Not yet.

Most Dead Bodies
in a Confined Space
Jean Marie Ward

"Just think, Muldoon — our very first X-file!"

I covered my ears, but I knew it wouldn't help. Sally's a cute bit of fluff, but once she starts talking in exclamation points there's no turning back. You're going to do what she wants you to do sooner or later. So you might as well take it and like it. I turned to the death trap at the back of the cavernous garage.

The corroded tin box looked like a mad scientist's version of one of those kiddie rides people rent for picnics. To operate this one, you wound a large crank, then convinced your marks that they'd win a prize if they could crawl through the open-ended cylinder in the centre of the box in 30 seconds or less. But once the patsies had clambered into the drum their weight tripped a spring that flipped them into the front of the box. Depending on whether the front door was closed or open, either they wound up "in jail" or they tumbled out on the ground giggling and disoriented.

That's the way it was supposed to work, but here something went terribly wrong. The first body sprawled almost upright in the open front bay as if flattened against the far wall by a giant fist. Her left arm reached skyward. Her lips curled back from gums dried to the colour of blood, frozen in a scream of ontological despair against the meaninglessness of existence and the consequent certainty of oblivion.

At least that's how Fox Mulder would've called it.

I wondered why nobody had heard her cry for help. More to the point, why hadn't anybody smelled her and the other withered and deflated bodies wedged into the open drum? I started counting before I realized what I was doing: one head sagged out of the opening on the left side of the drum, the soles of one set of feet indicated a body facing the other direction, one . . .

I stopped at four, coughing back the sour taste that rose up my throat. I told myself the tarry scent of oil-stained concrete mixed with mouse droppings and dust from the ragged sacks of birdseed stacked near the trap disagreed with my lunch. Except I hadn't eaten lunch.

"Alien harvesting?" Sally chirped hopefully as she tried to dodge around me to get a better view. Did I mention she identified with a certain red-haired tv character whose name also begins with "S"?

"Cheese Louise," Jerry groaned, hunching his shoulders and ducking his head as if he could make like a turtle and disappear for a while. "I should've never brought you guys into it. I just thought you oughta know what was happening."

"Yeah, a real humanitarian," I said. Someone hidden in the shadows giggled. "What are you and your cousin doing around here anyway? The boss already booted you off the property once. You know what'll happen if she catches you back here. It would go a lot better for you if you just got lost and left this to the guys in uniform."

Sally tried to pout. "Thomas Aloysius Muldoon, you're no fun at all. If we leave it to the uniforms, we'll never know what happened. We could be in danger too, you know."

"When was the last time you were in the garage, Sally? Hey! Get back!" I blocked her move towards the trap just in time.

"But somebody needs to examine the bodies," she said.

"Leave it to the experts. The last I heard, watching medical shows does not qualify you for an M.D. But all those cop shows you're addicted to should've taught you not to contaminate the scene of a crime. People think you've got something to do with it, and the real killer gets away."

Sally narrowed her eyes and tilted her head this way and that as if considering a particularly difficult problem: me. Moving in for the kill, she tangled herself in my arms and rubbed her temple against my cheek. "Muldoon," she purred, her breath ruffling my hair, "the truth is in there."

I know it's wrong. Sally's half my age, and I'm not supposed to feel these urges. But I do, and she knows it. "All right, but stay back. They might've had some kind of disease."

Behind me Jerry's cousin Minnie tittered again. A soft scrunching of paper told me she'd plopped herself on the feedbags to watch the show. Another one Jerry owed me — as if that little rodent would ever pay up.

I circled the killing machine, crouching and stretching to examine the box from every angle — not an easy thing to do since I was still trying to avoid looking at its contents. Small brown stains, still oily and slick, caught my eye. They were far enough away from the box for me to risk hunkering down for a closer examination.

Sure enough, the spots smelled familiar. "Chocolate," I said. "That stuff's poison."

"No way! That's Godiva," Jerry protested.

"Muldoon has a point," Sally said. "Every diet doctor I've ever seen on television says chocolate's bad for you. Not only does it clog your arteries, it acts like a happy pill on the human brain. But" — Sally shot me an apologetic glance — "strictly speaking, unless you're allergic, it's only poisonous to cats and dogs."

"Do the dead guys look like dogs to you?" Jerry asked.

"No, they look like victims of the Jonestown massacre, and I can think of only three possible explanations for that. One: it was some kind of killer virus, and we're all going to die horribly in less than five minutes. Two: a serial killer . . . or alien," I added for Sally's benefit, "is using the box for his own private morgue. The problem with that is nobody looks like they were stabbed or shot or strangled or dissected. Nobody's missing any body parts. The only thing that supports the morgue idea is that some of the bodies look older than others, which means they didn't all die at once.

"Which means you have to explain why they all crammed themselves, one after another, into this box to die. It must've stunk to high heaven, and it's not like *The Guinness Book of World Records* has a category for most dead bodies in a confined space. So what do you have left? Number three: poison or drugs — probably both."

Jerry's shoulders twitched up and down. "I dunno. They could've had their reasons. Me and Minnie used to play here as kids. Used to be a great ride — and free, too. Dead is dead, you know. Way we live, you can't let it get you down."

"Can't let it get you down?" Sally sputtered. "You mean you'd climb over a stack of decomposing corpses for a cheap thrill? What kind of ghoul are you?"

"Hey, it's not like there's anything else to do in this neighbourhood," Jerry said.

Minnie's black eyes glittered in agreement. Some of the corpses had Minnie's drab colouring and almost the same nose and narrow cheeks. They might've been relatives, but that didn't seem to bother Minnie. Instead Minnie swiped a hand across her mouth in a way that suggested she was getting hungry.

It's one thing to dream about investigating the paranormal and inexplicable abductions that happen to somebody else. It's quite another to discover a completely alien intelligence in your own backyard. Gives a whole new meaning to the phrase "trust no one". But Sally held her ground.

"It couldn't be poison," Sally said in a small voice. "One thing about the boss, she wouldn't leave anything that could do this lying around where people could get into it by mistake. She even makes the exterminator use that insecticide made from chrysanthemums.

"Muldoon . . . "

She sounded so forlorn I would've done anything to make her feel better. If I could've given her aliens, I would've. If I could've faked aliens, even better. But all I could do was look the dead in the face and see if I'd missed anything the first time.

Still trying to keep the immediate area clear for the professionals, I knelt down as close as I dared to the open bay. No visible spores, no dried froth around the mouth, no obvious sores — good, good and good. The body didn't even smell that bad. No worse than dried mushrooms anyway. Which probably ruled out poison as well as disease.

I forced myself to take in every detail. Nothing looked broken, but the way the body sagged made it hard to tell. Concave. Boneless.

So why was the corpse's arm still sticking in the air? I angled my head closer to the opening.

Damn.

I risked touching a knuckle to the crank. With a terrible groan, the drum lurched slowly, slowly, grinding and tumbling its contents together. I told myself Jerry was right. Dead is dead, and they don't feel a thing. The almost invisible seam in the back of the bay widened, and the body slumped to the floor.

"Hey, it still works!" Jerry exclaimed.

"Unfortunately," I said. "But only partway. That's the problem. Your friends went in for a ride. They tripped the spring like always. But the mechanism must be rusted. It moved too slowly, and they got caught between the cylinder and the bay. And, once they got caught, there was no way they could get free. Look at the wrist on the one in the bay if you don't believe me. And it's worse in here."

"Oh, no," Sally whispered, "they starved to death trying to get free. What a terrible way to die."

"Coulda been worse," Jerry said philosophically. "Hey, thanks for looking into this. I wasn't worried, you understand, but Minnie's not so tough."

Minnie laughed uproariously.

"Muldoon, we've got to do something," Sally said. "It's our garage. We can't just let that thing sit there. More people could die."

"Nah, it's pretty full," Jerry countered. His gaze wandered as if by accident to the bin where the boss kept the shelled nuts. "But as long as we're here, you mind if we grab a snack?"

Like I'd do anything violent with Sally around. "We shouldn't move the box or dispose of the bodies. We leave that to the professionals," I told her.

"And until they get here?" Sally asked.

"We wait. You don't believe in ghosts as well as aliens, do you?"

"Not really." But she snuggled close to me anyway.

The low, ominous growl of an idling motor woke me from a doze. The car door moaned as it lurched upward, compelled by an unknown hand.

The rumble of the motor swelled to a tornado's roar that consumed all other sound. Jerry and Minnie streaked from view. Scraps of paper, leaves, seed and other debris flew in every direction, as if even the inanimate sought to flee the twin white suns rolling inexorably towards the trap.

I squinted against the glare, spots the shape of fat carp swimming across my vision. Sally buried her face in my shoulder. I felt the pulse in her throat throb against my chest.

"Sally, Muldoon, what are you doing out here?" the boss demanded. She stomped in front of the still burning headlights of the Volvo and a made a grab for us. Then she saw the trap.

"Bad cats! Bad, bad cats!" The boss wagged her finger at us. "Eeek! What are all those dead mice doing there?"

About time she noticed.

The Impossibility of
Travelling in Time
Paul Kincaid

I came across my old time machine yesterday. I didn't recognize it at first; it was in a far corner of the loft, where it had clearly spent many years acquiring a camouflage of cobwebs and mice shit and mildew and all the other things that made it nasty to the touch. The funny thing is that I would have sworn my parents got rid of it ages ago, when fashions changed and I stopped using it. Most of my toys were gone, the collections begun with a single-minded obsession and dropped incomplete after a season or two, the clothes that I just had to have until next summer I found them unworn at the back of a wardrobe and cringed with horror. For some reason, though, they had held onto the time machine. I'm sure they can't have imagined it might one day be valuable; even now you'll find them turning up occasionally at jumble sales or in dimly lit antique shops, but no one's really interested in them any more.

I dragged it out of the loft, down the stairs, and set it up in the hallway near where the old telephone table with the red plush seat had once stood. Then I had to go and wash my hands immediately; I have grown fastidious with age. After that, I really only paid it any attention as I squeezed past it on my way up and down the stairs. There wasn't as much in the loft as I had imagined. An old cardboard suitcase, the straps already rotted, which contained a half-dozen stained and crumpled books I remembered from my childhood; plastic boxes filled with slides of seaside holidays balanced precariously upon a projector still in its styrofoam packing; a small box inside which, carefully wrapped in forty-year-old newspapers, I found my christening mug, a baby book in which details of weight and teeth and hair had been carefully entered for five or six weeks then abandoned, pictures of a toothless infant framed in what I presumed was genuine silver. Some of this went straight into the skip which sat on the grass verge outside the front door, but most joined the growing pile of clutter that waited at the foot of the stairs. When, late in the day, I finally and wearily lowered myself onto one of the stairs to survey the mess, I realized that, though I had thought I was clearing up the remnants of my father's life, most of what I had accumulated appeared to be my own. Here, filthy and jumbled though it was, I was contemplating all the signs of my life from birth up to the time machine, whose discarding coincided roughly with when I left home for university. Nothing of my parents from either side of those two decades remained, and there wasn't much of them left among the junk that was me.

I pulled the nearest box towards me and started leafing desultorily through its contents. A run of Classics Illustrated comics that I had collected when I was, what? ten? twelve? Even today, when I'm bluffing my way through a literary conversation over dinner somewhere, most of my knowledge comes from memories of those old comics. There were maybe a dozen American Civil War bubblegum cards interleaved in the comics. I'd collected them about the same time, and I once had the complete set except for Mechanicsville; I wondered idly where the rest had disappeared to, but I couldn't rouse much interest. Every few minutes I found myself looking up, straight at the time machine. The brass struts were tarnished, the leather seat had grey-green stains on the black, the rubber on the handles and control levers had perished. It had never been one of the top-of-the-range machines, but it had been good enough and for a year or two there I'd been inordinately proud of it. I'd polished it regularly, rubbed oil into its few moving parts, even, on occasion, stripped it down, every clip and screw counted and laid to one side in careful order then individually greased and re-assembled. I never had anything left over, and the machine never failed to work. It would probably work now.

I stopped myself. I picked up the box of comics and bubblegum cards, and stepping warily among the wreckage of my life, I carried it out to the van I'd hired. The summer sky was already darkening towards mauve and the first street lights had come on. If I didn't get everything loaded soon it wouldn't be worth trying to get home tonight. I pushed the box of comics into a corner of the van, then had second thoughts and tipped them into the skip instead. I looked down at them, the pages fluttering in the slight breeze, and thought of the times I'd read them, stretched out on the rug in front of the old two-bar electric fire with the plastic flame-effect logs that never worked. The one on top was Victor Hugo's *The Man Who Laughed*, the crude drawing making him look not unlike the Joker in the Batman comics I'd graduated to, in a move which even at the time seemed like a reversal of the natural direction, after giving up on Classics Illustrated. If we'd kept those old Batman comics they'd probably be worth a bob or two now, but those had disappeared long ago and it was these forgotten and probably worthless Classics Illustrated that had somehow been preserved. Like memories, you've no real control over what will and will not be kept out of the confusion of your life.

I went back inside, found the telephone buried under a small mound of rusting tools I'd found out in the shed and which I imagined might turn me at long last into a gardener, and called Mandy. "I'm going to have to stay the night."

"Peter, you promised."

"I know, but there's just so much stuff. I still haven't sorted most of it out."

"I thought you were going to dump it all. You said . . . "

"I couldn't. There's things here, I don't know, it just feels wrong."

I'm not sure she heard me. There was a crash, rendered indistinct and unthreatening down the crackly line, and I could hear her yelling something at the kids or the dog. I waited, staring across the suitcases and plastic bags cluttering the hall. The lincrusta that rose halfway up the wall had been painted grey sometime after I had left home. The striped wallpaper above that had a darker square where a picture had been taken down. I must have taken that picture down myself earlier in the day, but I had no memory of what it was. When Mandy came back on the line she sounded exasperated.

"Where are you going to sleep tonight?"

"I brought a sleeping bag. Just in case. I'll be fine, don't worry."

"I'm not. Tomorrow, then?"

"Tomorrow."

"You're sure?"

"I promise."

"You promised before."

"Tomorrow, Mandy. Honest. I just need a little more time than I bargained for."

After she put the phone down I held the handset to my ear for a long time, wondering why I'd done that. All this stuff, it was junk mostly, things I didn't remember or didn't want to remember. I could clear it into the skip in another hour, maybe less. A little longer to get the things I wanted to keep into the van. I could be home by midnight at the latest. I put down the phone and picked up the garden tools, carried them out to the skip and let them drop. Damn the garden!

Then I went to the van and found a plastic bag full of stuff I'd liberated from the kitchen earlier in the day: a half-full bottle of washing-up liquid, Brillo pads still in their box, things that were too useful to throw away. I took out a roll of J-cloths, a bottle of disinfectant and, the most unexpected treasure of all, a blue-and-white tin of Brasso which I couldn't remember seeing since I was kid. I manhandled the time machine into the kitchen and started to clean it. Firstly I brushed away the cobwebs, swept up things whose nature I didn't inquire into too closely, scrubbed at the mildew. Then I sat cross-legged on the floor in front of it and began slowly and painstakingly to polish up the struts and bars, becoming more thoroughly absorbed in the job than I had been in anything since childhood.

At some point I went out and got chicken and bamboo shoots and egg fried rice from a Chinese takeaway round the corner, and a four-pack of Heineken from the off-licence next to it. But later, when I'd finally finished cleaning up the time machine, I found most of the food, cold now and congealed, still in its foil trays. Two of the cans of lager were empty, though. I couldn't remember drinking them. It was well past midnight now, dark and preternaturally still. I fancied for a moment that the world was holding its breath in anticipation, then I laughed at my fancy, pulled the tab on another beer, hunkered down against the kitchen wall and stared at the last remnant of my childhood.

It had come up beautifully, as my mother might have said. The brass seemed to glow with a warm and seductive fire. I was tired. My eyes were gritty, my knees ached from being too long in one position, I felt light-headed from the lager, but I couldn't leave it. I couldn't even take my eyes off it.

I had known what it was just from the way my parents were standing. They were standing awkwardly, side by side, looking uncomfortable even then at the touch of the other. My mother wore her unsmiling face, and my father, turned slightly away from her, had what she always criticised as his "stupid grin". It was my fifteenth birthday and I'd been begging, cajoling, bargaining for a time machine for most of the past year. Everyone else had one. I promised to be good, to run errands, not to ask for anything else, promises I would forget instantly but which my parents never did. Now they moved apart with a clumsy flourish as if opening the velvet curtains on a stage, and there it was, in the middle of the kitchen, the old formica-topped table pushed to one side to make space for it.

Did I say "thank you"? My mother said I didn't — it was one of her regular complaints. I just don't remember. All I remember is the brightness of it, the cool, slick feel as I ran my hand over struts still with factory grease on them, the solid reality of something I'd come to think of as a dream.

"No you don't," my mother said, as I made to swing myself up into the saddle. "Not until you learn to look after it properly." She held out the flimsy little instruction book that came with time machines back then. For a long moment I couldn't take my hands off the handles, couldn't stop feasting my eyes on the shining brass, the little ivory rods that formed an intricate and somehow unfathomable pattern on the control panel.

It was a pattern that seemed to draw you down somewhere into a depth that couldn't exist. I could never stop staring into it, feeling myself falling down through time.

I shook my head suddenly, surprised to find myself sitting on the machine, leaning forward over the handles like a boy racer about to pedal his bike into hyperdrive. My parents were gone, of course. Long gone. The instruction book, read over and over with a thoroughness my schoolbooks never enjoyed, must have been thrown out years back. But the machine was still here, in this same, now-empty kitchen where I had first seen it. I ran my hands quickly over the controls, making sure everything was set at neutral, and realized what I was doing only after I'd done it. I should get off. I was a grown man, for heaven's sake; toys were for children.

But I wondered if I'd ever really left my childhood behind. Certainly that was what my mother said, when I started earning a living writing silly little pieces about Townswomen's Guild meetings and dog shows for the local paper. But then I wore open-necked shirts and a rather battered but much-loved sports jacket I'd found at an Oxfam shop, and my mother would never believe I was grown up until I wore a suit and tie every day to work. It didn't seem to matter much to her when I graduated to the *Manchester Evening News*, and she was already dead by the time I made it to the nationals. I suppose I'd reacted against her notion of what it was to be an adult all my life, but it had felt very grown up and very scary the first time I ever saw my by-line.

One of the things I'd found, when I'd been helping my father sort out her things after she died, was a small pile of cheap scrapbooks into which had been neatly pasted every single article that ever bore my name. The collection, all dated, stopped a little before the kidney failure finally killed her. She'd never mentioned it, and I still couldn't make it fit with the way she'd talked about journalism. If she hated my job, why did she collect my work? Once, when I'd got maudlin drunk, I told Mandy I was going to dig out my old time machine so I could go back and ask her. "If they had any sense they got rid of that years ago," Mandy said, looking at me in that pitying way which could, at times, make her seem uncomfortably like my mother. Well, now I had the time machine, my fingers lingering over the levers, and I didn't go. Because I didn't want to know the answer? Because I knew the answer? Or because, eight years before, when my mother had been lying puffed and glossy-skinned and barely conscious in an intensive care ward, I had more than anything felt a sense of release, and if I went back now I would be back under the same spell?

It was eight years ago, also, that Mandy and I had started quarrelling, those bitter little Sunday dinner-time exchanges like the ones I remember watching between my parents when I was small. It would be better to go back and put those right before they'd started. But I didn't do that either.

I got off the time machine at last and stretched. The seat was a lot more uncomfortable than I remembered. I picked up the last beer and took it through to the lounge where I'd laid out my sleeping bag more or less where the old settee had been. I suddenly felt cold, and crawled into the bag fully clothed, but I couldn't sleep. Still wrapped in the sleeping bag, I sat up against the wall and popped the can of beer.

I'd been into Cavaliers and Roundheads in those days. Not the English Civil War, you understand, but the romance I'd found in countless novels ever since I'd first discovered *The Children of the New Forest*, probably in one of those Classics Illustrated comics. So when I'd finally mastered the instruction book to my mother's satisfaction I persuaded my mate Ron that we should go and see a battle. We'd known, ever since we first met at infant school, that there'd been a skirmish here, on the site of the council estate. Everyone in the neighbourhood who had a time machine must have gone back at some point to watch it; we'd heard some pretty bloody stories in the playground, though there wasn't much in the way of detail and I don't think either of us had any real idea what to expect. Ron had got his time machine not long before mine. They were never very manoeuvrable, but we managed to set them up side by side and very carefully made sure we fed in exactly the same settings. I recall Ron's grin as we settled into our seats and then, when I gave the thumbs up, pushed the lever forward.

There was a filthy man with long, ragged hair rushing at me with a pole. I panicked and pulled the lever back. Ron was there before me. We never told anyone about that. I never even knew which side the man was on. He certainly didn't fit with my image of a dashing, satin-clad Royalist, but then he wasn't much like the crop-haired Parliamentarians either.

For a while after that we didn't actually use the time machines very much. I got the notion that we should be more prepared for when we were turning up, so I started reading our history textbooks with a little more attention. My grades improved, but not much else changed. Ron still had a desire to see the big dramatic moment. He had a thing about naval battles and kept trying to persuade me we should go and see one. I had to explain, more than once, that we'd never be able to get ourselves and our time machines out to exactly the right spot at sea. And if we did land on a ship it would be just like our Civil War experience again, and if we didn't, which was much more likely, we'd drown.

That turned out to be one of the problems with the time machine: getting it to somewhere where it was worth going into the past. Those early machines were heavy and clumsy, so mostly we just went to see what had been there on the sites where our homes now were. Once, when exams were coming round, Ron suggested that we go into the future and get the answers, but we couldn't even work out the best time and place to do that. I did get to see the dinosaurs one time, which was pretty special; and I also got myself into an early Beatles concert, when they were just starting out and played the local hall, but it was crowded and smoky and I didn't see much and I couldn't hear anything over the screaming.

So why, I thought, hugging my knees to my chest and sipping slowly at the beer, did I still feel such affection for it? I remembered my father's face when they gave it to me, that silly grin. What was it he was responding to? He never did say much. Maybe it was just a habit of silence, but I always felt he knew more than he was letting on. I never found out. When my mother died he was too set in his ways to become garrulous. And I didn't feel comfortable enough in his presence to ask about anything until after the cancer had started eating into his throat and he couldn't speak anyway.

I was in the kitchen again. The time machine looked too bright under the harsh fluorescent light. I was sure it would still work; I could go back and ask. It would be easy: just return to that silent time between my mother's death and the onset of the cancer, one of those long awkward weekends when we would come up to visit and find ourselves sitting there in excruciating silence while we tried to imagine what we might do to fill in the time before we went home. Dad, what were you smiling at all the time? How did you learn that silence in the face of mother's carping? Oh, I knew the answer to that one; I'd learned it for myself. An instinctual inertia that sometimes seemed to make things worse, but always felt like the safest option. And maybe the smile wasn't really as happy as I'd always wanted it to be? Maybe it was just silly, like Mum said.

The light was different. The fluorescent light was off and a dingy daylight was leaching into the room through the rain-spattered window. I snatched my hands away from the controls, then thought better of it and reached to pull the lever back to neutral once more. Too late, the door from the lounge opened. "You here?" Dad said, showing no surprise. "Awful day. Don't blame you for not going out. Let's have a little light on the subject." He threw the switch, then seemed to notice the time machine for the first time. "Good grief, where'd you dig that out from? What a waste of money that was. All that fuss, and then I don't think you ever used it, did you?"

"Yes," I said, getting over my shock at last. "Sometimes."

He looked older than I remembered. This was — what? — probably a year before they finally diagnosed cancer, but he was much more shrivelled and frail than I had allowed myself to see at the time. He coughed violently, then spat into the sink. I looked away, as I always had done. "Catarrh," he said. "I still can't seem to shake it." It wasn't catarrh. I knew that now, and I'd probably known it at the time.

"Yes, Dad," I said. Was it something in my voice that made him turn and peer at me that way? All of a sudden I was afraid that I was going to spill it all, the operations, the pipes in the throat, the wasting away, the horrible, horrible death. "Dad," I said. "Dad."

"Hmm? Did you really use that thing? Now, what did I come in here for?"

"Dad?"

"Ah, tea. Would you like a cup? I'll put the kettle on."

"Dad, why did you always smile so much?" It came out in a rush.

"Did I?" He smiled.

"Mum always used to call it your silly grin."

He stopped what he was doing, staring out of the window for a moment. I could see his ghostly smile reflected over the rain-sodden garden. "Yes," he said, "I remember that." He was silent for a moment longer, then looked around as if not exactly sure where he was any more. "Where did I leave the tea bags?"

"It's OK, Dad," I said. "I'll make the tea. You go back and sit down."

He turned slowly. Had he always moved so awkwardly? "Thank you, it's good of you." He started towards the door, then paused. "Chocolate biscuits, remember. I always have chocolate biscuits with my tea." He smiled again.

I waited, hardly daring to breathe, until he had closed the door behind him. Then, in abject panic, I jerked the handle back.

The moment I was sure I was back in the present I leapt from the machine and fled to the far wall. There I cowered, staring at the time machine. For a moment it seemed threatening, almost predatory. I pressed against the wall, but couldn't bring myself to go back to the sleeping bag. I was tired, that was all. There was already a hint of light in the sky. Sometime in the next few hours I would have to drive nearly the length of the country, back to Mandy and the kids. I wasn't in a fit state for that, but I could imagine what would happen if I didn't. I needed sleep, a few hours at least, enough to feel more in control of myself. But instead I went and picked up the beer can and shook it a little to make sure there was still some lager in it, then I returned to the kitchen and the time machine.

There must be some point I could go back to when I could make everything better. Not to stop him dying. I had a far too vivid picture of death in his smile. I knew nothing as simplistic as that could work. But some moment before the battles started, before everything was set in its course of criticism and silence. Before, I realised with embarrassment, I picked up the habits I'd carried into my own marriage.

I straddled the machine, touched each of the controls one by one, imagined how I would move them, just a little, that dial there, that lever. But nothing happened. There was nowhere to go, no one moment when everything became wrong. I wasn't even sure it ever had been as wrong as it felt: my father did always have that smile. Maybe it would be simpler just to go back to when Mandy and I had been happy. Because we *had* been happy, once. I could make sure that the little accumulations of disappointment and worry and ignorance and irritation never got to be a poison. Except, I'd not recognized any of them then; why should I be able to recognize them now? More likely, I'd just want to stay there, enjoy the good times. But good times end, and I couldn't keep travelling back in an endless hedonistic loop. Besides, could I displace myself from my own marriage? And, knowing what was to come, would I be able to enjoy the good times as much as I had?

It was definitely dawn now. I ran my hands over the controls once more, again making sure they were all set to neutral. Then I got off and turned the kitchen light out. In the pale glow through the window the time machine seemed smaller and less vivid. I started carrying the junk out of the hall to the skip. I dumped all of it in the end. The last thing to go was the collection of slides. I opened one of the boxes but found I couldn't face looking at any of the transparencies, so I just threw them all into the skip. I locked up the house and drove away with only my sleeping bag and some washing up liquid in the van. I stopped off briefly to leave the key with the estate agent, then headed south. I was halfway down the M6 when I remembered the time machine was still in the kitchen. The new owners were welcome to it. Any past it gave them access to would not be mine.

Private View
Ian Johnson

The Sea . . . The Sea . . . Would the sound never cease? She had closed the window, but she could still hear it, and it did not bring her the comfort it once had.

She sat hunched over the table, playing with the edge of a doily . . . apathetic. It wasn't this banal activity keeping her numb. It wasn't the washed-out light or the lethargic ticking of the ancient grandfather clock in the corner, either. No. These things *complemented* her mood.

Then . . . what?

She dropped the doily's edge, watched disinterestedly as it sank back into place. The table itself was polished dark, the surface of a hidden lake. The candle's light rippled upon it, ghostly. She looked down into her own face, and saw looking back at her the most watery of reflections. Alone, she looked back at herself. Loneliest of daughters.

The clock continued to tick, and the tide cast the sea inland and drew it out again, endless. The light dimmed outside, and melted wax pooled about the candle's flame. Her head began to dip.

It was then that the clock struck the hour. She sat upright, one hand going to her brow and the other to the locket that hung from her neck. She pressed her thumb into its engraving. An amaranth: the undying flower.

She looked out the window. She could see someone coming up the quays through the wan daylight. She watched him draw nearer, a large man in heavy fisherman's clothes. *He's expecting rain,* she realized, looking briefly out to sea. There were grey swells of cloud on the horizon.

He was closer now. His beard was like seaweed. His face was weathered, raw red, solid. She clutched her locket with a pale hand. Her breath clouded the glass.

She shivered, discovering for the first time how cold she was. Looking into the room, she saw she hadn't lit the fire all day. Next to the fireplace was an empty chair, and upon the seat a cushion. Dust had amassed on the armrests. Beyond the chair was a bucket that had collected rainwater from last night. It stood near to the wall. The wall's patterned paper was peeling. It had needed repairing for some time.

When she looked out again, the man had gone, and another afternoon of rain had begun.

The Stars Move Still
John Brunner

Prologue

Little by little the Imperial grip was slipping. World after distant world found allegiance to Argus burdensome, or — worse yet — pointless.

Moreover, what had been loyal fleets were starting to turn rogue, selling their services to would-be independent planets, even seizing them as private fiefs.

Causes — or, more exactly, somewhere to lay the blame — were sought by those who could not accept the truth: the Empire had become ungovernable. A king still ruled on Argus, but he had grown weary of his power and luxury, and now his sole concern was to restore that planet with its nine bright moons to the state it had had in legendary times: one castle, one spaceport, one town. The rest was to revert to wilderness.

Favourite of all explanations for the Imperial decline was subversion from the Rim, whither for countless generations the agents of Argus had been accustomed to exile mutants and those suspected of strange powers. It had become a fetish to preserve the human strain unaltered.

Now, though, ancient guilt preyed on the minds of the Imperials, so that they saw a threat where none existed. Some claimed that, out there where the stars were scattered thin, humans — or their descendants —

had at last begun to build their own starships. To what purpose? Maybe . . . conquest!

It was as the consequence of one more attempt to shore up the tottering edifice that Anza Cly was sent to scour the frontier worlds and purify them of mutated stock. This is in part her story. But it tells also of Hennig of the Twisted Foot, and of Elyucham and Rempus, and how a certain spark was struck that was to smoulder throughout the Long Night and finally break into a flame so bright it made the very stars seem dim.

Begin. Begin on Kah. It is a frontier world . . .

1

"Be upstanding for the noble Tiron, Hereditary Keeper of the Motte of Kah!" intoned the Grand Chamberlain. At once the chattering that filled the great hall died, and there followed a rustling of garments as the courtiers obeyed. Anza Cly judged there to be two hundred of them, exuding the indefinable aura of hangers-on forever trying to seem busy but with no real occupation save intrigue.

Tiron strove to keep his court in the Argian manner. It was in only this single respect that he appeared to have completely succeeded.

Unimpressed though she was by this near-parody, Anza too rose to her feet, aware how many glances she attracted. Not only was she the first emissary direct from Argus for more than a generation; she overtopped everyone else by a head and a half. She could feel the stares of the locals like insects on her skin, sense the unspoken resolve in all their minds to throw away their gaudy out-of-fashion garb and copy her drab, practical attire. By way of amusement, she decided — for she foresaw little else to entertain her on this farflung planet — that she would wait until they were all attired in ash and filemot, then commission a local tailor to deck her in the vilest of pinks and greens.

With purple and orange face-paint. Yes. Why not?

Now Tiron emerged onto the dais where stood his chair of state. She had researched him from what records were available in the chaos of the Argian system. Reports were still being dutifully filed from all the frontier zones, but expulsion of the administrative bureaux to the moons so that the king might achieve his ambition of restoring the planet to desert, prairie and jungle had wrought indescribable havoc. In respect of many volumes no data had been indexed for half a century.

At least, though, Anza had been given the correct name, and some presumably trustworthy details. For instance, she knew Tiron was aged sixty, and had held office for about a decade. She knew also that his proud title, Hereditary Keeper, was hollow; he was no kin to his predecessor, and unlikely to establish a succeeding dynasty.

Still, that was the way of things on these frontier worlds. Much the same could be said of the Praestans of Klareth, and the Dominatrix of Mallimameddy, and the Public Servant of Batyra Dap, to name but a few of the lordlings who had been tempted by their increasing isolation from Argus into considering secession.

She gazed steadily at Tiron, with the intention of making him feel uneasy. In that she succeeded. He avoided looking her way as he settled in his chair, and a gleam of sweat showed on his face, whose fat jowls bore testimony to years of too-rich living.

The courtiers, at a sign from the Grand Chamberlain, resumed their seats. Anza, however, moved not a muscle, and within seconds the rest of the company were visibly wondering whether they had done the wrong thing.

Now, finally, Tiron was obliged to acknowledge his unwelcome visitor. Inclining his head, he said, "We are here assembled, as you know, to greet the first envoy from Argus in a regrettably long while. Anza Cly, we bid you welcome."

It was her turn to nod, but she made no other answer.

"What, if we may know it, is the business that brings you hither? To be frank, we of Kah had begun to imagine that our petty local affairs were no longer of much concern down in the Hub."

The sharpness of the implied rebuke caused a susurrus of comment among the audience.

"What brings me?" Anza echoed reflectively. Her voice was deep and resounding, a sonic match for her dark hair, bronze complexion, statuesque frame. "Why, a report from the Fifteenth Frontier Fleet. It seems you mistook the character of its commander. He is loyal to Argus."

"Why should he not be?" countered Tiron. His tone betrayed alarm.

"Certain persons appear to imagine that he isn't. At all events, he sent an urgent message informing the Supreme Command about an offer he'd received."

Anza paused. Tiron knew very well what offer she was referring to. She was wondering how he planned to excuse his behaviour.

"I don't understand," was his bluff response.

"To be precise" — although Anza merely murmured the words, her murmur carried to all corners of the hall without assistance — "he stated that he had been invited to put his fleet at the disposal of Kah, with a view to reducing Aylshaw, Grovang and the Seam of Ho, of whose just taxes Argus would thereafter be deprived. The proceeds were to be divided between his fleet and Kah. This was the substance of Commander Zang's report."

Most of the listeners exclaimed in dismay. Anza's keen eyes picked out the few who merely feigned that dismay. Tiron was chief among them.

"Why in the galaxy should he have said such a thing? There's been a terrible misunderstanding! The proposal I actually made — "

"So you don't deny making a proposition to him?" Anza interjected.

"I did indeed, but it was to no such effect!" Tiron gestured to an attendant and was handed a glass mug. To judge by the red colour of the liquid within, the mug held fuming ancinard. Among the data concerning Tiron that had been sorted back on Argus was mention of his excessive fondness for that risky beverage.

Having downed a healthy swig, the Keeper of the Motte gathered his wits.

"I observed already that we hereabouts have felt neglected for some considerable while. Beyond the frontier, among the systems of the Rim, strange events are rumoured: mutants building starships of their own, for one thing. And besides" — he was regaining courage — "there are facts behind the rumours, incontrovertible facts! There have long been pirates in this volume, and slavers too. Of late they have grown dangerously bold. You mentioned Aylshaw; did you know a slaver landed there and took five hundred captives, mainly children? Naturally the authorities signalled for help, but it was to no avail."

"Did you dispatch ships of your own to assist?"

"Of course! But by the time we heard about the raid it was too late. So was the arrival of the Fifteenth Fleet. And what I said to Commander Zang, in fact, was no more than what still strikes me as most sensible."

He leaned forward.

"That slowness of response indicates a need for forces under local control, paid for by those who will benefit from their protection. Sending all the way to Argus for permission to raise extra taxes . . . With respect, it's no longer feasible. Together with Grovang, Aylshaw and the Seam of Ho, we form a readily defensible volume. So I appealed to the commander to consider the advisability of such a scheme. And that was all!"

Pleased by the ingenuity of his defence, he sat back with a smile of satisfaction and took another gulp of ancinard.

Now for a real shock! Anza repressed a smile.

"I thought that might have been the way of it."

Her words had all the impact she was hoping for. The company froze in astonishment, while Tiron — whose mind a moment earlier must have been full of visions of investment by the Fifteenth Fleet as a preliminary to his being tried for treason — simply gaped for several seconds. At last he forced out, "Well . . . Well, I'm overjoyed to hear you say so! Naturally! But what I still don't understand is how Commander Zang could have misinterpreted my intentions so completely."

"There's one extremely likely explanation," Anza said, striding forward to the clear space in front of Tiron's dais. Despite the fact that it was knee-high to her, her head was on a level with his when she turned to face the assembly.

"You are all aware of Imperial policy regarding mutants, are you not?"

There was a mutter of affirmation.

"It has always been accepted, I submit, as just and humane. Among certain ignorant and badly administered communities — one must admit the fact, albeit with distaste — those unfortunate enough to be born with altered germ-plasm have been brutally persecuted, to the extent that sometimes they were put to death even when they posed no threat to society but merely constituted a trifling burden on it. By contrast, the civilized and merciful attitude of Argus has invariably been: let them lead their lives as they choose, so long as it is far away from us. I trust that no one here would disapprove of that policy?"

Several of her listeners said loudly, "Of course not!"

"Yet!" Anza went on. "Yet what reward do we receive for our forbearance? Is it not the case that, out there on the Rim, those who ought to be our grateful cousins are turning rather into implacable enemies?"

There was dead silence. Scarcely anybody moved.

"You know the difficulties that the Empire faces! Were things a thousand years ago as they are today? A hundred, even? They were not! Keeper Tiron has mentioned the ravages of pirates and slavers. In the old days the kind of retribution that he appealed for from the Fifteenth Fleet would have been automatic, would it not? So why was it that Commander Zang misunderstood a practical suggestion, distorted it into an accusation of treachery and garnished it with the implication that Kah intended to secede?"

For all his addiction to ancinard, Tiron's mind was still blade-keen. He whispered, "You're implying that a secret mutant has ensnared us."

"May have," corrected Anza with a sidelong glance. "But it seems a feasible explanation. As you know, mutants have powers denied to the rest of us, including the imposition of mental conditioning that we — we normals — must employ machines for. It is my duty to establish whether such is the truth behind the present mystery. Mutants *must* be identified and exiled, or humanity will cease to be humanity!"

She let the point sink home before continuing.

"In this volume, do you know of, do you suspect, a world where the practice of exiling mutants is not being complied with? Bear in mind: they may crop up anywhere. So long as there is radiation, so long as there are native organic chemicals on all the myriad worlds humanity inhabits, there will unceasingly be alterations to our gametes . . . Well?"

She took half a pace back, settling her weight on the rear leg, and crossed her arms. Her piercing dark stare swept the faces before her like the beam of a fast-spinning neutron star.

At last, diffidently, the Grand Chamberlain said, "Well, it does puzzle certain of us . . . "

"What does, man? Speak out, in the name of Argus!"

Unaccustomed to being addressed in such brusque terms, the Chamberlain blinked and hesitated, but recovered in a moment. "Well, it is most strange that, of all the worlds in the Seam of Ho, the least hospitable should be the most prosperous. Despite engulfing ice and dreadful storms, Ho Five supports a population of a million, and exports not just the minerals one might expect but plants and even animals that cannot possibly have evolved there naturally."

"Are you sure," Anza said penetratingly, "that you are not merely yielding to disguised jealousy?"

Denials rang out on all sides.

"Then," said Anza Cly with satisfaction, "we must investigate Ho Five."

2

Born to a harsh world of gales and glaciers, Hennig of the Twisted Foot learned early that he must acquire skills to ensure acceptance. Life was a constant struggle. Only by tapping the deep heat of the planet had the pioneers survived here, coaxing seeds and life-spores brought from far away into forms that resisted the cruel climate, or adapted to the roofed-in valleys where the humans huddled.

Given his handicap, there were some who wondered why Hennig's parents had not reverted to the custom, long disused, of exposing their baby at birth . . . but never in their hearing. There were, his father insisted, more means to earn one's keep than muscle-power alone. His mother, likewise, said, "He is our child and our heredity is sound! His foot was twisted as he left the womb, and on worlds less poor than ours could have been straightened by a surgeon. Not knowing how, we dared not meddle more and risk worse harm."

To which his father would respond, "Don't *look* at him! *Listen!* You never knew such a child for asking questions! If he finds out half the answers that he's after, he'll wind up knowing more than you or I!"

Indeed. As soon as he learned that there were planets where sunlight might beam down all year, Hennig wanted to know why people had come to this chill world. But he was too young to understand when they said it had to do with a long-ago war. Nowadays his people were much too busy staying alive to think about fighting, so there were scarcely even any quarrels to hint at what a war might be.

Also he asked, "Why is our home called Ho Five?"

They recounted how, in the legends of another world, a certain pattern of stars in the night sky had been compared to embroidery on a robe. The story went that a woman named Ho had worked on such a robe for her invalid daughter, in hopes that the daughter would wear it at her coming-of-age party. Her neighbours mocked her, for she made the robe so stiff with shining metal thread, so thick with jewels, that no one could have worn it comfortably. That is, no one still alive and moving . . .

The daughter died before she came of age. The robe was put around her in her grave. "Now," said the mother, "tell me my daughter is not glad to wear the robe I sewed."

Therefore a constellation was called the Seam of Ho.

Hennig nodded gravely, mused a while, and eventually asked, "But why Five? If you have a Five, there must at least be a One, Two, Three and Four."

Whereupon his parents decided it was time to stop amusing him with legends and explain reality. He showed adeptness with machines at once. By the age of eight he could take quite complicated ones apart and reassemble them. By ten, his father had apprenticed him to his own trade of modifying and improving living creatures.

Then Anza Cly descended from the roiling welkin and began her witch-hunt for suspected mutants.

#

Intelligent as he was, and well informed for his years, Hennig could not begin to understand what was happening, for it made no sense. His frightened parents told him that the planet was surrounded by the Fifteenth Fleet, and a ship had landed at Ho Five's mountaintop spaceport so large it made their little freighters look like toys. They explained that their people were accused of mentally subverting the loyalty of the Keeper of the Motte of Kah, persuading him to launch a plot that would have resulted in the secession of all the local worlds from Imperial suzerainty. They cursed the cowards who had told Anza and her agents about the family that had kept a child with a twisted foot who now was brighter than he had a right to be. But the words bore no relation to reality.

What did was the grasp of the guards who arrested Hennig and his parents and took them to a strange hot place the other side of the clouds, along with scores of others, all of whom seemed to want to blame him for what had happened.

With impersonal efficiency the captives were stripped, physically examined, interrogated, drugged unconscious, and carried off to stars knew where.

#

"How many did we settle for in the end?" asked Anza Cly.

Commander Zang, in the control cabin of his flagship, stroked his beard and smiled. "Two hundred and twenty."

"Very good. You understand what you have to do now?"

"Of course. Arrest the next ship we cross that's bound towards the Rim and order her captain to dump them well clear of the frontier. They are to be set down on any non-Imperial world. If he can get a fee for them, he may."

"And afterwards?"

"Ho Five will come under the jurisdiction of the Keeper of the Motte of Kah. At least in theory. In fact, the whole of this volume will henceforth be under direct military control. I shall be empowered to levy local taxes, as required to support the fleet in being, without consulting Argus every time. As soon as possible, on the grounds that all the planets hereabouts were formerly beyond the Imperial frontier and mutants may well have been exiled to them so long ago that the records have been lost, I am to ensure that the other Seam worlds, and eventually Aylshaw and Grovang too, go the same way."

"Leading to the outcome Tiron dreamed of, only he didn't know how to set about it." Anza Cly sighed and stretched her long arms. "It's a harsh procedure, but essential. Do you have any ancinard on board? I feel one should drink to the successful accomplishment of the operation."

"Yes, of course!"

#

Following Anza Cly's departure to her next assignment, Commander Zang shook his head ruefully. He had never imagined that the Imperial

170

government still kept so sensitive a finger on the pulse of frontier affairs. All reports indicated that this crazy scheme of the king's to turn Argus back into a primitive planet had totally fouled up normal administration. He had filed a self-protective memorandum about Tiron's proposition purely in order to cover his own tracks, not expecting anyone to pay attention to it for at least a decade. The arrival of a special envoy in search of mutants had taken him completely by surprise. (*Mutants?* Why, the nearest this mission had come to producing one was that boy with the deformed foot! *Superpowers?* What a load of comet dust!)

Well, everything had turned out for the best. And the profit from two hundred and twenty slaves — or, making allowance for the crippled boy, two hundred and nineteen — would be substantial.

Now: Elyucham's slave-ship ought to be in this vicinity, so it was time to fix a rendezvous.

Zang felt no remorse. In these troubled times one had to make ends meet as best one could.

3

"Hey, you! Yes, I mean you — *Rempus!*"

On the stone-flagged street a voice rang out above the hubbub of a crowd which, despite heavy rain, had gathered for that exceptional event, a sale of slaves.

Within the Empire proper, trade in human beings had always been illegal. Those who had first imposed the rule of Argus step by step on other systems had shared the assumption of their forebears who burst forth from the legendary birthworld that machines could be devised to undertake whatever tasks a human could.

From the start, though, theory had proved irreconcilable with practice. During the pioneering phase there had never been quite enough people to build those machines; during the settled phase of Imperial power there had always been the wealthy and the greedy anxious to surpass the mechanical possessions of their rivals, and not a few of the poor and hopeless driven to abandon inhospitable planets, for whom drudgery near the Hub was preferable to misery elsewhere; while, once the underpinnings of Empire started to creak so badly that many machines could no longer be repaired, thousands of worlds resorted in despair to a solution they had once affected to despise.

By now, therefore, on sundry planets within the ill defined zone referred to loosely as "the frontier" — for instance, here on Pefferlosh — the chief concern of the authorities was to ensure that slave-sales passed off without incident . . . and that they shared the profits.

Rempus turned. He was no longer in his first youth, and his hair, beard and even eyebrows were salted with grey, but his sight was still keen. From beneath his wet hood he recognized who was hailing him.

With a grimace of disgust he made to pass on by.

"That's no way to treat an old friend!" the other cried.

Curt, Rempus said, "I'm not your friend. Not since you changed your trade."

Elyucham the slaver laughed: a burly fellow dressed in bright, water-repellent clothing that marked him out among the throng of locals.

"You bent the law in your time, Rempus, same as me! You can't have forgotten what I used to sell for you?"

"I was younger then," Rempus grunted.

"And I two decades younger still. I'd won my first ship in a game of shen fu and was eager to put her into service, but lacked cargo. You set me up in business, and I owe a debt I'm past due to repay. While I roam free from star to star, here you are still stuck on our home world, and none too prosperous either by the look of you! Well, I plan to square accounts at last. Come on!"

Elyucham seized Rempus's arm.

Reluctant, but unable to resist, the older man let himself be led into the market square, where slaves were huddled miserably beneath black awnings. Not only was the weather wet; it was windy, and the awnings flapped like Poowadyan bats.

"Don't let appearances deceive you," Elyucham exclaimed. "All these are going to the best of homes! Save one . . . See that boy with wide eyes and a twisted foot?"

"What of him?" Rempus growled.

"He's yours. A gift from me."

172

"I, own a slave? Elyucham, you're insane!"

"It's either you take him," Elyucham said deliberately, "or we dump him into space. I've found no buyer for him, and he eats and breathes as much as any child his age. Besides, someone with your skills can probably make him a new foot."

"To starcore with you!" Rempus freed his arm.

"Well, as you like. But if you fixed him up you could sell him for as much as I got from your eroteks."

"Don't mention them!"

"Why? Aren't you proud of your work any more? You should be! I maintain an interest in the goods I've handled, of whatever kind, and lately I learned that one at least of your teks is still in use . . . on Mercator!"

"That's right down near the Hub," said Rempus slowly.

"It is indeed. You know, if you'd had the courage of your convictions, you could be selling your marvellous creations to the Argian Court. I always said you had the talent . . . But I see you're not listening. Oh, well. We space tonight. The boy will be with us. Briefly."

He shrugged and turned away.

"Wait!" Rempus said anxiously. "You really mean to . . . ?"

"Was I ever other than a man of my word?"

Shaking back his hood, the older man looked into the younger's face. He said at last, "No. That at least I have to grant you. Very well."

"I knew you'd come round in the end!" Elyucham crowed. "Here, boy! Yes, you — Hennig of the Twisted Foot! This man is your master from now on! You serve him well, or I'll come back and dump you on an asteroid!"

#

"This is my home," Rempus said gruffly, opening the door of a two-floored house surrounded by weed-infested gardens It was badly in need of repair; its roof sagged and streaks of green ran down its stone and timber walls, marking the points at which its eaves shed rain most readily. "Come in. Take off that soaking gown."

It was all the boy had on; even his feet were bare. But he removed it obediently, his face impassive.

173

"There's a heater yonder that works most of the time. Hang your gown nearby. I'd call someone to bring a towel, but I live alone. My wife is dead, and my four children went to space. I don't hear much about them any more."

For the first time Hennig showed a spark of interest. "Were they taken away, like me?"

"No, they set off to make their fortunes somewhere else: two first, and then the other two. They said ours was a world without a future. Perhaps they were right. At any rate, the machines that used to make existence bearable are breaking down left and right and we can't pay for engineers to mend them, or for spare parts. My kids said they had to seize their chance, in case ships stopped calling here altogether. I don't think that will happen soon, myself — though I must admit Elyucham's is the first in several months. And what a cargo! What straits we are reduced to! *I don't want to own a slave! I want my machines to work again!* Alas, I lack the wherewithal."

Hennig's wide, thoughtful eyes surveyed the room. It had once been impressively well equipped, but now half the wall-panels hung ajar, and the circuitry beyond was in a tangle. Pipes stuck out at unlikely angles; tools were scattered on low tables; dust was everywhere.

"At least your world is better off than mine," Hennig muttered.

"Better off? How can that be? No, don't explain at once. You're apt to catch your death of cold!"

Hennig shook his head. "I've never felt so warm in all my life, except aboard the slave-ship."

"Warm?" Rempus blinked. "I'm almost shivering. The wind today . . . Well, in that case I guess I *may* be doing you some kind of favour after all. Better here, at least, than in the chill of space. In that room over there is a chest where I still keep some of my children's clothes. From sentiment, you know. Help yourself. Then I'll fix us something to eat."

The boy started to move, then checked. He said, "Who are you, sir? What do you do? I heard Elyucham say you could give me a new foot."

"I'm sorry." Rempus stared at the floor. "But, as well as being a criminal, Elyucham is a dreamer and a fool."

"The universe seems to be full of them," Hennig said, and limped into the next room as he had been bidden, not staying for the rest of his question to be answered.

#

But answered it was, as evening fell. Rempus had lived alone for many years, and it had been long since he had entertained a guest of any kind. After they had eaten he produced a flask of wine, from which he let Hennig take a sip, and on the rest of it he grew garrulous.

"Yes, when I first met Elyucham, longer ago than I care to remember, I was doing strange and stupid things. I'd trained, you see, to make . . . Do you know what teks are?"

Grave, paying total attention, the boy shook his head.

"Well, they are luxuries. On a world like yours I don't imagine there have ever been resources to spare for them. They're not so much built as grown. They can repair themselves, or as you might say heal, and also they behave in ways you don't have to spell out in order to teach them. You know a machine can do only as it has been told. Teks are different. The kind I mainly used to build can be coupled to a human nervous system, so the owner feels as though he has new perceptions and new organs."

"New feet?" Hennig whispered, glancing at his own. The right one was shrivelled into the shape of a claw, the toes doubled under and capped with calluses.

"There are other ways to tackle that sort of problem," Rempus said, forgetting for the moment that his claim had not held good on Pefferlosh since well before Hennig was born. "No, my teks were chiefly in demand among the rich and bored who had little to do except eat, drink and make love, and felt they weren't enjoying it enough."

"Can you show me one?" Hennig ventured.

Rempus gave a bitter laugh. "I sold the last of mine long ago. I still have my equipment — in the basement — but each one takes a year to make, and people can't afford my prices any more. Even when I started out there wasn't much of a market on Pefferlosh, so I needed to sell them offworld. As an experiment, I'd designed a new model, and Elyucham saw its commercial possibilities, so . . . "

He broke off. Although they had enjoyed a ready sale, the eroteks he had built in his young days had been — still were — officially illegal. Tek-making was an Imperial monopoly, jealously guarded. Better to say no more; he was talking to an offworld stranger, and a child at that.

"Well, there'll be time in days to come to discuss such matters. Right now I guess I ought to let you sleep."

"You haven't told me my duties," Hennig said stonily. "It was made clear on the ship: I am never to know what has become of my parents. They were taken, too, but traded to other slavers whom we crossed in space while I was kept in store, and Elyucham said he has no idea what worlds they may have gone to. All I know is that, if I want to stay alive, I must work hard and hope one day to be set free. So kindly issue my instructions."

Through a blur of wine-fumes Rempus finally realized what he was hearing. This was not, nor had Hennig's earlier statements been, the normal speech of a ten-year-old as good as orphaned. He and the rest of the cargo must have been conditioned during the trip to fit them for their future state.

Rempus's eyes filled with tears, and his mind with rage. "If ever I set eyes on Elyucham again . . .!"

Hennig looked politely curious.

"Oh, never mind." Rempus forced his stiffening limbs upright. "Well, here's your first order. Go back to the other room, the one that used to be my daughters', with the chest of clothes in it. Make up the bed as best you can with what you find. I've drunk too much to tell you everything, but you should be able to figure things out for yourself better than a tek, and I've built some that were at least that smart . . . Sleep well and in the morning talk to me again."

"Yes, sir," Hennig said respectfully. "What about?"

"I'll tell you then! Turn in!"

"Yes, sir."

But Hennig's posture was so doleful that Rempus had to hasten after him and put an arm around his shoulders.

"Poor child!" he whispered. "I never thought to meet anyone again as lonely as I've become myself! Well, you and I together, Hennig, we'll get along, I'm sure. And one day — one day! — we'll spit in the face of a universe that's been so cruel! Dream of it!"

"Yes, sir," the boy said once again. "I will."

4

Very soon — as things transpire on the galactic scale — the operation of which Anza Cly had been a spearhead brought results. The Imperial grasp tightened afresh on system after frontier system; trade resumed as ships whose captains had been daunted by the threat of piracy returned to their familiar starlanes; slave-raids, though they continued, grew less frequent, and now and then captives were rescued and restored to their homes. Not unconnected was the fact that two fleets which had turned rogue re-pledged their former loyalty. As though awaking from a nightmare, folk on the outer worlds reverted to their ancient and accustomed ways.

It wasn't hard. Argus had reigned supreme for millennia. Only the most dedicated scholars were aware that matters had once been differently arranged, and even among that select elite scarcely any cared to ponder the prospect of them being different in the future. For all its faults, the Empire had endured; visions of its total collapse were too dreadful to contemplate.

Yet and still, there were rumours of continued trouble. Making shift as best they could amid the chaos of their expulsion from Argus proper, Imperial officials met and fretted. One case in particular . . .

"Murder!"

"Ah, who knows what the population is? A census has been unfeasible since . . . " Here was inserted the earliest date the speaker knew could go unchallenged, and it was always several centuries ago. "So one more murder here or there . . . "

"But a starfleet commander on planetside leave . . . ? On Delcadore, what's more! And under most extraordinary circumstances. Cast your eye over the summary."

"Hmm. I see what you mean. What state are the records from that volume in?"

"Appalling!"

"Isn't that the story of our lives? Well, since you insist . . . "

#

Reports of that kind came belatedly to Argus. Unless the mutants of the Rim had invented one, there was not and never had been any means of communication faster than light, save physical dispatch of one of the uncountable starships humanity had inherited by accident on their early ventures outward from the birthworld. It was held that not even the long-lost Masters of the Ship had known that secret. Why otherwise should they have ordained such a colossal horde of ships, enough to have sustained the Empire through millennia — to say nothing of the wastage suffered during the early period of expansion?

Some, indeed, conjectured that the mysterious source which sowed the ships among the stars might still be operating. How else to explain why, no matter how great the losses due to wars and accidental damage (the ships could mend themselves, but only within limits, and humans had devised weapons against which their recuperative powers were of no avail) — how else to explain why nobody had ever been able, even at the height of Imperial domination, to count the ships in service? Taking a census of humanity: admittedly that was out of the question, though in the past it had been tried with some success. On the other hand, there could be at most about one-millionth as many starships as there were people, and even that was hard to credit, given that plenty of planets near the Hub had populations a billion strong. So why . . . ?

But there was a counterargument that ran as follows:

We know their source must be close to the birthworld, lost though the latter is. Yet we have searched Imperial space, inward to where the radiation strikes us dead, outward to where stars straggle into the intergalactic void. We haven't found a system spawning starships.

Remains the Rim.

Could we have been so stupid as to exclude the source from our domain?

Or — and is this not more likely? — could some of those we have expelled for mutancy not have begun to build their own starships, which we cannot? How many of the ships we draft into Imperial service to replace those lost in battle — commandeered from pirates, for example — may in fact be *not* from the old original stock?

Paranoia generated further paranoia. Might not some of those ships be boobytrapped? Think of the fleets we could have sworn were loyal that nevertheless turned rogue and rove the starlanes now as pirates! If they were mutant-built, who knows what mental seduction their crews might have been exposed to?

Worse yet: If the Masters of the Ship are in fact still pouring forth their vessels, hurling them to where more and more are being found today — is it because they plan to make a comeback? Have they concealed their planet? Are they plotting to return and conquer us?

Notions of that kind found fertile soil in the minds of people who, sequestered on the moons of Argus, were the best-informed in history . . . yet, paradoxically, also the most ignorant. There is no more pitiable state of ignorance than theirs: swamped by a plethora of half-understood information, mating scrap with scrap and breeding a false conclusion.

Still, certain of the facts were sound. And one was this.

#

There was little call for working crew aboard a starship. Those who manned Imperial ships of the line were of the dregs: conditioned to behave like guards or soldiers when the need arose, otherwise maintained in a state of futile pleasure with drink and drugs and sex and such amusements. Time-expired, they were dumped on any willing planet — usually for a handsome fee — and tolerated for the sake of the monstrously exaggerated yarns they could spin about their adventures while aspace. Not in the whole duration of the Empire had more than a tenth of one per cent of humankind, at any time, been outside the envelope of local atmosphere, so any spacefarer was an exotic.

But the case of the officers was different.

Hailing for the most part from worlds close to the Hub, where luxuries undreamed-of on the outer worlds were taken for granted, they were invariably intelligent, underprivileged, and ambitious. Had it been possible to condition them like the crewmen, there would have been no problem . . . but conditioning destroyed initiative, and the galaxy was vast, and new predicaments were constantly arising where only judgment and initiative would serve — not knee-jerk reflex.

179

Accordingly, the officers were pampered. Their long tours of duty were counterbalanced with generous periods of groundside leave: months for the junior ranks, years for the senior. It was a risk, of course, that some might find a planet they fell in love with and would no longer wish to quit for the hazards of the service; if so, however, it was unambiguously borne in on them what future advancement they had thus renounced.

At any rate, that had been the way of things in the past. Nowadays life aboard an Imperial ship was often preferable to what could be found planetside.

Delcadoré was a marked exception. There the old traditions were kept up. There the height of luxury could still be found — and, what was more, reserved to service personnel. True, one-half the planet was a starfleet base, and sometimes damaged vessels splashed down in the wrong ocean and there was a crisis . . . but it hadn't happened for a hundred years, and everything had always been swiftly restored to normal.

Coming from the background that he did, Commander Zang had dreamed of retiring on Delcadoré ever since he'd first set down there as a junior lieutenant. He had assiduously cultivated the acquaintance of the powers that were, learned that only the very wealthiest of retired officers might dream of settling here — and dedicated himself to acquiring the necessary fortune.

He had almost attained his goal. He had been able to build an island nearly as large as the senior admiral's, although he was four steps lower in rank; after his last-but-one tour he had commissioned a design for a house to be erected on it; he had come back and back until he was practically a native — insofar as there were "natives" on a service world apart from the dregs who had been born to sweat in the starship maintenance yards. The hulls, and their mysterious drivers, might be self-repairing, but the equipment human beings had added was not, including notably the armament. So, at any given time, a good half of Delcadoré's population was composed of service personnel and crews in transit, plus a fluctuating horde of gawping visitors.

Now Zang was barely a decade away from fulfilment of his ambition. And he had a whole year to relax, amuse himself, and figure out how best to exploit his status. He was, after all, an active officer, who had commanded ships in battle. Many of the admirals and commodores who constituted "society" on Delcadoré had either inherited their rank or been awarded it by decree from Argus, then had deputed their responsibilities to underlings. Zang was no underling. And if, as rumour had it, he had now and then transgressed the border of the law, had it not been to get the better of pirates and slavers, deprive them of their misgotten gains? More power to his drivers, then! Hard times called for hard measures! (So said those who held the sway on Delcadoré, perhaps remembering occasions when they would have dearly loved to do like Zang, had they not seen too little profit in the outcome.)

All, it seemed, was well with Star Commander Zang on the private island where for the duration of his leave he had taken up residence in what he thought of as a hovel, despite its size. The builders were at work by night and day on his permanent house, but their activities did not disturb him. They were machines programmed to operate in silence, under the supervision of not just one tek tuned to his mind — the senior admiral had boasted as much — but two.

Zang was very proud of owning those teks. They had been abominably expensive, and dire predictions had been uttered about his ability to control them, but he scoffed, for so far everything had gone precisely as had been ordained.

He had confiscated certain slaves from the consignments that had passed through the volume he controlled. Exhausted by their enjoyable attentions, he dismissed them and dozed off, alone in the bedroom that formed the entire upper floor of his temporary shelter — a structure as large as many family homes on poorer planets.

He was to be rudely woken.

#

It was his professional reflexes that aroused him.

Superbly silenced though they were, the machines delving the foundations for his home communicated vibrations to the bedrock, and to Zang this was reminiscent of the barely felt hum of a smooth-running starship.

The vibrations had stopped.

181

He sat up, drowsy from last night's ancinard, and raised his arm in a gesture that on Delcadoré called forth light in any building at any time of day or night.

Nothing happened.

He muttered a curse. Something was wrong. Badly wrong.

Groping in the darkness for a gown he had discarded, he shouted an order. Had there been a power failure — and even on Delcadoré failures were not unknown, especially in the vicinity of a construction site — his human attendants at least ought to respond, and make haste to find out what he wanted. Instead, there was silence.

Then, abruptly, the silence was broken by the noise of something smashing — something large, metallic, falling from a height.

Hitherto Zang had been merely alarmed. Now he felt a pang of outright fear.

He sought a way of escape. The door, which he located by touch, was normally power-operated, but should have been openable manually as well. All his strength did not suffice to budge it.

There remained the windows. They occupied one whole wall, overlooking the building-site. Until the power failed they had been opaque, but they were shifting towards transparency as the crystal they were made of reverted to its default condition. Outside, the sun was rising.

Relieved, Zang rushed to gaze out, thinking he might at least attract the attention of his teks. They had been attuned to respond to him and no one else.

The sight that met his eyes filled him with horror.

The foundation-pit, designed to house the elaborate and costly service machinery he had specified, was almost finished; it was ten times deeper than a man was tall, and already his temporary building could have been dropped into it twice over with room to spare. What had in fact fallen into it was his entire team of excavators, together with the metal girders that served as gantries. It looked as though the structure had given way simultaneously on all sides.

No, not quite. On the far brink of the pit remained two of the conveyors used to carry away rubble. Even as he looked, however, one of them rocked and heaved, broke loose, and slid to join its fellows down below.

Zang uttered a shout of disbelief. For he saw, revealed as the conveyor fell, one of his teks. Having managed to dislodge one conveyor, it was now turning to the machine's companion, releasing the necessary fastenings, letting cross-members clatter to the ground. Zang could not hear them, but he could imagine the noise they made.

Furiously, pointlessly, he battered at the window. It was proof against his fists and against anything he could spot when, panting, he glanced around in search of a means to smash through it.

Then, horrifyingly, the house gave a lurch.

It rested on struts. Obviously, one or more had been severed. It had begun to tilt towards the pit . . .

Behind him, a voice said mildly, "Commander Zang?"

Spinning around, Zang saw nothing save familiar furniture, ornaments, household equipment.

"The same Commander Zang whose forces once deported so-called mutants from a planet called Ho Five?"

"Slaves! Come here!" Zang shrieked at the top of his lungs.

"Your servants will not answer," said the voice. "They have been . . . released."

Zang's gaze darted hither and yon, seeking once more a possible source for the voice. But it seemed to come from everywhere and nowhere. It was a projection of the highest quality.

"You cannot but recall the episode in question," the voice continued inexorably, its light inflection never wavering. "No doubt you also remember what became of the alleged "mutants"?"

"Of course not!" Zang retorted with a flash of his normal spirit. "I kept no record of captives like that. They had been decreed mutant by the authority of Argus. It was no concern of mine what happened to them."

"Not even when you sold them to Elyucham?"

The house gave another lurch. That did not frighten Zang half as much as the question. But he put up a bold front.

"I did no such thing! As was required, I arrested the next ship bound for the Rim, and transferred to her commander jurisdiction over — "

"Save your breath. You sold them to Elyucham. For what fee? Enough to build an island here on Delcadoré, was it not?"

This parody of a friendly chat was wearing down Zang's nerves. His voice rose to a shout.

"Who are you? What do you want? A share of the take?"

"No!"

Abruptly the unseen speaker's tone deepened and became resounding. It was like the voice of eternal judgment.

"All I seek is justice! You were most thorough when you covered your tracks. Not a trace of what you did survives in the official record save maybe at third — tenth — a hundredth hand!

"But it endures in the memories of those you sold!"

Zang stood like a statue, his guts chilled, sweat pearling down each crease and cranny of his flesh. His lips writhed but he could form not a single word.

"Of whom I'm one." The intruder's tone was casual again. "Long ago, you may even have known my name. If you don't remember it, no matter. Suffice it to say that retribution has finally caught up with you."

Another support gave way. This time the house not only lurched, but canted, so that Zang fell back against the window, unable to climb the steeply slanting floor. At his back — he could see from the corner of his eye — the pile of metal loomed. Fumes were starting to rise from it; the machines' powerpacks were shorting out and sparks were flying. Fire might erupt at any moment.

The voice said conversationally, "You have doubtless deduced that your other tek is cutting through the house supports. If you're superstitious — and I gather many in the starfleets are — now is the time to talk to yourself and call it praying. When this shack slips into the pit, you will almost certainly be burned alive."

"Stop! Wait! I can pay — "

But the final strut snapped, and the house slid, hesitated, slid again, and crashed with a tremendous racket onto the mass of wrecked machinery.

Seconds later, the pit was like a smelter's furnace.

5

"His screams," said Detective Wirt, "are the last sounds decipherable from the recording."

Looking down on the pit from which most of the flame-seared wreckage had now been extracted, seeming ill at ease under open sky, Forkellen, the investigator from Fleet High Command, said, "And that is all you have to tell me?"

Bridling, the Delcadoréan snapped, "It was a miracle that sufficient recorders survived in the house-walls to tell us even this much! On most planets there'd have been nothing but circumstantial evidence!"

"On which one may sometimes rely on something more secure than recorders that are so easily tampered with . . . "

Forkellen did not wait for an answer but flashed on the air before him a complete display of the data thus far accumulated.

"So! The victim should have been as secure here as aboard his flagship. Yet somebody negated his defences, suborned his teks, and arranged for his shack to fall into that pit, where it caught fire with him inside. What happened to the teks, by the way?"

"Programmed to self-destruct, apparently," said Wirt, displaying all the near-instinctual distaste of ordinary folk for teks' dismaying in-betweenness. "It looks as though they jumped into the fire."

"Hmph! Well, what about the human servants?"

Wirt avoided the other's eyes. "They've — uh — disappeared."

"You can't be serious! Someone in Zang's position would never trust servants that weren't properly conditioned! Even the rudimentary treatment slave-traders give their captives is enough to stop them running away, if not to make them fight to the death in defence of their owners."

"We're still searching," Wirt said defensively. "They may yet turn up."

"'May'!" Forkellen drove fist into palm. "Is this all I'm ever to hear from you? 'May'? What about some concrete facts? For example, is there any truth in the allegation that Zang sold deportee mutants to a slaver?"

Wirt pondered a moment. Which was worse, the immediate wrath of this investigator from the High Command or the later fury of his superiors on Delcadoré, whose reputation would be besmirched were it to come out that they had welcomed a slave-seller into their midst?

"If you don't co-operate . . . " said Forkellen meaningfully.

That settled it. Wirt whispered, "He was remarkably well off for someone of his rank."

"Ah, now we're getting to the core of the matter, aren't we? If it were the case that he'd acquired illegal assets, they would be forfeit to the Empire. Moreover, persons instrumental in exposing his wrong-doing might lay claim to a proportion of them. Do I make my point clear?"

Wirt gulped and nodded.

"Then we understand each other," Forkellen declared with satisfaction. "Praise to the stars, this means we can at last make headway. Clearly, here on Delcadoré, there must be someone who is jealous of Zang's prosperity yet afraid to expose his evil doings because he too — or she — is involved in similar illegal enterprises. Suppose . . . "

He checked abruptly, narrowing his eyes.

"You do realize a report will have to be dispatched to Argus?"

Fervently Wirt said, "Not only do I realize that but a courier is already on his way."

Forkellen seemed about to explode, but mastered himself. "I could have wished that you'd awaited my arrival," he said eventually. "Still, that will save me a bit of trouble. Now, tell me: who on Delcadoré might have had an interest in eliminating Zang?"

#

It was not Forkellen's lengthy dossier, full of slander and innuendo, but Wirt's preliminary report that attracted most attention. For a starfleet commander to have been murdered: that was bad enough. But for his death to have been brought about by someone apparently bent on revenge for his dealings in slaves: that was far more disturbing. Not a few extremely high officials had, if not personally bought and sold human beings, at least taken a quid pro quo for turning a blind eye to such traffic. On countless of the worlds to which the news filtered through, rich men and women slept less easily despite redoubling their security. If servants might break their conditioning . . . But how could one manage without them? So many machines, whose work they had been called upon to replace, were simply not repairable any longer!

Not a few petitioned Argus direct for extra forces to keep down the slave-trade, hoping perhaps that, if there were any more avengers on the warpath, they would be less likely to turn their attention to volumes where diligent countermeasures were in force. Whatever effect such moves might have had on the general public, they had an impact on the

Imperial bureaucracy. Senior officials judged it advisable to comply where possible, given that otherwise those farflung systems where the Empire's grip was weakest might think once more in terms of secession.

Besides — and this held such terrifying implications that the officials deemed it necessary to inform the king himself — if, instead of being safely banished beyond the frontier, mutants were being sold for slaves, some could well have been traded on towards the Hub. Might they not be agents of subversion and decay? Whose trusted servant might not prove to be possessed of unknown powers, biding his or her time before revealing them?

The king, however, although he enjoyed a large personal retinue and might be as much at risk as anyone, devoted scant minutes to the matter. He said pettishly, "I don't know how much more of this I can put up with! Ever since your move to the moons it seems I can't rely on my deputies the way I used to! I'd expect you to remember more about Zang's sector than do I. Apparently, alas, I'm wrong . . . "

Those waiting on him shuffled and looked embarrassed, but the reason that the king remained the king was that his ancestors, *par excellence*, had known how to keep track of warp and woof, and he had inherited some traces of their talent.

"What about the woman who exposed the mutants in the first place — the tall one I was so sorry to lose from my Court? Has anybody found out whether she has light to cast on the affair? No? Well, go away and do it and let me get on with my design for the southwestern continent!"

#

But where was Anza Cly? More immediately: where were the reports she had continued dutifully to post, as and when a courier could be found heading towards the Hub? Someone vaguely remembered that when last heard of she had been entering a volume concerning which the records were more than averagely overdue for sorting and filing, but that was precious little to go by.

In the upshot, they had to search for months on end, and still had not located the report they were after when, as luck would have it, a fresh one arrived from her. It informed them that yet another batch of mutants —

this time, a thousand strong — had been identified and deported. After a brief rest, Anza Cly proposed to make for Y Ly Ging, whose heiress, a minor, had accused her uncle, the Interrex, of plotting to secede. This might, Anza stated, merely be a ploy to secure dominion of the planet and its dependencies; it might, on the other hand, be yet one more sign of mutant-inspired subversion.

A fast ship promptly departed for Y Ly Ging bearing an order under the king's own seal — he had never seen it, but that was the way of things now — telling Anza Cly to relinquish her current assignment and head for Delcadoré.

On reading the missive she became extremely angry.

But complied.

6

"Welcome back!" wheezed Rempus to the young man who had been first his slave, then his apprentice, then the means of restoring his fortunes. The house was still the same, but it was in perfect working order again — had been for a couple of decades — and teks for sale were growing in the basement. Why, Rempus often wondered, had he never hit on the idea of designing a tek whose only purpose was to supervise production of more teks? The initial outlay had been repaid twenty times over, even at today's low prices!

Rempus added, "Your fame, by the way, precedes you."

Hennig smiled. "What are they saying about me?" he inquired as he dropped into a familiar chair, peeled off the undetectable prosthetic that concealed his twisted foot, and rested it on a low stool, exactly as though he had never been away. "Not, I trust, realizing that it is me they mean."

"Oh, of course not!" the old man chuckled as he poured wine into crystal goblets, then stiffly raised his own in a silent toast. Wiping his lip, he went on. "Well, the tales grow more and more fantastic. It's known that the authorities on Delcadoré failed to find Zang's slaves, let alone any suspicious character who might have been the killer. Around this nubbin of fact, amazing rumours have grown up: for instance, that you must possess a ship capable of eluding Imperial detectors, in which you carried the servants off the planet."

"Yes, I've heard that one," Hennig confirmed, and sipped his wine. "Apparently, for the first time in several centuries, they're actually undertaking research on Delcadoré, trying to figure out how it's done. I wish them joy."

"Ah, but did you hear where you got your ship?"

"How do you mean?"

Rempus leaned forward, his rheumy old eyes bright with malicious amusement.

"It's from the Rim, of course! It's human-built!"

"Really?" Hennig grinned broadly; he had grown up into rather a good-looking young man, and his teeth were superb. "Well, I suppose it was to be expected. though you'd think that that stale old notion would have died for lack of evidence. While I was on Delcadoré I heard how they are continually sending out people to investigate such yarns, always without success. They've been doing it for centuries, of course, so I guess it's become a habit."

He drank again and set the goblet aside. "They are, though, convinced I own a starship?"

"According to what reaches here: completely."

"That's good. I have to keep them on the wrong track as long as possible. Of course, the day may come when I have to acquire one."

Rempus sat as bolt upright as his aged bones allowed. "Ah, even with the income we now earn from teks, that's too much to hope for, isn't it?"

"Oh, I'm not asking you to provide the wherewithal. What I have in mind . . . No, it's too soon to talk about it. That plan's not finalized."

Rempus hesitated. He said at length, "What about your other plans? The more immediate ones?"

"Those proceed nicely," Hennig murmured.

"May I hear about them? Or would you rather — ?"

"Old friend, if the day comes when I feel I can't trust you, I'll abandon my self-imposed mission and drink myself into an early grave."

Suiting action mockingly to word, he poured more wine but, even as he made to sip again, his face clouded. "I'm already tempted, I confess. I learned on Delcadoré that revenge is not sweet, as I once imagined."

Rempus gave an effortful shrug. "Well, you've struck one blow to avenge your parents and their friends."

"Yes, and a successful one. Even so, it's not enough. I shall go on as long as I can force myself to action. My next trip will be to Kah."

"I thought you meant to take on Elyucham next. With every passing day that he's at large, more people's freedom is at risk. You said as much yourself when you first broached your scheme to me."

"That's true. However, Elyucham is out of reach."

"You mean he's dead already?"

Hennig gave a harsh laugh. "I would he were! But no, he flourishes, and doubtless will be back here soon. Right now, though, he's on the trail of an interesting rumour. It seems the Interrex of Y Ly Ging wishes to dispose of certain troublesome elements of his population — specifically, those who grumble under his yoke and want him replaced by the Heiress Apparent. And to have them snatched from one of their clandestine meetings by a slaver strikes him as a tidy and profitable solution to his problem."

"Subtle," said Rempus with reluctant admiration.

"Indeed. Especially since a slave-raid would give him the best possible reason to have a few Imperial ships come garrison his system, ready to put down further discontent. It is of course entirely probable that the captains of the said ships see a future, in taking service privately with Y Ly Ging, as profitable as Zang's. Has it been reported on Pefferlosh that a remarkable number of line ships have been lost recently in battle against underwhelming odds?"

Rempus stared. "No, it hasn't, but I see what you're driving at. You mean senior commanders are being bribed to let subordinates desert?"

With a wry twist of his lip Hennig replied, "Amazing, isn't it, what incredible tales one hears while travelling around the galaxy?"

Draining his goblet anew, the younger man briskened and rose. "Let's take a look at the new teks, shall we? I'd like to know how my latest modifications are working out."

Later, having pronounced himself well satisfied, Hennig mused aloud, "You know, there's something I find even more amazing than the rumours that run the starlanes."

"That being — ?"

"How stupid people have become under the Empire. Everywhere I go I find them surrounded by useless machines that could be mended in a few

hours or days, like yours that I fixed when I first came here. But everybody says the same: 'Oh, that was imported, nobody here knows how it
works, we can't get parts for it any more . . .'"

"Was I not the same when we first met?" Rempus sighed. "The years I
wasted because I couldn't see what you saw instantly, child though you
were!" He gestured at the tek which supervised his little underground
factory and added, "I owe you more than I can hope to repay."

"Never say that," Hennig countered. "You gave me what I chiefly
needed: hope. And now, of course . . . "

Instead of saying more he embraced Rempus warmly.

"Hennig," the old man muttered, "if people have grown so
lazy-minded, how come they hatch ingenious plots like — ?"

"Like the Interrex of Y Ly Ging?"

"Oh!" said Rempus. Then, more loudly, "*Oh!*"

#

"Things are slipping from bad to worse!" grumbled Tiron. He drained
his mug of ancinard, held it out for refilling, and glared at his Grand
Chamberlain as though challenging him to disagree.

Which he did, albeit diffidently. They were in the Keeper's private
quarters, where one might speak relatively openly — that is, within the
limits Tiron allowed. They were not alone, but the slaves in attendance
were well conditioned and literally would never think of repeating what
they heard, even to one another.

"With respect, matters appear to be going rather well. Kah is now the
de facto power in this volume; Aylshaw and Grovang will shortly be as
subservient to us as the Seam of Ho already is — "

Tiron cut him short. "That's not what I'm talking about! I'm talking
about what you can see right here!" He gestured, and the Chamberlain
obediently surveyed their surroundings.

In truth, they constituted a depressing spectacle. The walls of the
chamber were drab grey; once they had been a constant blaze of colour,
for hidden circuitry displayed on them any of a thousand views, from this
planet and elsewhere. Machines had responded to the occupier's softest
whisper, producing food and drink, fresh garments, warmth, light and

191

music. Even the furniture had been malleable; for instance, one needed only to doze off in a chair for it to turn automatically into a comfortable bed.

The furniture remained, but it no longer changed. Some of it was stuck in awkward in-between states. The seat allotted to the Chamberlain was one such item.

He sighed and admitted that Tiron had a point.

"I'll say!" the Keeper barked. "And I've gone to such lengths! I do as you once suggested" — at this the Chamberlain flinched visibly — "and keep a watch on the spaceport, make announcements inviting anybody who knows how to fix this sort of thing to come here right away, good pay assured, a permanent post for the right candidate. What good has it done? None whatever! I had high hopes of the last fellow who showed up because at least he sorted out some of the kitchen appliances and the food's been better since. But he spent nearly a month right here in my quarters, and you can see what I have to show for it. *And* he'd have insisted on being paid if I hadn't made it clear what sort of fee I think a failure's worth! As for these spaceheads I'm forced to rely on instead . . .!" He held his mug out for more ancinard, but his hand shook and a few drops spilled.

At once the Keeper was beside himself with rage.

"I'll have you lashed, you cross-bred offspring of a Sirian ape!" he shouted at the girl who held the flask. "I'll have the skin whipped off your flesh, and your flesh whipped off your bones!"

The girl trembled a little, but showed no other reaction. Contemptuously Tiron said, "See what I mean? There isn't even any pleasure in punishing them! They just put up with it! What good is punishment if you can't see the culprit suffer?"

"Did you ask, 'What good is punishment if you can't see the culprit suffer?'"

His words had been echoed in a mild, unfamiliar voice. The Keeper and the Chamberlain started and glanced around.

"Which of you said that?" Tiron rapped at the slaves. There were four, all girls, all pretty, all compliant.

But the voice had been male.

There was a dead pause.

Then, suddenly, the slaves seemed to rouse as from long sleep. Staring about them as though they failed to recognize their surroundings, they turned in unison to leave the room.

"Come back!" Tiron bellowed, struggling to force himself out of his chair. But he had become grossly fat in the past two decades, and by the time he was on his feet the last girl had closed the door behind her.

At some stage a manual lock had been fitted. The two men could hear it snick.

Paling, the Chamberlain leaned his weight against the door, but it had been installed by a Keeper who went in fear of assassination.

"There's no point in trying to break it down," said the mild voice. "Doing so would be to waste your last few minutes of endurable existence."

The two men stared wildly about them, but the voice was coming from no discernible source.

"Do you remember a certain Commander Zang?" it went on conversationally. "I imagine you do. I take it you also know what happened to him.

"Well, something similar is going to happen to you."

"What in space are you talking about, whoever you are?" Tiron raged, seizing a metal ornament and brandishing it like a club.

"I was among a group of so-called mutants seized from the planet Ho Five and sold for slaves. My inquiries have established that it was you, Ser Chamberlain, who named my world to the despicable Anza Cly. Her time will come, by the way.

"And you, of course, Tiron, profited from this crime. Not only did you lay the blame for your plot to secede from the Empire on perfectly innocent people, you also bought some of the captives from Elyucham — whose time will also come, and soon. Among your . . . No, I can't say 'present slaves', because they've just been freed . . . Among your *recent* slave-girls is the daughter of one of them."

"Wait a second." Tiron had gathered his ragged wits. "I recognize that voice. It belongs to the man who tried and failed to fix the machinery of this apartment!"

"I wondered how long it would take you to work that out," came the gentle reply. "Of course, I'm not here — not even on this planet any more.

193

And, to deprive you of one last consolation, the recorder plates set in your walls will not show any evidence that I ever *was* here. All they will repeat, over and over, is a single truth: that one of you directed Zang and Anza Cly to my home planet, and the other connived at and profited from the resulting crime."

"This means automatic machinery somewhere," Tiron said to his companion in a low tone. "Grab whatever you can find and start breaking everything in reach. We might be lucky."

But, before they could begin, the furniture came back to life.

Sliding silently across the floor, two armchairs struck them behind the knees, forcing them to fall backward. The arms folded around their bellies and began to squeeze. In moments they were gasping for breath.

"Don't waste air on trying to shout," advised the voice. "No one will hear, or, if they do, they won't come, or, if they come, they can't possibly open the door. And don't expect to die quickly, either. You will be extremely thirsty, and maybe even hungry, before the life is crushed out of your repellent bodies . . .

"Oh, one last thing. You asked what good punishment is if you can't see the victims suffer.

"I can't see you. I don't want to. Perhaps that's the difference between us. All I know, much though I'd rather not, is that this is *necessary*."

#

On Delcadoré, where as yet more machines were functional than not, Anza Cly was roused from sleep by an urgent call from Investigator Forkellen.

"What do you make of *this*?" he demanded, filling her quarters with visual projections and feeding depositions of evidence into the sound-circuit.

She studied them, slowly and thoroughly.

At last he grew impatient and growled, "I'm waiting for an answer."

Shrugging her broad shoulders, passing long fingers through her tousled hair, she said, "That the Keeper of the Motte of Kah was no great loss to the Empire. If I were back in my old department at Argus I'd take immediate steps to ensure a more competent successor, but — "

"It's none of my business how those accursed bureaucrats run their affairs!" Forkellen roared. "I have my own to look after! But doesn't it seem to you as though there's a connection with the Zang case?"

Anza gave him a reproving glare. "Did you rout me out of bed just to have that confirmed? Of course it does! And" — with a flash of steely anger — "it makes it clearer than ever that, when he sold those mutants to a slaver, Zang committed a far more fatal error than you and your kind so far seem to have realized!"

7

On Y Ly Ging, a planet of small cities scattered amid forests so beset with gorgeous blooms that they might have passed elsewhere for public parks, it was not customary for the ruler — be he Rex or Interrex — to deal in person with those who served his ends, especially not offworlders.

In this instance, however, it had been deemed inadvisable to entrust even the smallest detail of the transaction to a remote communication channel. All had been done by conditioned couriers and word of mouth, no mention of the scheme being made save in secure environments.

And now came the final, climactic meeting. So pleased was he by what had transpired, the Interrex had consented to honour with his physical presence the person who had restored his grip on the populace by beheading the monster of insurrection that had threatened him.

In a sunny yellow bower atop a giant tree, with white clouds scudding past beneath a pale blue sky, Elyucham sat awaiting him, alone. Now and then Elyucham remembered that this ought to make him nervous. Then all fear was swept away by the renewed realization that he had attained a lifelong ambition:

He was dealing on equal terms at last with the ruler of an entire planet.

Not bad, Elyucham kept thinking to himself. *Not bad for someone who started out by winning a starship at shen fu!*

Leaves rustled that were not leaves but an impregnable defensive wall disguised as leaves. Elyucham started to his feet. An elderly man appeared, dark-eyed but white-haired, acknowledging his presence with a nod.

"Resume your seat," the Interrex said, himself relaxing into a chair the other side of a table whose top was made from a single Loudor gleamshell. Elyucham had been admiring it; it was such as one might trade a starship for. "Let there be refreshment."

Cups of wine — nothing so coarse and dangerous as ancinard — and dishes of nuts and Sirenian plums appeared on the table, not materialized but placed there by servants garbed with invisibility. One could tell by the way the dishes flickered as they were set down.

How strong a guard does the Interrex boast in this bower? wondered Elyucham, but it was impossible to tell without the kind of detector he had been forbidden to bring.

Justifiably. He had not objected.

The Interrex raised his wine-cup. Hastily the slaver imitated him, and they sipped simultaneously.

"Congratulations on the success of your raid," said the Interrex as he returned his cup to the table. "All but a handful of the ringleaders were taken. It will be decades before they create another such organization, and in the interim I shall have picked off the rump. But it was not to compliment you that I agreed to this meeting."

"I know," said Elyucham boldly. "It was because I insisted."

The white-haired man shrugged. "Your insistence is hollow. You should have been content with your pay. You should have left at once and fulfilled your obligation to scatter your captives among so many distant systems that there will be no chance of them ever reuniting."

"Then why didn't you order me to go at once? I would have done so — very likely." Elyucham selected a plum, sank his teeth in it, and was at once annoyed with himself because its purple juice ran down to stain his beard. Still, it was utterly delicious. That was why Sirenian plums had spread throughout the galaxy.

Now and then he wondered where Sirenia might be.

"I think perhaps . . . " The Interrex sounded puzzled, but he was ever full of guile. "No, tell me first — not that your insistence made any odds, as I have said — tell me why you were inclined to run the risk of being caught in our system by Imperial forces, which at this moment head for Y Ly Ging at emergency extreme."

Elyucham was about to toss aside his plumstone and lick his fingers; instead, the stone was deftly removed and an invisible damp napkin was plied around his hands and lips. Pretending he was used to such luxury, he deferred his answer until the task was over. Then he said, "Do you really want me to explain?"

The Interrex tensed his hands on the arms of his chair. "Did I not say so?"

"Very well. But you're not going to like this." Conscious of being briefly in the ascendant, Elyucham leaned back and held out his wine-cup for replenishment. "It's because, during my career as a slaver, I've learned something about you planetary rulers. You and I, at bottom, are no different."

"You dare to claim — !"

"I do!" Elyucham flared. "Despite being surrounded by unseen guards who could strike me dead in half a second, I dare to speak the truth! I too hold power of life and death over countless human beings. At this moment I hold power over *you*. For" — his voice dropped — "if I do not regain my ship by sundown *it will not leave*! It will still be here, with all its cargo, when the Imperials arrive . . . You don't want that. Particularly not since Anza Cly came by."

The Interrex said slowly, "You're a clever fellow."

"Clever enough, when my interests are served. What I wanted — what I'm now enjoying — is the chance to speak on equal terms with the ruler of a planet. I'll be content with an hour, and I shall treasure the memory until I die. Shall we not drink another cup and chat a while?"

A grudging smile spread over the Interrex's face.

"Agreed!" he said with sudden force. "More wine!"

#

Later:

"Why *did* you consent to this meeting?" Elyucham asked.

"If I must put it into words . . . " The Interrex pursed his lips and set his fingertips together. "Why, I suppose it's because I meet so few offworlders. Those that I do are all subservient; they're ambassadors and envoys without a shred of independence. They're far too like the people I must treat with every day, who bow and scrape unceasingly. A person like yourself, on the other hand — "

"A person like myself," Elyucham cut in, "if he'd turned up on Y Ly Ging, would be among my cargo by now! And you wouldn't have it any other way, would you? Any more than I could tolerate a mutiny among my crew!"

His broad grin was met by the Interrex's frosty smile. They understood each other perfectly.

#

Later still:

"A while ago you mentioned Anza Cly. Are you acquainted with her?"

Elyucham shrugged. "Not exactly. But, way back when, she called at Kah, and as a result I closed a profitable deal. Not directly: through Commander Zang. You know him?"

"Knew him," the Interrex corrected delicately.

Elyucham blinked. By now the wine was affecting him. "Oh?"

"You hadn't heard that he was dead?"

"I've been out of this volume for a good few years. Now the Imperial grip has slackened so much, I spend half my time beyond the frontier. There are worlds out there desperate for able-bodied settlers. Sometimes I get more from them than . . . But don't worry! Financial considerations will not influence my disposal of your rebels. They'll be scattered over twenty systems . . . What happened to Zang? I recall him as quite young."

"Ten years away from retirement, at least. But, as the story came to us . . . " And the Interrex recounted it, not without malice.

Elyucham's hand no longer held his wine-cup so steadily. He muttered, "Someone seeking revenge, you say?"

"That's correct." The Interrex spoke unblinkingly. "In respect of slaves lifted from Ho Five. And it would appear that a similar fate has lately overtaken the Keeper of the Motte of Kah. Did you know him?"

"Not personally," Elyucham admitted, and made haste to add, "Though I have been on Kah."

"There must be tens of thousands every year who can say the same. Does it not strike you as surprising that, despite the falling-off in most galactic trade, there are still so many private travellers on the starlanes? More itinerant workers than before, of course, more pilgrims and more deportees. But nonetheless there does remain a thriving traffic."

"Maybe one day I'll opt for it myself," Elyucham said, striving to turn the conversation with a joke.

The Interrex leaned towards him, his eyes like chips of naked space. "I think you may not have the chance," he whispered. "Has it not occurred to you to wonder who suggested that I get in touch with you?"

The slaver sat immobile for a second. It had not. All of a sudden he was wondering why.

"No? Then I will tell you! It was Anza Cly! Who bears me no good will! In her eyes, I'm guilty of having let a coven of mutants gather round my niece, working on my mind — yes, even mine! — until the notion of seceding from the Empire spread like plague!"

Despite the pleasant warmth of the day, chills had begun to creep up and down Elyucham's spine.

"I *don't know* why I let you meet me here today!" The Interrex jumped up and paced the floor. "For all I can tell, the mutants that you took aboard your ship are still working their — their foul *magic* on me! Maybe that's the reason!"

He spun around and snapped his fingers. Instantly his guards and servants were visible. There were nine of them, six fully armed.

"Go back to your ship at once! Scatter those rebels as you promised! But make sure you do it before the killer who slew Zang and Tiron catches up with you as well!"

Elyucham rose slowly to his feet, desperate to seize one last advantage.

Abruptly he saw it, and spoke it, though it was to give him nightmares.

He said, "It was Anza Cly who recommended me to you?"

"As I told you!" barked the Interrex.

"What did she say?"

"Oh! Oh, that you were as honest as any in your line! I think she'd only heard of you, never met you."

"That's the case." Elyucham drew himself upright. "But, if you think about it, Ser Interrex, you may come to wonder whether *she* is as honest an agent of Argus as she claims!"

On the basis of which petty triumph, he stormed out.

8

At the house where teks grew in the basement:

"I may be old," sighed Rempus, "but it seems to me you're growing reckless. The neat way you disposed of Zang, by making sure he bought our teks to supervise the building of his home — that was masterly. You were systems distant when he died, and record-keeping throughout the Empire is in such a state that nobody could possibly have connected you with the affair. Even if they'd found some clue concerning Hennig of the Twisted Foot, there would have been no link . . . Oh, I'm sorry!"

Hennig shook his head, leaning back as usual in a chair facing the old man's — very old now, for time had taken its toll of both of them, and he himself was acutely aware of advancing into middle age without, he felt, ever having enjoyed youth. Unconsciously he stroked his hair back; it no longer sprouted so low on his forehead as it had done.

He said, "Not the keenest eye, not the most sensitive detector at a spaceport, can possibly have registered the fact that I'm deformed."

"That I believe . . . More wine?"

Again they were drinking a celebratory flask to mark the wanderer's return. For once the weather was fine. It was near sunset, and there were brilliant crimson smears across the sky. Scents floated on the evening breeze.

"And yet — and yet . . . " Rempus sounded troubled. "You exposed yourself on Kah."

"I was long gone before Tiron and his chamberlain met their just deserts."

"That may be so, but actually to have entered the Keeper's apartments . . . "

It was no use. Rempus could read that from Hennig's expression, as stony as the one he had worn when Elyucham first brought him to Pefferlosh. Sighing, he resumed, "Well, that leaves two. Will you live long enough to deal with both?"

"You expect Elyucham to outsmart me?" Hennig countered. "When I set so ingenious a trap not only for him but for the Interrex, and both of them walked into it?"

"That trap has not yet closed," Rempus reminded him sombrely. "And there remains the matter of Anza Cly . . . Are you sure she is equally guilty? You've never met her."

He hunched forward, coughing.

"Oh, yes." Hennig's tone was judgmental. "If anything, she's more guilty than the rest. She's obsessed! She's devoted her career to driving mutants from the Empire, heedless of what families she's torn apart, what worlds have never recovered from the slur of being termed a mutants' haven . . . You know what became of the planets in the Seam of Ho. Multiply that by a hundred and you'll have some inkling of the evil task she's spent her life on."

He drained his goblet at a gulp. "Only death will stop me from sending her the way I've sent Zang and Tiron, and the way Elyucham will go next!"

"When?" Rempus's voice was a mere whisper.

"Very soon. Very soon indeed. But I want him to suffer for a while before we meet again."

"Boy — " Rempus caught himself. "Hennig, I mean. Not so long ago you were saying that revenge tastes bitter!"

"You're right." Hennig's tone itself was bitter. "I didn't allow for it becoming habit-forming."

#

As his crew had observed, ever since his encounter with the Interrex, Elyucham had walked as though afraid of being followed. Not being conditioned as the slaves were — for the same reason as starfleet officers could not be — they made vulgar jokes behind his back about what he was afraid of happening behind his back.

Furthermore, they taunted him with being an Argian agent when, instead of doing as had been agreed — not with the Interrex — and selling off what captives he could to any chance slave-ship crossed in the interstellar gulfs, he persisted on a course towards the Rim, declaring that, if no one else could be found to take the lot that way, he would.

To which they mockingly inquired, "Since when did you become a mutant-lover?"

Only when he reminded them that this ship was adapted so that it could dump mutineers into space, leaving only the captain, those loyal to him, and the cargo, did they sullenly accept that now was not a time for joshing.

Not even to his closest subordinates did he admit what was preying on his mind.

It was the matter of Zang's and Tiron's servants.

Zang, he knew, had bought in many of the prettiest women captives. A few more had gone to Tiron, or so memory indicated — though it had been a long while ago, and so many individual slaves had passed through his hands he no longer recalled more than a fraction of them . . .

Glancing down at his ample belly, prodding it with hands that had grown pillow-plump, he acknowledged the impact of time.

Nonetheless! Nonetheless the question remained: How was it that Zang's slaves, and Tiron's, had broken their conditioning? He sold his goods with warranty; they were mentally disciplined during the voyage away from their home world. He himself relied on the same technique to ensure that he was attended night and day, in space and planetside, by two discreet and watchful bodyguards.

He had trusted them all his life. But if someone had found out how to make them rebel . . . ?

This present bunch must be disposed of before they infected the rest!

The days were long past when even Rempus, his old friend turned enemy, had had to admit he was a man of his word. Activating all the inboard speakers, he roared an order.

"We're going to dump the cargo! To starcore with the Interrex! We'll sell them for whatever we can get and be well shot of the mutated bastards!"

There was a pause. Eventually there came back, in a voice that sounded relieved, the hesitant query: "As you say, Captain. But — where?"

"The nearest planet where we won't be hassled!" Elyucham called up star-charts, scanned them. "Pefferlosh!"

"That's not the nearest — "

He cancelled the objection with a shout.

"I say it is and that is where we'll make for!"

"Very well — *Captain!*"

Elyucham sat back in his command chair, sweating. He wiped his brow with his sleeve.

Only by degrees did he begin to wonder: *Was that a wise decision?* He came to doubt it. By then, of course, it was too late to change his mind. Doing so would have convinced his crew he must indeed be crazy.

All unknowing, he had walked into the subtlest of snares.

9

"Welcome back to Pefferlosh, Elyucham!"

No longer the hale and handsome fellow he had been when he had accosted Rempus on this very street — where the flagstones were no softer underfoot, though profit from allowing slaves to be sold there had financed improvements to the nearby market — the slaver turned to show a haggard face above his beard.

"Who in space are *you?*" he snapped, glancing around in search of the bodyguards he had arrived with.

They were nowhere to be seen.

Yet nothing else in this crowded, sunlit street had changed.

"We enjoy good weather, do we not, this summer?" said the . . .

Stranger?

Elyucham had to blink, and blink again. He knew he had been addressed by a man of about forty; he knew he was looking at him, could reach out and touch him — yet a different image kept recurring:

A boy, near-naked, with a halting gait . . .

"I see you recognize me," said the — other. "Once, years ago, you even knew my name. Do you recall it?"

And waited, within arm's length.

Transfixed, unable to move, Elyucham husked, "I think you may be . . . Wait! It's coming back!"

"Wait as long as you like," said the man who confronted him. "I'm in no hurry. Nor is anybody hereabouts."

Elyucham glanced from side to side — and, incredibly, he found it true. Of a sudden, the customary racket of the crowd had diminished to a dull deep drone, and all about were moving with dreadful slowness, as though they plodded through deep mud compounded of time.

The very air he sucked into his lungs felt sluggish.

He forced out, "Yes, of course! You're Hennig of the Twisted Foot!"

And glanced by reflex downward. But the man's two boots matched.

"You owe your life to that remembrance," Hennig said. "For a while, at least . . . Now, come with me."

"But I have business in the market!"

"Not any more. Those whom you called your slaves do not sit huddled under awnings. They have gone away. Moreover, their would-be buyers are unhappy, for the sale has had to be cancelled through lack of merchandise. If you don't follow me I think they'll catch you instead and try to sell you. Not that you'd fetch much of a price." Hennig's voice was level, casual, yet tinged with menace.

The grumbling of the crowd rose in pitch, and the slow forms of robed and hooded people quickened. Certain bad-tempered faces turned Elyucham's way, eyes widening with recognition.

"I'll come with you!" Babbling, the slaver caught the nearest to a friendly arm.

"I thought you might" — composedly. "Well, then, this way."

#

"This is the home of an old friend of yours. Remember?"

Elyucham stood, fists clenched and trembling, in the middle of a room none too large, but pleasant, and with all its equipment functioning. He could tell because he had been here long ago, and recognized the hum that resounded from its walls and floor meant there was a tek factory in its basement.

"Where's Rempus?" he forced out.

"Dead."

"Dead? When?"

"A scant ten days ago. A shame! He had hoped to live long enough to see you driven from the starlanes."

Elyucham fought to bring his whirling mind under control. He said, "I'm sorry he's gone. We . . . Well, was a time when we were close."

"You remember how you sold . . . correction, how you *gave* me to him?" said Hennig, dropping into a chair and peeling off his right boot.

204

Revealed was a callused claw which he rested, with visible relief, on a low stool.

"Not," he added, "that it was much of a gift, in view of your plan to save air by dumping me in space."

A hundred truths clashed together in Elyucham's mind like stars colliding. He burst out, "You lured me here because I agreed to take your family from Ho Five! But it was under orders from Argus! I did it in the line of business — you can't compare me with Zang or Tiron!"

"So you heard what happened to them, did you? From — by any chance — the Interrex of Y Ly Ging?"

There was a moment of total silence, save for the murmur of the city and the half-heard burr-burr-burr of the spaceport's takeoff alarm.

"That marks your ship fleeing offworld," Hennig said when the noise had sufficiently registered. "I felt it best to deprive you of your means of escape."

Elyucham stood stone-rigid for a moment. Then he recovered his normal bluff manner and sat down in the chair that had been Rempus's.

"So you set up my deal with the Interrex, did you? Well, I don't know how, and I don't want to. All I can say is that, if my time has come, it might as well be here on my home world. I can't say I'm sorry I took your people away because, after all, I did so, albeit indirectly, under orders from Argus, and all of us are ultimately dependent on the Empire, within and without the frontier. It's the Empire that makes the laws, and it's the Imperials who find out how to break them . . . Grant me this, at least!"

He leaned forward and spoke in a wheedling tone. "As things have turned out, did I not cede you to a kindly master?"

"You sound," said Hennig crossly, "as though I lured you here to treat you as I treated Zang and Tiron."

A horrifying suspicion crossed Elyucham's mind; it could be read from his tormented face.

"You mean — ?"

"I mean precisely this! Admittedly, I spread the word — never said otherwise, even to Rempus — that you were to be my next target. But — oh, space *alive*! You're less than comet dust to me! I didn't bring you here to punish you! What satisfaction would it give me? You're no more than clay. You're what circumstance has made you — a villain striving to survive at the expense of everybody else.

"But you can say that of every planetary lordling! You did, I think. My guess is that you said it, or near enough. Did you enjoy your conversation with the Interrex — on equal terms?"

Hennig's tone was like a lash. Elyucham's mouth worked but no words emerged.

"No, *you*" — Hennig raked him with ineffable contempt — "you've had one role in all of this."

"What's that?" It was a breathless whisper.

"You've served as bait. And now, shut up. My prey is nibbling at you. I have cast my line well."

There was another silence, broken this time by a noise more ancient than the Empire, so archetypal that it triggered shivers down all human spines.

A rap at the door.

Hennig rose.

"Come in," he said. "I knew you'd make for here. Come in, Anza Cly."

And something shifted in the basement where the teks were grown: something that made the house's whole foundation tremble.

Before the door had time to open, the air was full of threat.

10

Abruptly the room seemed small. This woman dwarfed it, who looked as though she could have picked up Hennig in one hand and Elyucham in the other, despite his grossness — and, should need arise, use them to batter down its walls.

Erect, stern, wary, she confronted them one long tense moment.

Then, quite unexpectedly, she laughed.

The transformation was incredible. Sandal-shod, she wore an ankle-length cloak; it was of a black to match her midnight hair. With a twist of her torso she shed it and stood naked, hands outstretched with palms displayed in token of no threat.

"So you are Hennig," she said musingly. "I congratulate you on the trap you set for Elyucham. It worked perfectly. Doubtless you hoped the same of the one you set for me."

Rising slowly, sounding uncertain, Hennig said, "My bait has brought you here."

Once again, from underground, there was a stir that made the whole house tremble.

"I beg to correct you," Anza said with a faint chuckle. "Not your bait . . . but *you*."

There was a vacant couch nearby. She dropped onto it and crossed her legs, adding, "Call off the tek you slaved so long to build. It isn't up to its intended task."

"I say it is!" Hennig erupted to full height and snapped his fingers. A trapdoor in the floor that led to the tek factory shook to a battering from below. Elyucham, who had unknowingly set one foot on it, shrieked aloud and darted to skulk in a corner.

"You forgot to release the bolt," Anza murmured. "Do you want it broken?"

"I . . . "

For a long second Hennig stood there stupefied. Then, like a guilty child, he flicked the bolt with his crippled foot and the trap flew wide. The tek emerged.

Few of the galaxy's uncountable population had ever seen one. It was a boast among those rich enough to buy them — as, indeed, among those who worked at their making — that even possession of a tek must indicate unusual strength of mind. They were so indescribably *other* that it was easier to say what they were *not* like than what they were. Easiest of all was to turn away and vow one had seen nothing.

And this tek was among the very strangest. Moving like an animal, it wasn't one, or even similar. Grown like a plant, it wasn't one, or even similar. Powerful as a machine, it wasn't one, or even similar. Conceived by human beings, it wasn't one, or even similar.

It emerged onto the floor of the room and stood (except it didn't *stand*) there, shimmering.

Elyucham, who had bought and sold his fellow creatures for a profit, stared at it with horror-widened eyes, then hid his face and moaned aloud.

As though she had read Hennig's thoughts, Anza Cly said in a tone of clinical detachment, "You were right. This slaver, loathsome though his trade may be, is not cast of the same metal as Commander Zang, who could consign men by the tens of thousands to their deaths in battle and grew so drunk with egotism that he never flinched while being attuned to the teks which he acquired to build his house — didn't even give them a second thought.

"Nor, though he'd like to think so, is Elyucham as vicious as the planetary lords who also see their subjects as a means to profit: Tiron, for instance, or the Interrex of Y Ly Ging. Elyucham's greedy and unfeeling, but at bottom he is just a creature of his times — and times are bad!"

While she spoke the tek was analysing her and concluding that she must represent the target it had been designed to attack. It closed in cautiously, like a Loudor graball hungry for a meal of moths. Extrusions reached out that *were not* limbs or tentacles or antennae — and yet *were*. Still she betrayed no hint of fear.

Hennig stood blank with shock and disbelief.

"You spent years devising this tek on the basis of what you thought you knew about me, didn't you?" Anza's tone was conversational. "You designed it to trap someone who had devoted her life to a foul, unpardonable crusade: the persecution of mutants, their kidnapping, their hounding far beyond the Empire's borders."

"Yes!" Hennig cried, his fists clenched so tight that his nails bit deep into his palms. "Why not? Talk of mutants is an Imperial lie! It's an excuse to legalize the slave-trade! There *are* no mutants — not in the sense that they're endowed with superpowers!"

The tek was stooping over Anza now (except it wasn't *stooping*; it didn't move like any human or animal that one might say was stooping) and its protuberances (that were not like limbs or antennae or tentacles or — or anything!) were brushing her skin, but she remained unshakably calm. Hennig could not believe the evidence of his own eyes.

Elyucham had kept his covered, and was shaking with sobs of terror.

Then, for all the galaxy as though it had been baffled by an insoluble problem, the tek grew still. Once motionless, it was no longer so impossible to grasp with one's perceptions. It resembled — the image flitted across Hennig's mind — it resembled a symbol for the Empire, which had expanded for millennia and had frozen, and must now decay.

Anza let the impact sink in, then rose smoothly to her feet, eluding contact with the tek by a dexterous dropping of one shoulder. She confronted Hennig sternly, like a reproachful teacher.

"Why didn't it . . . ?" Words failed him.

"Work as intended?" Anza supplied. "Why, because you disbelieved — still do — a crucial truth.

"Mutants exist. I'm one.

"And so are you."

#

It was as though the thunder of all the stars in the galaxy had invaded Hennig's head. He stood petrified for what felt like half eternity.

At last:

"I'm a *mutant*?"

He raised his crippled foot and looked a dumb inquiry.

Anza threw back her head and laughed aloud.

"Space alive, the mutants that the Empire fears don't show it in their bodies, but their minds! It seems I have a great deal to explain. Sit down and relax. I'll just take the liberty of returning this tek of yours to where it came from, because immobilizing it so close at hand is becoming a bit of a strain . . . "

She let it become attuned to her nervous system, the task it was intended for, and scowled at it. At once it — slithered? sidled? — *went* back to the basement. It even closed the trap behind it.

"I don't believe it," Hennig muttered. "I don't *want* to believe it!"

"That's more truthful. You see . . . Oh, Elyucham is still here. You! Get out! Spend your declining years in some less disgusting profession! Of course, you have no alternative, inasmuch as Hennig sent your ship away and her crew will assuredly not risk returning to Pefferlosh. But never forget that you were right in what you told the Interrex: planetary lords and slavers are morally indistinguishable, and they're both nauseating!"

Elyucham fled.

"*Did* he say that to the Interrex?" Hennig whispered.

Anza shrugged. "How should I know? I wasn't within an octant of Y Ly Ging when that unlovely pair met. But, if I have a talent, it lies in being able to foresee from insufficient evidence what's bound to happen. It may presage an eventual transcendence of time. If you look in the pouch of my cloak you'll find a flask of ancinard. Pour some for both of us, sit down, and *pay attention!*"

Hennig remained stubbornly immobile. He said at length, "You've accused me of being a mutant. I want proof, even though you admit as much about yourself."

"You never guessed I might be?"

"You know I didn't!" — kicking the bolt back in place to seal the trapdoor, with his crippled foot as before.

"Well, if you overlooked it in yourself . . . " Anza sighed. "There was one question you never asked yourself."

"What?"

"How did you take the conditioning off all those slaves — Zang's and Tiron's — and, this very day, off the bodyguards without whom Elyucham would never have dared venture on the streets?"

"Why, I consciously designed my teks to . . . " Hennig's words died. Not without malice, Anza waited until she was sure he knew how wrong he was. Then she said in a gentler tone, "I'm sorry, Hennig. But you didn't — consciously. All you know about teks is what you learned from Rempus. How I regret that I never met him, for he must have been like us."

"You're calling him a mutant too?" cried Hennig.

"Him, and his predecessors. There may not, as yet, be human-built starships, but I think there will be, because teks have at least one thing in common with them. They are neither alive, though they heal themselves, nor purely machines, for they don't have to be told step-by-step every last thing they have to do. They were, in fact, devised as a substitute for slaves when the need for more machines than we could find the time to build first presented itself. But that was back in the age when planets like yours in the Seam of Ho were still uninhabited — back when Kah, which is where your family came from, was so far beyond the frontier that it was considered suitable for deporting mutants to."

Hennig swayed. "You're claiming that my ancestors — ?"

Anza raised one broad dark hand. "Hold hard. You have much to learn, but it's not your fault that you're so ill informed. You were lied to as a child, I'm sure. Were you told why your forebears were driven to colonize Ho Five?"

"Because of a war!" Hennig cried.

"No." The word hung heavy in the air. "No, because of a witch-hunt against mutants centuries before we realized we must disguise our talents. Before most people were prepared to consider the possibility that the Empire would inevitably fall.

"Do as I said and bring some goblets. Then sit down, relax, and pay attention."

11

"Suppose there were no teks," said Anza Cly. "Can you conceive of someone — nowadays — inventing them?"

Hennig hesitated. Long ago, in this very house, he had told his mentor how unimpressed he was with contemporary humanity, surrounded by broken-down machines that he could mend in a few hours. It had been that talent he'd applied on Kah — the world, he had just been assured, of his own ancestors . . .

He said sharply, "Most of us seem content to wring our hands over what our ancestors produced when it breaks and we can't fix it. Are you implying it takes mutants to improve our state?"

"I am indeed." After sipping her ancinard, Anza cradled the goblet in both hands. She had not bothered to resume her cloak, and her presence in the room — dark, bare, and massive — was redolent of unspoken referents: his own first evening here with Rempus, deep space, the gulfs of time. "Or those the arrogance of Empire has *branded* mutants . . .

"You see, longer ago than you or most of humankind would credit, it became clear to certain persons that the Empire could not last forever. Those who imagine that it will — who strive, even now, to convince themselves it must — it's as though they think the galactic wheel has ceased to turn.

"And yet the stars move still!"

The impact of the phrase sent shivers down Hennig's spine. It was a literal truth; it carried, too, the force of a poetic one.

"Those whom I spoke of," Anza Cly went on, "were the first to be deported Rimward from the Hub. They were dubbed 'mutant' to furnish an excuse for the Empire to get rid of them. In those days, of course, the

211

Imperial fiat did not run to Pefferlosh, or Kah, or Y Ly Ging, let alone the Seam of Ho. Successively, the same policy has been applied here. As you know, I've preached it and enforced it. Would that there had been an alternative course, but . . . Your disdain for ordinary humanity, by the way, is wholly justified. Ever since we chanced on the cache of starships that enabled us to burst out through the galaxy like Loudor pollen, it seems that very few of us have invented anything. This may have some connection with the fact that, although our total gene-pool is vast, on any single planet it is relatively tiny and dangerously inbred.

"Even on Argus itself! Indeed, right now the proudest achievement that the King of Argus has to boast about, despite his high and honourable ancestry, lies in returning his world to its state ten thousand years ago — one stronghold and one spaceport and one town!

"I was at the Court of Argus. I didn't believe, not in my heart of hearts, that the Empire was doomed until I had to watch that sorry scene."

She drank deeply, savagely, of ancinard.

"Then I was informed of what I am, by someone I won't name, who was himself not mutant, but who taught me what I now believe.

"The only hope for humankind lies not among those who passively enjoy the benefits that have flowed from our accidental inheritance of alien starships . . . but among those who were expelled towards the Rim.

"Because, although originally the policy of banishing mutants was a cheap political device, it came to be taken literally, with the result that those who truly did display new talents — talents such as our species needed when it was faced with the task of administering planets by the hundred thousand — also got expelled.

"Your ancestors among them!"

#

Hennig's face was troubled. He said at length, "But my parents . . . "

"There are mutants, and there are *mutants*. The only kind I owe loyalty to are those who will provide fertile ground for a new civilization after the Empire's downfall. And they have talents like yours."

Hennig raised one arm as though to ward off a blow. He exclaimed, "But I don't believe I have a talent! Oh, I did learn how to mend machines

212

and genes when I was young, and Rempus did say I learned more about making teks in a year than he, as an apprentice, learned in ten. But that's not proof!"

"Proof lies in what you did with what you learned," said Anza firmly, "and what you did that you cannot have learned."

"Do you mean — ?"

"Yes, I'm back to the subject of slaves. Pour, and keep on listening."

Her goblet full again, she made no move to drink, but sat back with her dark gaze fixed on Hennig's face. "For how long has conditioning been known?"

"I've no idea."

"It may," said Anza solemnly, "have been the last invention of unmodified humanity: a means to mould the mind into obedience, so cheap and easy even slavers use it. Do you accept that?"

Hennig gulped his liquor, nodding.

"It would be typical, wouldn't it? In particular, it would have been the most useful of all tools in the establishment of Empire."

"Wait, wait! I'm sure neither my parents nor — "

"You're right. There was no need by then. Only slaves and suchlike are still routinely conditioned. Everybody else takes it for granted that the Empire always was and always will be.

"But the first genuine mutants to be expelled from Argus's domain... Well?"

"Those who were resistant to conditioning?" Hennig whispered, clasping his goblet tightly.

"Correct. And among them were a few that had a talent infinitely more threatening."

"That being — ?"

"The power to undo conditioning in other people. The one you have."

#

After a long pause Hennig exhaled gustily. "I thought — "

"I know what you thought. You thought you'd figured out how to dispose tidily of Zang but for one point: he had human slaves. Out of sympathy for those who shared your plight of having been stolen by slavers, you didn't want to harm them. Most commendable!"

"But — "

"You arranged to sell him two of your best teks — and, by the way, they were amazing. They were lightyears ahead of what anyone else has contrived. But you can't teach me, can you, how to program a tek to eliminate conditioning from human beings?"

"I . . . "

Hennig's voice faded and he shook his head.

"Yet" — Anza's tone was full of sympathy — "*that's what you did.* Literally without thinking. All the time you were working on the latest versions of the teks Rempus originally developed to reinforce the erotic impulse in a human being, you were printing them with the drive toward free will. It matched in, naturally. But it proved so powerful that it liberated Zang's slaves to the stage where they were able to invent new identities and vanish into the crowd. Not even Investigator Forkellen and Detective Wirt caught on."

She checked. "You may not know those two names. Take it from me: they hate you! But the point is this: you grew more confident. You applied the methods you had learned while building teks under Rempus's guidance — I *wish* he'd lived long enough for me to meet him! — and applied them so well that you were able to exploit them in a completely mechanical context: Tiron's apartments."

"I . . . "

"Did, or did not, the four slaves who were present leave without instructions before the Keeper and the Chamberlain were killed?"

Hennig's mouth worked. No sound emerged. Sweat beaded on his forehead and his hands clutched air.

"Exactly. Unaware, you'd built into your killer circuits others that release all slaves from bondage. You couldn't help it! Any more than you could help making Elyucham's bodyguards run away today, or slowing passers-by on the street beside the market to give yourself enough time to persuade him to come here. You so hate the idea of servitude that you've turned your gift into a reflex. But . . . "

She leaned forward, elbow on knee.

"You think you laid a trap for Elyucham at Y Ly Ging? I beg to differ. *I laid one for you!*

"Because by then I knew you would come hunting me. I'd finally found out something I should have guessed long ago: Zang cheated me. I'd been successful in a score of missions, and I suppose my guard was down. Until today you imagined you knew what I was up to. Now what do you think?"

"I think," husked Hennig, "you've been trying to ensure that true mutants are removed beyond the frontier, because if not, as Imperial power declines, they will inevitably be massacred."

"Precisely. Their, and our, future lies in the volume where humanity can continue making progress, rather than their being dragged down by the slow slide of the Empire. I don't believe our cousins of the Rim — struggling as they are against the demeaning opinion of themselves that they've inherited from the way they were treated inside the frontier — I don't believe they've yet done anything as constructive as inventing starships.

"But this I do know."

She drained her goblet and set it to one side. "I know that out there something's happening which implies progress, and advancement, and perhaps in the long term the first truly human civilization. We were trapped and deceived by the discovery of alien starships into re-running all our old mistakes. If someone from ten thousand years ago were to come to me and say, 'Nothing in the Empire is or ever has been new, it's just a repetition of what happened on the birthworld' — I'd believe it! And I look to mutants, those who cannot be conditioned, to build something new, something truly galactic, after the Empire has become, if not forgotten, then irrelevant!"

She fixed Hennig with a starbright glare.

"Zang I would fry on a nova — slowly — and rejoice! A hundred parsecs past the Seam of Ho there's a world that needs somebody like you, and thanks to him they've been waiting for you for a generation. Given the stock that colonized Ho Five, it *had* to breed a mutant like yourself who would fit in and take control . . . I don't mean conditioning control. I mean: add the last piece to a planetary puzzle. Instead, you've squandered your amazing talent on a quest for vengeance. You must give it up. I don't think it suits your taste, even though your elimination of Zang and Tiron was what drew you to my notice."

"I said as much to Rempus," Hennig muttered. "And added that I'd not expected it to be habit-forming. I've devoted three-quarters of the time I've so far lived to my revenge. If I've done any good as well, it's been by accident."

"And don't you think our species has need of people who do good, instead of ill, by accident?"

Anza Cly was smiling, bright teeth gleaming in the darkstone background of her face.

"I feel," Hennig whispered, "as though I were still ten — as though I've just entered this room for the first time and don't even know what teks might be."

"They're a dead end." Anza spoke with curt authority. "It's up to us, and only us, to civilize the galaxy — and I do not mean prolong the misery of Empire. You are needed, Hennig, on the Rim, where mutants have been shipped along with those who are not mutants but plucked up courage to speak out against some tyranny or other and got sold to slavers for their bravery. Go there, and help them free their minds! There should be a drop left in this flask . . . "

Accepting his refilled goblet, Hennig said, "I wish I could believe the things you've told me. But they feel unreal, as though you've drugged this liquor."

"Have I not been drinking cup for cup? You're in your right mind, if a little tipsy. Well?"

He pondered a long while, and ultimately shrugged. "No matter how much I want to believe you, I still have to say: How can I, on your unsupported word?"

"You share the paranoia of Elyucham and the governors of Argus," Anza sighed. "Well, fair enough. So, for half my life, did I. What changed my mind? A vision from what I take to be the future. There's someone — or maybe it's a some*thing* — trying to reach out to us across the aeons, and when it finds a person with the ability to hear its message it has the power to convince. I shall never, so long as I live, forget what I saw. Space knows how it will appear to you, so I won't tell you any more. Lean back, close your eyes, and open your mind by making it a blank. Then wait."

"That's all I have to do?" — doubtfully.

"That's all. It wants to show you truth. I feel it."

#

Abruptly Hennig was seeing in ten dimensions — twenty? Thirty? How many dimensions could accommodate not just the familiar picture of the Empire as a force in its own right, but the hopes and fears and suf-ferings of every individual who endured its arbitrary jurisdiction?

He was seeing — no: it was as different from seeing as a tek from a ma-chine or animal: he was *sensing* all of that.

Beyond it: he was aware of their ambitions, frustrated on every level by others whom they'd never met, as though a constant war were being waged on levels below, around, above everyday reality. (Yet the misery of having one's best imaginings defeated was not less than real . . .)

But in the distance (not in space, not in time — or was it a blend of both with something other?) —

His mind was flying apart and yet he stayed himself, aware, perceiv-ing —

A long way off, something was rousing: huge yet gentle, as capable of fear and hate as anyone, gifted with illimitable power to put both right, and yet resigned, because that was the order of things in what had been its . . .

Past?

It no longer recognized past or future. It simply *was.*

And among the other things it was . . . was human.

It hunched among the stars, and overloomed them. Its posture felt fa-miliar (for he was not only viewing it but being it, it was Hennig and Anza and Elyucham and Tiron and all the people who had ever lived and more) and it was —

Foetal.

It was also the curve of that quadrant of the galaxy that humans call *the* galaxy, and of course was not. Not under the sway of Argus had the outward urge been sustained, nor could it be by any trivial Empire. It had therefore faltered. And, now Hennig came to think of it, the Argian do-main (were one to look at it from intergalactic space) might well be matchable to the curve of an unborn baby's back . . .

Reason and logic fought in Hennig's mind against an overpowering sense of truth. They lost. The force of an image like that one could not be gainsaid. He had glimpsed new futures in the womb of Empire. And beyond what had been shown him . . .

A face. Far off, yet absolutely sharp, as though viewed through the wrong end of a telescope. Hennig could afterwards remember nothing of it — not even whether it seemed male or female — save that it was inexpressibly alluring and haloed with light (was that the right word? was there a word?) while its expression . . .

Its expression blended absolute power with absolute contentment.

If it smiled (and he thought it did) it was because he, of all the quintillions who had gone before, had suddenly become aware of it . . .

Hennig cried out. But he could not have said whether it was from terror or from joy.

#

A long while later he discovered he was staring up at the ceiling of the same room — yet despite having known this house since childhood, he found everything he looked at different in ways he could not define — and between it and him was the calm, dark, sympathetic countenance of Anza.

Who said, "I'm sorry. I didn't realize you were already so receptive."

"What? What?" Shaking, Hennig forced himself to his feet, and she steadied him with strong dark arms.

"You saw the Conjurer, I think."

"I . . . " Sweat was pouring into his eyes. "I don't know. I did see someone, but I don't know who."

"A long way off?"

"Yes!

"Handsome?"

"I suppose so . . . I can't tell! I only know I saw — "

"Someone whom you dared not disbelieve?"

Hennig let his hands drop to his sides. "Yes!"

"So did I" — in a low tone. "So do many of us. Some think he must be the one who will be the first to get the point of the joke that is the universe."

"I don't understand!"

"Who can, beset with misery and suffering? We're simply convinced that somebody will come, in a thousand or ten thousand years, who gets the point, and what is more will know how to explain it to the rest. But also he will juggle with the stars as easily as children playing ball."

"You're trying to tell me" — Hennig stood in what had been Rempus's main room where at age ten he had spent an hour as naked as Anza was now, unable now to remember what had and what had not changed since he first saw it — "that the universe is a joke?"

"Think of a better explanation," said Anza Cly, donning her cloak and restoring her flask to its pouch. "I know what I'm obliged to do — go back to breaking hearts and wrecking families by branding persons mutant who may not be, just in case, like you, they reveal their talents when subjected to the proper pressure. You hated me and were prepared to kill me. You have killed other people. You must expiate that, whether or not it turns out to be funny.

"Goodbye. I hope we'll never meet again."

"Wait!"

It was too late; she'd gone.

Hennig broke down weeping.

Nightfall closed around the house, and rain.

#

But in the morning he remembered something that she had — said? might have said? well, *he* had said:

"The time may come when I have to acquire one . . . "

That being a starship.

He made for the spaceport and, as though it had been fated, found a disillusioned would-be slaver who was sick of wandering the starlanes but had been cheated in his hope of reaping fat profits from Elyucham's sale here. He liked Pefferlosh no better and no worse than sundry other worlds, but was prepared to trade his starship for a house in running order and retire.

The basement factory did not appeal, but he agreed it was a selling point for those who might come after. In the meantime, would Hennig kindly oblige him by disposing of his disturbing creations?

219

Unregretfully Hennig did as he was asked. When their components had been recycled, he had a new home that could bear him into space.

"Where must I go?" he wondered . . .

And realized that he knew: a hundred parsecs past the Seam of Ho, where others of his kind were waiting for him.

With fresh and great respect for Anza Cly, he went.

Epilogue

Like blight-struck branches on a mighty tree, the edges of the Empire were eroding. Still its vast fleets imposed its rule, sometimes pausing between a planet and its sun to remind the natives how easily they cut off light and heat by casting shadows, but oftener and oftener the star commanders did so in the interest of themselves alone. With every year that slipped away the clutch of Argus weakened, weakened . . .

It might take millennia for the Empire to die, but the end of Empire was assured.

By Hennig's time, and Anza's, though, the seeds of the first truly human culture to infect the stars had sprouted in the minds of those who knew. Not feared, and not suspected: *knew* the truth.

And mostly they dwelt on worlds whither since time immemorial had been deported mutants — mostly so-called, but with a leaven of the genuine.

Their strain was thus distilled like ancinard, and concentrated. All of them, always, could resist conditioning; some, like Hennig, could remove it. That spelt freedom of the mind.

Lost talents of invention re-emerged. Then new ones came: the power to see through time, to move an object without touching it, to read another's thoughts, faintly at first and on the level only of emotion, afterwards more subtly and more fully.

At last there dawned the epoch that begat the Conjurer, who knew the universe for the bad joke it is, and saw its point.

But that's another story.

The Young Woman
in a House of Old
Vera Nazarian

The young girl lived in a big stone house with ivy-covered walls and with old men and women who were all her kin.

When she was a very tiny little girl, she remembered adult faces looking down at her as she lay in her crib, warm wrinkle-framed eyes of tired aunts and grandmothers and cousins and second-cousins and great-aunts and uncles-twice-removed and great-great-grandfathers, and even creatures so old and wrinkled and small that she mistook them for dolls until they moved and she saw that they were ancient kindly goblins and gnomes with white cobwebs for hair and eyebrows.

Her parents were no longer in this world, she was told, and instead here were her closest kinfolk, all taking care of her.

The little girl had no one to play with in the big house. She did try to play with the grandmothers and the cousins and the aunts, but they all had rheumatism or gout or bad knees or asthma or shortness of breath, and tired soon after. They never ran to catch the ball she threw, and did not even walk to retrieve it more than a couple of times. Nor did they laugh too loudly, only smiled at her with weary fondness. Some tried to trick her out of playing games that required physical exertion by telling her intricate stories, but fell asleep before they ever finished them. Many of them offered to read to her, but there is only so much reading-to a little girl can tolerate.

And so she went outside in the tree-lined streets, and sometimes she met other children who lived in the neighbouring houses, and together they played lively games of chasing balls and hiding from one another in the overgrown alleys and narrow passageways between houses.

The little girl ran around and played in the sun, and when the shadows grew long towards evening, she returned like all the other children to her own house where the old aunts and uncles sat at the dinner table. There she took her place, and ate the hot dinner, and took part in the grown-up talk.

The older people always talked to her as though she were of an age to understand the table conversation even when her head barely reached the top of the table. And somehow it indeed came to be that she understood them perfectly and even formed opinions.

"What do you think of the current weather?" they asked her. And she smiled back shyly and slurped her soup. "I think the heat is too much for the roses. That's why they curl up and wither before fully opening. And the wind is unusually dry for such early spring."

No one ever told her that slurping was impolite. Indeed, many of the aunts and cousins and grandfathers slurped too, loudly and tastily, as they ate their soup. Some of the really old ones often picked up their bowls and drank the soup as though it were tea, spilling much of it on their withered chins. The white-moustached goblins poured much of it in the thicket of their beards and down their napkins. As dinner progressed, lights were turned on in chandeliers. Evening shadows turned deep blue to displace the golden pinks of the fading sunset.

Then came tea. It was poured from fine porcelain pots, and creamy desserts were served by other old cousins. Everyone laughed with shaky old voices, and the conversation grew as animated as it could be, considering the elderly participants, and eventually there was more fragrant tea. The teapots emptied, and soon someone would call for another pot, and, you guessed it, there was even more tea, pots and pots of it, of different varieties and crops, from India, the Caucasus, Sri Lanka, with the rich dark leaves and the flavourings like oil of bergamot, or citrus or even some dried raspberries tossed in.

The little girl got tired of it after a while, full to bursting with the pastries and the hot soothing tea, and yet no one ever told her it was time for bed. So she sneaked away, pushing her chair in quietly, and ran to the library where the lights were dim. Here, she dug around in the musty stacks, and selected books with big decorative covers and cursive type that looked like it was a part of the border design. Those were usually the kind to have pictures, and she stared and pretended she was in the pictures, pretended to be the beautiful woman or man or creature drawn with such bright colours and wearing such sweeping robes, caught at a moment when the wind lifted their hems and tangled gauze sleeves and veils and billowed them like sails.

Time then became endless and blurry, its passage convoluted, so that some pictures took forever to examine, while some pages flew past her at the speed of thought.

And then it was very late indeed, and she noticed that all the lights in the house were out except for the faint brown-gold nightlights in the hallways, as the old grandmothers and uncles and cousins had gone to their beds, and all the doors were locked.

The little girl went to wash her face and brush her teeth and braid her hair into a looser soft braid for the night, and with a glass of water she came to her great bed that filled most of her room. She put the glass on her table, pinched the wick in the lamp with a pair of pincers to extinguish the flame, and then rushed to jump under the safe covers that now spread over her like magical layers of a warm protective ocean.

Unlike her cousins and aunts and grandfathers she did not immediately fall asleep but lay there in the warm semi-dream state and allowed images of godlike women and men and creatures to blossom in her vision. Sometimes her eyes remained open for a long time, and at other times she closed her eyes and observed things against the velvet backdrop of her eyelids. The images stood up before her in faraway brilliant colour — lands of incredible sunsets and green forests, with running water in mountain pools, with crashing ocean waves of silver against a brilliant white sky, with beautiful ancient ruins and temples of goddesses and fair gods, with flying beings like angels and yet, with other beings, that were like darkness, which struggled with the angels, and

223

which . . .

She finally slept, and the next morning she carried the dreams with her. She did the same thing every day and looked forward to the following evening.

#

The girl grew and reached school age. One clear early autumn morning, two of her aunts accompanied her on her first day to school, and then left her there. The girl was told to be good and to listen to the teachers, and to pay close attention. She was also told that here in the school she would be referred to as Miss Marianne Mornay because that was her given name. The girl sounded out her given name and it seemed nice but a bit odd, since no one had ever called her by that name before. Indeed, the idea of having a name was a bit odd too, because in her old stone house with ivy-covered walls her aunts and grandmothers and cousins never mentioned their own names. It was rather unnecessary since everyone always seemed to know who everyone else was referring to.

"Miss Mornay," said her teacher, a serious middle-aged woman with glasses and auburn hair taken up in a tight bun, so that the girl started at being directly addressed. "Miss Mornay, here in school you will learn how to read and write and count. You will also learn history and the arts and the sciences. You will play with your fellow students only during recess and lunch, and you will obey your elders promptly."

And, with that, school started.

The girl whose given name was Marianne Mornay attended her classes, and sat at a desk next to other students her age, and when the day was over she came back home where her grandmothers and cousins and uncles had the dinner ready, and everyone was waiting for her so that they could begin eating.

"I am going to learn how to read and write and count!" said Marianne, when asked how her day was.

"That is wonderful, Dear," said an elderly cousin, and several of the old aunts and grandfathers and goblins and gnomes with white eyebrows echoed the sentiment.

Then the soup was served, and the dinner-table conversation started.

The next morning the girl was back at school, and the teacher showed them the first three of the letters of the alphabet, and drew them on the blackboard with dusty yellowish chalk. The letter "A" was made up of three lines, two propping each other up, and the third lying flat and trying hard to keep them apart from the middle. Marianne held her pencil in her fingers and tried to draw the three lines just so.

Next to her another little girl who was addressed by the teacher as Miss Lily North, with pale blonde hair, much lighter than her own, was having a bit of trouble. Her three lines did not seem to connect properly, and the middle line was always lopsided.

"Here," said Marianne to Lily. "This is how you do it." And she drew the three lines just so, exactly how the teacher had drawn them on the blackboard.

On the other side of her sat a boy with dark hair and clever cool eyes. "Show off," he said to Marianne.

But Lily only smiled to her and said politely, "Thank you."

"Dummy," said the dark-haired boy to Lily.

But Marianne and Lily ignored him, and instead they listened to the teacher who showed them how to draw the next letter.

When school was over and Marianne had come home, she told everyone in the old house how she had learned the letters "A", "B" and "C". The old ones applauded, and a grandmother with spectacles patted Marianne on the cheek as she poured her the soup.

Later, as tea was served, Marianne slipped away after only one fragrant cup in order to run to the library. Here she selected her favourite book with great colourful pictures, and for the first time she did not look at the pictures first but at the squiggly lines underneath that she now knew to be writing.

She looked at them, and sometimes she found the letter "A". Often the letter "A" came at the beginning of lines and sometimes it was very big and colourful, with green vines creeping around its edges and crimson roses peeking around its top.

"A," said Marianne. "A, A, A," she read over and over, quickly turning the pages while excitement built inside her so that she suddenly wanted to know what all the other squiggles were. Then she looked closely and found the letters "B" and "C" hiding among the squiggles. They popped up unexpectedly, like treasures. And once she knew they were there she saw them on every page in many places.

Marianne could hardly contain herself, and went to bed early so that she did not have to wait 'til tomorrow to learn the next letters.

The next day Marianne's class learned "D", "E" and "F", and as the week progressed there were more and more letters, and the teacher showed them how to put some of the letters together to make magic in the form of words.

Marianne was one of the quickest in the class, and she drew the prettiest letters just so, exactly as the teacher. Next to her, Lily had trouble with some letters, and Marianne was happy to help her draw "G" and "C" so that they did not look alike. During recesses Marianne and Lily sat beside each other often on the steps of the school, and they drew the letters together. Sometimes Lily would get tired and she'd draw a stick person instead and giggle.

The dark-haired boy who sat in class on the other side of Marianne, and whom the teacher called Mister Robin Noggins, often ran by with his friends and stuck out his tongue at Lily and Marianne. Sometimes he threw a rock that clattered at their feet, and at other times he pulled Marianne's braid of chestnut-brown hair.

Once during lunch, as Robin Noggins came by and dropped a bug on Lily's head, Marianne stuck out her foot just as he was running past them, and Robin Noggins fell down flat on his face in front of them and started to cry. He'd skinned his knee and torn his sock, and got himself a big red bruise covered with playground dirt.

The teacher came quickly and shook her head at the three of them. Lily had gotten up and was screaming and batting at her blonde hair to get the bug off, Robin was wailing on the ground where he now sat, and Marianne remained in her spot with a glowering look.

"I don't know who did what, and which of you started it," said the teacher. "But all three of you are going to stay an hour after school and do your homework right here with me. Now, go inside and clean your knee with soap and water, Mister Noggins. And, Miss North, leave your hair alone, there is nothing there. As for you, Miss Mornay . . ."

But the teacher did not have anything to say, only looked at Marianne reproachfully. "Really now, I'd have thought better of you, Miss Mornay," she finally said, at which Marianne blushed.

After school, Marianne, Lily and Robin remained seated at their desks and worked on their letters, occasionally staring meanly at one another. In the front of the class the teacher sat in her chair reading, her spectacles having slid down to the tip of her nose.

When the hour was over, they were excused, and Marianne rushed home. This was the first time that she had not been home in time for dinner, and she knew that her old aunts and grandmothers and cousins must be terribly worried.

And she was right. The house was oddly quiet and everyone was seated silently at the dinner table before empty dishes — not empty as in eaten, but empty and squeaky clean as though dinner had never been served. The soup had grown cold in the kettle, and some of the oldest grandmothers and aunts were nodding in their chairs. The goblins slept with their faces down on the tablecloths, and one or two were snoring softly.

As soon as Marianne had entered the room, everyone woke up, however, and one old granny said, "Ah, there you are, Dear! Where have you been? Do you realize the soup has gotten cold! And it is not even gazpacho or that newfangled vichyssoise soup but string bean, pea and carrot, which means that it needs to be eaten when piping hot. Well, never mind now!"

Immediately an old cousin got up and began to ladle out the cold soup to all, and as though nothing happened, and the usual conversation started up.

"I am sorry," muttered Marianne, but only one grandfather heard her, and he nodded at her and winked, and then dipped his spoon into the soup bowl and began to slurp hungrily.

Later that night Marianne sat in her usual place in the library. She held a book in her lap, and she could read most of the words in it. But tonight she was unable to concentrate, and instead continued to think about her old grand-aunts and cousins and great-great-uncles and all the rest of them. What if she were to be late again for an hour, and what if something happened and she was really *really* late? Or, what if she did not come home at all? Would they all go hungry on her behalf?

The next morning during breakfast, Marianne said to a second-cousin and uncle, "Cousin, Uncle, please promise me that if I am

227

late coming home again you will go ahead and have dinner without me?"

"Why would you be late again, Dear?" said the uncle with a toothless smile as he buttered his muffin and then added a large spoonful of apricot-pineapple preserves on top.

"Well," said Marianne, "I don't know. What if the teacher makes me stay after school again?"

"That wouldn't be a good thing at all," replied her second-cousin in a tremulous voice as she poured milk into her bowl on top of some sugary cornflakes and loudly scraped the sides of the bowl to stir it.

"But what if it happens?" persisted Marianne. "Would the two of you please make sure to let the others know that it's OK and that you should just eat without me?"

"Oh," said the uncle, biting his muffin, "I suppose we could do that, couldn't we?" And he nudged the second-cousin. "Could we?"

She started in alarm and dropped her spoon into the cornflakes. "What? What did you just say?"

"I said, we need to make sure to let the others know that she — that she — " The uncle looked back at Marianne and said, "What was that again, Dear? What are we supposed to say?"

"Oh, never mind," said Marianne, frustration breaking into her voice. "I won't be late again, I promise."

"Late?" said the second-cousin. "Who is late?"

The uncle just shrugged and scratched his wrinkled cheek. He continued to chew his muffin and smacked his lips loudly.

#

In no time at all the school year drew to a close. Marianne could now read all the words in her primer with a fluent speed that left most of her classmates behind, except for Lily and Robin. Lily could read very well indeed because Marianne always made sure she could, and Robin was not going to let two girls get ahead of him. In addition to reading and writing, they also learned numbers and counting and formulas with mysterious x and y values they had to solve for. They used rulers to make all kinds of interesting angles, and protractors to draw circles, and even started on degrees. There was also history, where Marianne suddenly recognized references to some of the Godlike people in the books at home, and knew now that many of them had been real people who lived a long time ago, and that the books simply portrayed them as divine because this is what often happens in history books to people who are popular or strong or brave. In addition to history, they had art, where everyone got to draw objects and still lifes, and where the teacher let them look at even more amazing books filled with pictures of ancient white marble statues and intricate paintings of the great masters.

Marianne could draw very well just like she could form the letters, and she was better than everyone else when it came to drawing faces. One painter called Rembrandt interested her in particular because he portrayed old people with deep lines in their faces and dark brown shadows and darkness and dim lighting. No one else drew such real-looking old grandmothers and grandfathers, and for a moment Marianne thought some of them looked awfully familiar. Indeed, the more she thought about it the more she came to the conclusion that some of the old relatives living in her house were just like these people in the paintings. They had the same depth of wrinkles and the same shrunken skin and deep hollows.

Marianne took her sketchpad and her art pencils home with her and during dinners, when everyone was gathered, she made some quick drawings of an aunt or a cousin or a grandmother. Since it was now summer and school was out, she had plenty of time during the day to stop in various rooms of the house and draw a napping white-haired goblin here and an old granny there, while in yet another room she found two or three withered uncles and a gnome playing dominoes, and a cousin or two reading in the library.

By the end of the summer, her sketchbook was full, and the only thing left to do was to return to the library every night or lazy heat-filled afternoon, and to read and look at pictures that she already knew so well, and to dream of ancient times and faraway places all over the world.

When school resumed and Marianne brought her sketchbook to class, the teacher took a long careful look at the images and then stared back at Marianne. "Hmmmm," said the teacher. And then added, "Very well done, Miss Mornay. You appear to have a great facility for character portraiture. I will put you with the advanced class this year."

Marianne blushed with pleasure, and later showed the sketchbook to Lily and even to Robin, who had stared over her shoulder for so long that she had thought she might as well let him peek.

"Why did you draw all these old people?" asked Lily. "It is really all very good, of course, but why did you draw them?"

"These are my aunts and uncles and cousins and grandparents," said Marianne. She was a bit taken aback by the question.

"How come they are all so old?" said Robin in a sharp, snotty voice.

Marianne shut her sketchbook with a snap. And then she said, "Sorry."

"It's OK," said Lily, and smiled her usual kind smile. They all forgot this in a matter of minutes, but Marianne could not. The pleasure at the teacher's comment was somehow diminished now, and Marianne suddenly no longer wanted to draw anything at all. In the next art class she drew a boring still life with roses in a vase.

And she continued to think about what Lily and snotty Robin had asked when she got home. Why did she have so many old relatives? Where did they all come from? What kind of a house was this, anyway?

As everyone ate dinner, she wore a frown on her face, and even some nearsighted cousins noticed.

"What's wrong, Dear?" a couple of them said with warm concern.

"Nothing," replied Marianne.

"Well, then, have another piece of potato pie, Dear," said a grandmother with a pretty lacy collar around her skinny neck.

And then Marianne cleared her throat loudly and gathered her courage. And she asked everyone at the table: "Excuse me, but why do I have more than two grandmothers and grandfathers? And *who* are all of you?"

The question resulted in silence. Old wrinkled faces stilled in amazement, in surprise, all flavours of it. One or two grannies adjusted their hearing aids, and at least three great-uncles set down their spoons or forks and put on their spectacles as though that was going to help them hear better.

"Ahem, Dear?" said one goblin at the end of the table, his voice so shaky and weak that he had to put his withered hands around his mouth to be heard. "What was it that you said?"

Marianne bit her lip. "Who are all of you?" she said again. "Why do you all live here with me? Why do I live here?"

"What kind of a silly question is that, Dear?" said one great-aunt. "Why, we are here because this is our house! Goodness, where else would we be?"

"Don't call me 'Dear'!" exclaimed Marianne. "My given name is Marianne! Why don't you ever use it? And why don't any of you have given names of your own?"

"Well, of course your given name is Marianne," said a grandfather, scratching the top of his balding head. "We all know that, don't we?"

"Of course we do," replied several cousins, nodding.

"So why should we have to use a given name when we all know what it is?"

"Exactly," echoed two aunts.

"Would be a waste of words, wouldn't it?" muttered a second-cousin twice removed.

"Say, what's the main course there?" said another tiny aunt, and immediately the dinner-table conversation resumed where it had left off. Meanwhile the old uncle on the right of Marianne patted her hand, saying, "There, there, Dear. Main course will cheer you up in a minute!"

"I don't need cheering up," whispered Marianne. "I need to better understand! For example, Uncle, what is *your* name?"

But the old man had already turned his attention back to his plate and with shaking hands was cutting a piece of lamb chop into little easy bite-size pieces.

#

The school days stretched forward without end, and Marianne lost track of the many things she was learning. Several times Lily invited her home for dinner, and to study together, but Marianne always declined politely, saying that she had to be home that night. More than once there had been splendid birthday parties and her classmates asked their friends to come, and sometimes she was invited. But always Marianne would think of a good excuse why she could not go. No one at home had ever told her she could not attend; she just *knew* she could not.

On such nights she would come home and brood after dinner, sitting alone in her room or the library, while the evening shadows progressed. She imagined the children playing together and opening birthday presents, mountains of them, and running and laughing. Not that she wanted these presents in particular; she just wanted to be there when it was done, to hear the gasps of wonder, and the ripping of bright gift paper, and to imagine what was inside.

Once Marianne asked during dinner when her own birthday was and why did they never celebrate it.

"A birthday?" said one great-grandmother, pouring a cup of tea. "Why, what a lovely idea!"

"Why, yes, indeed," replied many of the cousins and uncles and great-grandfathers.

"We will have a birthday party!" said an aunt.

"What a splendid thought!"

Marianne frowned amid their clamour, and then she said, "No, that is not what I meant! I want to know *when* my birthday is! I didn't say I wanted to have a party! I want to know how old I am, and on what day I was born, and how it was, and about my parents — "

"How about tomorrow?" said a second uncle. "We can have the cake ready, don't you think? And there will be time enough to have presents!"

"Why, of course there will be presents, what kind of a birthday party doesn't have presents, silly?" said a cousin.

They went on and on. But Marianne was not listening. A cold strange feeling she had never had before was filling her, and she felt a vertigo, a stifling sense of futility.

And so she left them all arguing about the flavour of cake icing and the colour of the ribbons, and she went to her room. There she sat down and thought.

In the morning Marianne went to school, and during recess she told Lily that she was getting a birthday party of her own, and that Lily was invited. Marianne thought with a strange wicked glee that she was just going to have Lily show up at her house unannounced and see what came of it.

"A birthday party?" said Robin, who happened to be walking by just then. "Hey, everyone, Marianne's having a birthday party! And you're all invited!" he said very loudly and stuck his tongue out at Marianne before running off.

"Oh, hush!" said Marianne, but it was too late.

And so, as a result, later that night a group of schoolchildren knocked at the door of the old stone house with ivy-covered walls.

The door was opened by one of the grannies, who then opened her eyes, too — wide in surprise — and said "Goodness!" before letting everyone in.

The children walked through antique corridors and into a dining room filled with old aunts, grandmothers, great-uncles, second-cousins, and others. Marianne stood near the table, and there was a large two-tier birthday cake decorated in lovely off-white roses made from butter icing and covered with candles.

"Happy birthday!" everyone cried, tremulous old voices mingling with bright young children's voices — flat notes mixed with sharp — and gifts were deposited one by one on the side-table nearby.

"Oh, what lovely children!" exclaimed one great-aunt, and she pinched Robin Noggins on the cheek. Robin grimaced but stood his ground, and Marianne noticed that he had brought a present too, although it was a small one, and he stuck it discreetly behind the other boxes.

"Let's have tea and cake!" exclaimed a great-grandpa. "And then we can play!"

At his words, two cousins in aprons carted in a tea service with several china pots and lots of other pastries and finger sandwiches. Marianne stared with amazement at the extraordinary delicacies that were piled on the tea-cart. But she did not have time to gawk, because she was handed a silver cake cutter while a portly second-uncle waddled up and lit the candles on the cake, and then Marianne was told to make a wish and blow the candles out.

Marianne stood and thought, and for a moment her mind was perfectly blank. And then it came to her that what she really wanted above all else was to *know*. And with that in mind she took a big breath and blew out all the candles, while Lily and her classmates and the others clapped, even Robin.

"Now, cut it! Cut the cake!"

And so she did, cutting huge creamy pieces, and seeing that the insides were filled with vanilla custard and strawberries and sponge cake and flaky cake and marzipan and berry preserves and all kinds of amazing things. Two cousins helped her cut the rest of the cake, and although the pieces were all enormous there was enough for everyone in the room.

Soon everyone had settled around the room, in easy chairs and at the table, and tea was poured and more cake was consumed in large quantities. Lily had settled near two of the grannies, one of whom was now braiding her pretty blonde hair while the other was pouring her more tea. Robin was talking to three of the great-uncles twice and thrice removed, who were telling tales of sailing ships and wicked one-eyed pirates and stolen gold, and they had pulled out their domino set and were setting up a game. The other children were also preoccupied with an old cousin or aunt here, or an uncle or grandfather there, who told them stories and patted their heads, and gave them spontaneous squeezes and hugs. Marianne sat down next to a tiny wizened granny goblin, who smiled at her and chewed a piece of soft cake with her gums. "Happy birthday, Dear!" she whispered. And then, as though just remembering, "Why, aren't you going to open your presents?"

In that moment there was a chorus of voices in agreement, and Marianne had no choice but to start tearing the pretty paper boxes and pulling the ribbons. Inside, she found dolls and books and even a music box from Lily. Robin's small present contained a pencil set of fancy watercolour pencils.

"Thank you, thank you, thank you!" Marianne repeated to all as she opened the gifts. She had expected a fiasco, but instead this had turned into an odd but amazing birthday party.

The hour had grown late, and eventually it was time for everyone to go. The children lingered, many hugging the old great-aunts and second- and third-cousins, and receiving pecks on the cheeks from great-grandmothers and grandpas. Lily in particular hugged one of Marianne's grandmothers, saying, "You are just like my own granny Beth!"

Robin conceded to a hug from a great-grandfather, and blushed when his hair was ruffled.

Eventually they were all out the door, and Marianne and the old relatives stood on the ivy-covered porch, waving goodbye.

Marianne took a big breath and a profound inner smile filled her, all the way down to her toes. "Thank you, Granny," she whispered to the nearest old one at her side. "Thank you . . . "

"Why, Dear," the granny replied, "thank *you*! Those were all such lovely children, your friends. I am so glad to have seen them, they seem so familiar. I think they all remind me of you."

#

Time swept along so fast then that summer and winter came one after another, with no time for spring or fall.

Marianne was growing taller, and she was learning all kinds of things in school. She learned about ancient invasions and world wars and religions with many chaotic gods and one just god, about deserts and cold ice-covered lands and the reasons why rain fell and what made wind and about the wonderful new energy called electricity and how the earth was a ball that hung in a vacuum and revolved around the sun which was nothing but an average star in a universe filled with billions of billions of stars just like it. She learned that human beings had probably originated from other animals called primates and how those in turn came from tiny amphibians that came out of the ocean. She learned that science was the study of patterns in the universe, and she learned the methods that science used. And although there were so many things, so many amazing details in her different classes, and no one really mentioned this, it began to seem that so many things in the world were connected along various lines of meaning and pattern and organization.

At night, after her homework was done, she hungrily read the books in the library, and had gone through several of the shelves there, reading the books from cover to cover. There were books on history and travelogues and philosophies of ancient wise men translated from long-forgotten and long-dead languages. And there were books of stories and novels that told one long complicated story of selected human lives.

Strange intangible things were in those stories and novels — things that science seemed to pass by, maybe because these things were unquantifiable. Science had no true methods for organizing emotions and predicting behaviour, although it tried. There was no way to catalogue loyalty or friendship, nor to predict love. No way to measure or avoid fear and despair, and no cure for loss, no salve for anger, no consolation for anxiety. And yet all these things that slipped through the cracks of school studies, they were all here, analyzed and portrayed in the stories and novels, underneath the trappings of history or adventure.

Marianne filled her mind and her dreams with the intangibles, and there was always room for them right beside the numbers and the dates and the historic figures and the scientific details of the natural world.

Marianne thought about her own intangibles, and her own feelings and curiosities and her own fear. Because deep down there it always was, a fear of that which made no sense, of her own tiny microcosm in which she had lived since earliest childhood.

Why, for example, did her best friend Lily live with a mother and a father, and why did Robin, now a gangly teenager, have a younger sister? And why was it that Marianne lived with so many old relatives who were, to tell the truth, mostly senile, and who seemed to subsist on nothing more than the food they grew in the garden behind the house, and if so, where did they get all those things they had for dinner every night, such as chicken and beef? Was there an old age pension coming to some of them? Yet why did the mail never come to their house? Whence did the money come to buy new clothes for her growing figure and to buy school supplies? And who in the world were these shrivelled, grotesque, vaguely human creatures that could barely speak for their age, and how was it that after all these years none of them had ever required a doctor?

And finally a question occurred to Marianne that was the most disturbing of all. She asked it at dinner one evening, sitting in a chair that was much too small for her, since she was now a budding young woman, and all these old grandfathers and great-aunts and cousins and shrivelled gnomes appeared so much smaller than her.

"My dears," said Marianne, clearing her throat after her first swallow of asparagus cream soup, "if I may ask, do any of you require a doctor for things such as aches and pains? And this is a very difficult thing for me to say, and possibly impolite, but how old are all of you? And — and — I wish you all the grandest health and many many long happy years, but when was the last time anyone in this house . . . *died?*"

She expected there to be an immediate silence, and there was. Only a couple of the most shrivelled, most hard-of-hearing gnomes and great-aunts at the end of the table continued to clatter silverware against dishes.

Everyone else had stopped eating and talking and was staring at her or at each other. And then a cousin twice removed coughed into a napkin, and said, "My Dear, what an interesting question indeed. Aches and pains? Why, there are always aches and pains, and it's normal for old people to have them, is it not? Though, if you drink plenty of fresh hot tea and eat your vegetables, and take long walks every morning and evening, and if you laugh a whole lot and breathe deeply, then I dare say the aches and pains can be quite bearable. Really, my rheumatism goes away after breakfast, as soon as I take that walk!"

"You know, you are so right!" said an aunt. "I hardly get achy at all if I drink plenty of liquids every day."

"I don't know about you ladies, but a nice full pipe does the trick for me," said a great-grandfather with a hoary long beard and whiskers splattered with asparagus soup. "I smoke a full pipe, and pouff! No more bad knee for the rest of the night!"

Marianne stared at them all with the usual sense of inevitable frustration, as the various aunts and cousins and goblins with bushy cobweb-eyebrows started to tell their own stories. And then, just as she thought that it was hopeless to get any sense out of them, one great-great-aunt said, "Goodness, doesn't anyone get sick enough around here to have to stay in bed? How odd!"

"Yes," said Marianne, and forced herself to be brutal. "How odd indeed. Did anyone here ever get so sick that they stayed in bed for a long time? And did they then continue to only get sicker and sicker, and never recovered, and eventually died?"

Silence returned. Their faces were all puzzled, but some of them bore evidence of thinking very hard and in earnest.

"Died?" whispered a granny in a frightened tremulous voice, echoing Marianne. "Someone died here? Did anyone ever die?"

"You know, I don't know!" said one very hard-of-hearing uncle in a very loud voice. "By golly, I don't think anyone's died! Why, what an idea!"

"Well, yes," said another uncle, raising his brows with the effort of remembering. "And to think that I've been here forever, and I am older than a rock! I've never seen anyone die!"

"Me neither!" cried a gnome cousin.

"Nor me!"

"How odd and amazing!"

"Indeed, considering how long we've been here!"

Marianne took the opportunity to ask. "And how long exactly would that be?"

"Goodness," said a great-cousin, "I have no idea, but it must be very long indeed, since I don't remember being anywhere else but here."

"Neither do I," said a grandfather. "I've always been here in this house!"

Marianne stared and thought, and felt sorry for the looks of fear and confusion in all their sweet old faces, and the cold abandoned dinner on their plates. She felt vaguely guilty for having brought this up, but she could not stop now.

"Do you not remember being young?" asked Marianne.

They looked at her silently.

"Is it possible," said Marianne, "that all of you are dead already? Maybe — could it be — are you strange corporeal ghosts?"

"Oh!" exclaimed a great-aunt. "How terrible! How awfully frightening, and I certainly hope that's not true! I don't think I am dead, and I certainly don't want to be!"

"But how can I be a ghost?" said a third-cousin and lifted his fork to brandish it in his bony shaking hand.

Marianne rubbed her temple, and bit her lip. She just didn't know what to think, and it was obviously making everyone upset. "I am so sorry, my dears . . . " she managed to whisper at last. "I love all of you very much, and I don't think any of you are dead or ghosts, really, and I wish for you all to be happy and healthy always. It's just so very odd, this — this house of ours."

"Ah, Dear, well, we love you very much too, you know," said one dazed granny, finally breaking into a smile of relief. "Don't we?" she added, and was echoed by a chorus of old voices.

And then another granny got up and came to Marianne's side and kissed her soundly on the cheek with a loud smack.

Marianne felt a sudden unquantifiable intangible. It came in the form of tears welling in the corners of her eyes.

#

The years went by swiftly after that, like blinks of an eye. Marianne finished school, and she and her friends were all grown up. Lily became a lovely young woman with soft unblemished skin and a slender figure. She was to go to a university, and her family was proud that she was going to become a teacher herself. Robin was a tall, serious young man with dark hair and a strong face, and he no longer made fun of Marianne or Lily but instead spent afternoons in the summer in long talks about interesting intellectual subjects. He too was to attend a college all the way across the country, and planned to become a scientist.

Marianne herself was now a dark-haired, tall young woman with an intense expression in her inquisitive eyes and a pair of spectacles that she now had to wear because her weaker vision required it. On the evening before he was to leave for college, Robin came to Marianne's house to say goodbye to his friends, and to let them know that he would not see them for the next four years unless he came home on the holidays.

Lily cried into a napkin and Marianne tried not to, and bit her lip, and then Robin was gone. He did promise to write, and he did, over the next several months, then years. Meanwhile, Lily went to the university and studied to become a teacher. Marianne thought about them both, and about how neat it would be if she could also go to college. But to do that would have meant leaving home, and leaving behind all her old relatives in this house with ivy-covered walls.

"Go to college, Marianne!" Lily wrote her in many letters, repeatedly. "You were always smarter than me, and it would be a shame if you didn't — there's a world of things you could do! As for your old relatives, do what we did with my grandma Beth. Have a nurse come in to look after them, or else there are always the old folks' homes and nice convalescent homes and elderly retirement communities. Really, you have many options. Grandma Beth is now living in Cherry Hill Gardens, a very nice facility, and we visit her often . . . or at least as often as possible."

Marianne thought about it as she came home every night from her day

239

job at the local library, where she shelved books and watched the stacks to make sure everything was in place.

And once she asked during dinner, "My dears, how would all of you feel if I went to college?"

A familiar silence came to the dining table, the same kind of silence that had come only two or three times before in Marianne's life, when she had asked them her most difficult questions.

"To college?" said a toothless cousin. "And where would that be, Dear?"

"I am afraid," said Marianne, "it would probably be very far away and I would have to move to another city."

"But," said an uncle, "would that mean you would leave us?"

"Well, yes," said Marianne. "But not for long! The program is only four years, and I would come home on all the holidays!"

"Four years!" said a great-grandma with amazement. "Oh, what a very long time!"

"Where would you sleep, Dear? Your room would be so empty without you there . . . "

"And how would you eat all your vegetables without us making sure you do?" put in an aunt thrice removed.

"And how can we be sure you're all right?"

"Your dinner plate would look awfully lonely on the table with you not here," said a goblin grandpa. "Terribly lonely. I don't know if I'd be able to eat my own dinner, seeing it."

Marianne pulled at a lock of her hair in frustration, and then said, "I will miss you all terribly, dears, but what I am more worried about is how will you do without me being here. Will you make sure to start eating dinner? And what if something happens to any one of you?"

More silence.

"Well, I guess we'll just have to manage somehow," said a cousin eventually. "Won't we, I suppose?" and she looked around the room at the other old folks.

Everyone started to nod, and the conversation resumed as it normally did.

The next morning Marianne gathered her courage, and took a day off work to ride the train downtown and make arrangements for a day nurse to drop by the house that afternoon and make sure the old people were comfortable. And then she rode the train for several hours and arrived at a beautiful university campus in a nearby city, and made enquiries about admissions. When she was finally done, and took the train back home, it was very late and dark. Much later and darker than it had ever been.

As she walked up the path to the ivy-covered front porch, Marianne noticed that all the windows of the house were dark, and the front porch light was out. On the front door was attached a large envelope with a note from the nursing clinic. Marianne took the note as she entered the house and turned the hallway light on. The note was from the nurse and it said: "Dear Ms Mornay, I certainly hope this is the correct house, and if this is not Ms Mornay, then pardon me and disregard this message. As instructed, I arrived at 4:30pm promptly and knocked for a long time but no one came to the door. However, knowing that some old people can be infirm and hard of hearing, I tried the door and forced it open, and then I went inside. This is a very large house, but no one was here, and I checked every single one of the rooms on all the three floors, and the large dining room, as I was told it is a favourite gathering place. I am at a loss as to what to do, and will be leaving another message tomorrow at the clinic where I may be reached. Yours truly, Beverly Halden, R.N."

There was a cold feeling inside Marianne as she walked through the dark house, turning the various lights on, and finally came to the dining room.

The room was dim, smelling of melted candlewax — dim except for two small candles in the table centrepiece that had burned down to the bottom, and by their flickering vestiges of light Marianne saw all of her old relatives. They were seated around the dinner table, most with heads down, some leaning back in their chairs, and many snoring. The kettle of the usual soup stood ice-cold, and the plates were clean and unused.

"Good evening . . . " said Marianne.

And at the sound of her voice they all started to wake up.

"Dear, there you are!" cried a granny and hobbled over towards Marianne. "We were just waiting for you so we could start eating."

And then Marianne screamed. A fit of madness had come to her, an impossible storm that had to have an outlet, and so she screamed and tears ran down her face in a torrent and she could not stop, not even with the terrified old faces all around her, and the soothing hands with withered skin as they came to console her.

"No, no, no!" shrieked Marianne, beating them away, hearing her voice as she had never heard it in her life. "Where were you? And why are you all here now? Why, why, why? What —?"

She beat her chest with her fists, and pulled at her hair in an attempt to wipe her nose and she cried, "Why didn't you have dinner without me? Why, why, why? Didn't you remember what I told you, that I would be gone all day, and that you must eat and drink and live without me? And where were you when the nurse came?"

And then Marianne sat down on the floor and she wailed anew, "Oh, God! What have I done to be burdened with this? Why me? What do you want of me, you crazy old seniles? Why can't I go about my own life? Do you expect me to come to dinner and be here with you for the rest of my existence? Do you expect me to rot here forever?"

"What has happened to you, Dear?" said one great-aunt, also beginning to cry. "Why are you so upset? And why are you so late to dinner? The corn chowder is all cold, you know." And she sniffled dejectedly.

"No!" screamed Marianne again. "You crazy old . . ." She held her head and she shut her eyes tight, and she was choking on her own tears.

And in a moment between breaths she heard sounds of sobbing coming from all around the room as old great-aunts and -uncles and second-cousins and grandmothers and great-great-grandfathers and cousins twice removed and shrivelled goblins with dried-apple faces sat down or stood around her, crying, weeping, shuddering, like old elm trees and maples sighing in the winter wind.

The sound of their absolute desolation reached Marianne, and she held her breath. It was a sound of cold deepest December, the sound of midnight and the sound of the twelfth hour.

And Marianne took deep breaths and with an immense force of will she stopped crying. Then she took one long last juddering breath and she whispered in a voice made thick with tears, "I am sorry. I did not mean it . . . I am so sorry . . . my dears."

And at the sound of her lifeless resigned voice they came to her, coarse lukewarm palms stroking her hair and withered chests hugging her, the smell of old dried violets and soap and ancient tobacco on some, the whiff of vanilla and flour on others, the faint echo of lamb's wool and oak, and the soft cobwebs of pale goblin hair touching her at the edges of time fading away into the mists of memory.

"I'll never leave you, I promise," whispered Marianne to them all, cradling old heads with paper-thin skin and sparse hair, and stroking bent backs and fragile shoulders.

"Never," she added, getting up and starting to light the candelabras around the room.

#

Four years later, Lily had graduated from university, and Robin was on his last year of an extended program in physics. Robin wrote to Marianne unfailingly, and he came to visit on many holidays, and Lily also.

One summer afternoon, Robin knocked on the door of the old stone house with ivy-covered walls and, when Marianne came to the porch, he smiled at her shyly and asked if he could speak to her about an important matter.

As they passed through the hallways of the house, the sleeping gnomes and withered grannies woke up in their rocking chairs and waved to Robin gently, then resumed their naps. Marianne stole shy glances at Robin, since she did not see him for several months at a time, and each time she did he looked more handsome and confident. Robin's hair was so very dark and his profile noble and gentle. He was dressed a bit formally today, with a suit and tie, and Marianne, who only had a summer dress on, was wondering what he was up to.

In her room, Robin closed the door, then all of a sudden it seemed he had nothing to say, except that his breath had quickened, and his face was paling and then blushing.

"Marianne," he said then softly. "My Marianne."

And Marianne laughed suddenly, because for the first time it occurred to her that her given name sounded very much like the name of Maid Marian, the beloved of Robin Hood from the old legends. And here in front of her stood Robin Hood himself, dashing and beautiful and kind.

But Robin Noggins, her silly childhood friend, her Robin, was not smiling. "Marianne," he said, and his voice was alien in its intensity, "I love you, Marianne, my dearest friend. Will you be my wife?"

Marianne heard the wind of summer blowing the pale satin curtains at her window. And she felt the kiss of the sun upon the nape of her neck.

Here was her Robin, ready to take her away.

Marianne came forward, and she put her hands up, and she took her Robin and held him and her fingers slipped around his neck while her head lay resting against his chest.

"I love you," she whispered. "I love you, my Robin."

And she stayed that way, pressed against him, for a long glorious span of moments, while a distant grandfather clock in the hallway rang the hour.

Robin reached deep into his coat pockets and he brought out a ring with a pale transparent stone that carried in it sparks of the sun. "This ring is yours now," he whispered. "Once it was my grandmother's. We can live together and dream and do the things we've always wanted. If you like, we will have children, or we can travel the world, or do whatever you like, but we will be together now, my Marianne. Say yes, and we can be off tomorrow, on a trip of a lifetime! I know how you've always wanted to see the world!"

"For some reason," said Marianne softly, "I've always thought it'd be Lily. I thought you loved Lily that way, not me . . . "

Robin laughed. "Ah, but I always loved both of you, Lily as a sister, and you as the one for my heart."

"Like the letter 'A,'" whispered Marianne.

And when Robin glanced at her upturned face in surprise, she explained. "Remember when we learned to write the letter 'A'? There are three lines, two always coming together, and one always piercing the two to keep them apart. At one point or another in our lives, Robin, we've served as any one of the three lines. At first you were our foil, between Lily and me, when we were children. And now . . . I am afraid that Lily was never good at drawing that middle line and now you are asking her to be the foil, to stand between us and serve as our balance."

Robin's face became very still and he continued to look at her. "I am not sure what you mean, Marianne . . . " he said.

"I mean," she replied, "that maybe it's best that I be the foil, and I be

244

the balance. I love you so much, my Robin Hood, and I love Lily, and I know you love her also. Go and marry her, Robin. Because in my life I've discovered that I can only be that middle line. I will always stand firm and loving between you, not to separate you but to prop you up. Otherwise your two lines will just fall into each other, and there will be no letter 'A' at all."

"What are you talking about?" exclaimed Robin. His fist clutched the ring and his other hand bit into Marianne's shoulder painfully.

"I can't marry you, Robin," she said, while water pooled in the corners of her eyes. "I can't go off with you into the great wide world, and I can't have children, nor grow old with you — or with anyone. Go on and live your life, and marry Lily, and the two of you come and visit me sometimes, between the passage of the years."

"Marianne!" he cried.

"You will have lovely children," she whispered. "Light and dark coming together. Now, go, my dear, my dearest dear, and give a great big hug and kiss to Lily, on my behalf."

And, saying that, Marianne let go of him, and put her hands down at her sides and just stood there, watching his familiar agonized eyes that she'd known for so very long.

"Why?" he whispered then, one last time, bewildered and grown dark and pale and heavy in spirit.

But Marianne just stood there in silence.

Robin turned away and he walked out of the room, closing the door silently behind him.

#

Later Marianne found out that Lily and Robin did indeed get married, and they were travelling the world together before settling down to a life and daily routine in a distant university city. She did not see them again for many years.

Marianne continued to work at the library where she was eventually promoted to head librarian, and she spent long days in a world of books.

Every day she came home promptly for dinner, which was always waiting for her, and the old cousins and grandmothers and great-uncles and -aunts and the goblins and tiny shrunken gnomes laughed and smiled at her, seeming to be more boisterous every day.

Marianne sat down at her place, and adjusted the spectacles on her nose, and then smilingly began slurping her soup. She only slurped the soup when eating dinner at home, since she had learned it was impolite to do that outside in company, but she also knew it would be impolite not to do it with the old relatives around her.

And sometimes, after a very long day, as she finished her second or third cup of after-dinner tea, there would be an old goblin at her elbow, and she could almost hear a muttered "Thank you, Dear."

"Thank you for what?" said Marianne involuntarily, but the tiny shrivelled creature winked at her and nudged her arm gently and then said softly in the general noise of the table conversation: "Thank you for being you, my dear. Thank you for being here. Thank you for being. There's no one else, you know, only you. No one else for us. Like the letter 'A', your favourite one. You are the horizontal line, the foil and the strength and the succour."

"What do you mean?" Marianne would say in alarm, in wonder, but the old gnome would have turned his back on her and be poking around on his plate, his mind wandering.

#

And so it went on. Time flew by, and the dinners and the years melted into one. The world was changing all around, and the young woman Marianne was now stately and middle-aged. The library was a place of ageless wonderful daydreams for her, and she worked, then came home to her own library with its old books filled with cursive writing and magical pictures of godlike women, men and creatures out of legend. Sometimes she would find pictures of Robin Hood and Maid Marian, and with a pang she would remember old intangibles unquantifiable by science. And she would pause and wonder, and then turn the page of history and legend gently.

The old stone house with ivy-covered walls seemed to be in a pocket outside of time. It was always the same inside, with the smells of fresh cooking and sounds of old voices raised in tremulous laughter, soft shufflings of old slippered feet against wooden floorboards — the same feet and the same voices, for no one ever left here, and no one ever died. Indeed, it seemed that every day there were more and more of them, old relatives whom she had never seen or remembered seeing before, old women and men with gentle comfortable faces and half-senile kind smiles, and very little memory of anything else.

Maybe they came here from other places, Marianne wondered, because she thought at one point she saw Lily's grandmother Beth, whom she recognized from a photograph she had seen once a long time ago.

But really it no longer mattered. They were all hers now, and since no one else wanted them, or maybe because they had no other place to go, not even unto death, she would be there for them. Someone had to do it; and now she knew it, recognized it for what it was. She always did make a good bottom rung and middle line to keep things in balance — not because she had to but because she could.

Indeed, after the accumulation of years the young woman was now fading and feeling tired and old herself, with shortness of breath and pains in her joints. Often she sat with a book on her lap and watched them giddy with energy, as her old ones frolicked in the rooms of the house, galloping in abandon, with wrinkled faces set in permanent smiles.

"I love you, my children," she said when no one could hear her, the young woman who was so very old, and fading by the second.

And yet fading meant gentle regrets but slipping away was a different choice altogether, and there was to be none of it here.

For she was so young, so very young at heart always, just as she will ever be for them, in the house of old.

About the Contributors

Lou Anders is an editor, author, and journalist. In 2000, he served as the Executive Editor of Bookface.com, an internet company which provided books and short stories for free online reading, and before that he worked as the Los Angeles Liaison for the Titan Publishing Group. He has published over 500 articles in such magazines as *Dreamwatch, Star Trek Monthly, Star Wars Monthly, Babylon 5 Magazine, Sci Fi Universe, Doctor Who Magazine* and *Manga Max*. He is the author of *The Making of Star Trek: First Contact* (1996) and the editor of the anthologies *Outside the Box* (2001) and the forthcoming *Live Without a Net* (2003). Currently he is at work on two more anthologies and a novel.

David V. Barrett sold his first story to BBC radio in 1984. A former schoolteacher, intelligence analyst for the British GCHQ and the American NSA and journalist, he has been a freelance writer since 1990. He edited the sf anthology *Digital Dreams* (1990). All his other books have been nonfiction, including *Secret Societies* (1997) and the critically acclaimed *The New Believers: A Survey of Sects, "Cults" & Alternative Religions* (2001). In addition to writing, he is currently researching for a PhD in Sociology of Religion at the London School of Economics.

Keith Brooke spent a long time as a promising young sf writer, with three novels published in the early 1990s (*Keepers of the Peace, Expatria* and *Expatria Incorporated*) and over fifty short stories published around the world since 1989. Now he's a promising *mature* writer and an online publisher, having launched the web-based sf, fantasy and horror showcase *Infinity Plus* in 1997; *IP* now features the work of about sixty top genre authors including Michael Moorcock, Stephen Baxter, Kit Reed, Ian McDonald, Vonda McIntyre and James Patrick Kelly. He is co-editor with Nick Gevers of *Infinity Plus One*, an anthology based on the website. His latest books are: the novel *Lord of Stone* (1997; revised edition 2001); a collection of short stories, *Head Shots* (2001); and *Parallax View* (2000), a collection of stories written with Eric Brown. Hiding his identity behind the pen-name Nick Gifford, he likes to scare children, with the novel *Piggies* due in 2003 and another in 2004. Keith lives with his young family in the English seaside town of Brightlingsea. You can find out more about Keith and his work at www.keithbrooke.co.uk.

John Brunner died in 1995 at the World Science Fiction Convention in Glasgow, UK. He was the author of countless works of science fiction and numerous fantasies, thrillers and poetry collections. Among his classic sf novels are *The Whole Man* (1964), *The Squares of the City* (1965), *Quicksand* (1967), *Stand on Zanzibar* (which won the Hugo Award; 1968), *The Jagged Orbit* (1969), *The Sheep Look Up* (1972) and *The Shockwave Rider* (1975); his series of stories collected definitively as *The Compleat Traveler in Black* (1987) is generally regarded as representing the best of his fantasy. John was also a significant worker for humanitarian causes, founding the Martin Luther King Foundation in the UK. The editors of *Strange Pleasures #2* are proud to present John's hitherto unpublished novella "The Stars Move Still", which would have been lost entirely had it not been that a copy of the manuscript had been lent to John Grant by the author shortly before his death.

John Grant is the author of over fifty books — both fiction and nonfiction — and a winner of the Hugo, World Fantasy Award, Chesley Award, Locus Award and others. He is best-known in the fantasy/sf world for *The Encyclopedia of Fantasy* (1997), done with John Clute. Other major nonfictions include *Encyclopedia of Walt Disney's Animated Characters* (1986; revised editions 1992 and 1997) and *Masters of*

Animation (2001). His most recent fictions, both published in Fall 2002, are *The Far-Enough Window* and, with Bob Eggleton, *Dragonhenge*. Under his real name, Paul Barnett, he is Commissioning Editor of Paper Tiger, US Reviews Editor of *Infinity Plus*, Consultant Editor to the publisher BeWrite, and author of the monthly "Alan Smithee's Diaries" column for the webzine *Crescent Blues*. He is married to Pamela D. Scoville, Director of the Animation Art Guild; they live in New Jersey. Visit his website at www.hometown.aol.com/thogatthog and the officially sanctioned fan site at www.dawleybank.freeserve.co.uk.

Dave Hutchinson was born in Sheffield in 1960. After getting a degree in American Studies at the University of Nottingham, the only job he could find was as a journalist, which, if nothing else, probably proves that God has a well developed sense of humour. He has published short stories — including four book collections — and a novel, *The Villages* (2002). He lives in North London with his wife, Bogna, and their three cats.

Ian Johnson was born in Walsall in 1982. The younger of two children, Ian has been an enthusiastic reader and writer since childhood, often illustrating his own stories. He has a particular love for fantastic and modernist fiction. He was diagnosed with Asperger's Syndrome in 2001. Ian currently lives with his family in Telford, UK, and is working on the second draft of his first novel. "Private View" is his first published story.

Paul Kincaid is the administrator of The Arthur C. Clarke Award. He is the co-author of a book on the American Civil War, and a collection of essays and reviews called *What It Is We Do When We Read Science Fiction* is forthcoming from Cosmos Books. He has contributed to a number of reference books on science fiction, and writes regularly for *The New York Review of Science Fiction*, *Foundation*, *Vector* and other journals. His last work of fiction was shortlisted for the BSFA Award.

Nick Mamatas was nominated for the Bram Stoker Award for horror for his short novel about the Civil War Draft Riots, *Northern Gothic* (2001). His fiction has also appeared in slick mainstream mags like

Razor, science-fiction webzines including *Strange Horizons, Speculon* and *Horrorfind,* and underground literary journals like *The Whirligig.* Nick grew up in a bad part of Brooklyn and now lives in a bad part of Jersey City. He saw The Ramones perform nine times.

Vera Nazarian left the former USSR as a refugee at the age of eight and arrived in the USA a month before her tenth birthday by way of Lebanon, Greece, and Italy. Since figuring out the English language and managing to sell her first short story at the age of 17, she has published numerous works of short fiction in anthologies and magazines such as the *Sword and Sorceress* and *Darkover* series edited by the late Marion Zimmer Bradley. She has seen her work translated into French, German, Spanish, Italian, Dutch, Czech, and Hungarian. She is an active SFWA member. Her debut novel, the mythic fantasy *Dreams of the Compass Rose* (2002) has received widespread critical acclaim. A second novel, the epic fantasy *Lords of Rainbow* is forthcoming in 2003. Vera is currently at work on another standalone fantasy novel and two unrelated trilogies, one sf and one fantasy. Visit her official website at www.veranazarian.com.

Fay Sampson was named because her sister said the fairies brought her. She has a leaning towards the fantastic. She studied mathematics, exploring imaginary numbers, or any other world following logically from a hypothesis.

Her first children's book was the near-future *F.67* (1975), based on work with refugees and in Africa. *The Watch on Patterick Fell* (1978) won the *Barco de Vapor* award. Her Celtic fantasy *Pangur Ban* (1983, reissued 2002) was shortlisted for the *Guardian* Children's Fiction Prize, as were *Chris and the Dragon* (1985) and *A Free Man on Sunday* (1987). Among her adult fictions, the *Daughter of Tintagel* sequence (1989-92, omnibus 1992) tells the story of Morgan le Fay, critiquing distortions of her original legend. *Star Dancer* (1993) weaves fragments from cuneiform tablets into the story of Inanna, Sumerian goddess of love and war. Fay has also contributed stories to Arthurian anthologies.

Research for novels led to a history of the Celtic churches, *Visions and Voyages* (1998), and the Anglo-Saxon *Runes on the Cross* (2000). Her latest children's fantasy is *THEM* (2003).

She lives in a 16th-century cottage in Devon, UK, with writer husband Jack Priestley. She enjoys discovering the stories of her ancestors and walking the moorland and rivers.

Sarah Singleton was born in 1966 and awarded an honours degree in English by the University of Nottingham. She lives in Wiltshire, UK, county of long barrows and stone circles, with husband Brian and daughters Fuchsia and Poppy. Her debut novel *The Crow Maiden* was published by Cosmos Books in 2001. She has published short stories in magazines and anthologies including *Interzone*, *QWF*, David Hartwell's *Year's Best Fantasy*, *Legend*, *Enigmatic Tales* and *Strange Pleasures #1*, with others forthcoming in *Spectrum SF* and *The Third Alternative*. She is trying to learn to play the violin.

Jean Marie Ward edits *Crescent Blues*, an online magazine covering genre fiction and related arts, games and media. She is also a frequent contributor to other nonfiction magazines, including *SciFi Weekly* and the *ASFA Quarterly*. "Most Dead Bodies in a Confined Space" is her third published story and the first to be anthologized. She is currently writing a nonfiction book about the fantasy/sf artist Jean Pierre Targete.

N. Lee Wood was born in Hartford, Connecticut, but now divides her time between the UK and France. Although she has been writing since her youth, her professional life took numerous diversions — she has been a trucker and a surgical technologist — before Ursula K. Le Guin suggested she attend the Clarion Writers' Workshop. There she met a number of professional writers — including Norman Spinrad, whom she later married — and with their encouragement started taking her writing seriously. Her novels to date are *Looking for the Mahdi* (a New York Times Notable Book of the Year and shortlisted for the Arthur C. Clarke Award; 1996), *Faraday's Orphans* (1997) and *Bloodrights* (1999). She has just completed a murder mystery and is working on an historical novel about Eleanor of Aquitaine. "Balzac" is one of her rare short stories.

9 781894 815086